Divided Loyalties

Stories

Nilofar Shidmehr

Published in Canada in 2019 and the USA in 2019 by House of Anansi Press Inc.
www.houseofanansi.com

22 21 20 19 18   1 2 3 4 5

Library and Archives Canada Cataloguing in Publication

Shidmehr, Nilofar, author
Divided loyalties / Nilofar Shidmehr.

Short stories.
Issued in print and electronic formats.
ISBN 978-1-4870-0602-0 (softcover).— ISBN 978-1-4870-0603-7 (EPUB).—
ISBN 978-1-4870-0604-4 (Kindle)

I. Title.

PS8637.H49D58 2019   C813'.6   C2018-904720-8
                            C2018-904721-6

Library of Congress Control Number: 2018958252

Book design: Alysia Shewchuk
Typesetting: Sara Loos

 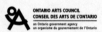

Canada Council   Conseil des Arts
for the Arts   du Canada

ONTARIO ARTS COUNCIL
CONSEIL DES ARTS DE L'ONTARIO
an Ontario government agency
un organisme du gouvernement de l'Ontario

*We acknowledge for their financial support of our publishing program
the Canada Council for the Arts, the Ontario Arts Council, and the Government of Canada.*

Printed and bound in Canada

MIX
Paper from
responsible sources
FSC® C004071
www.fsc.org

For the apple of my eye, my daughter Saaghar,
with new hope for unification

Contents

Sakeen

SAKEEN THE HOUSEMAID WAS rarely free to play with us, even at parties. She had to prepare dinner, serve it to the guests, and clean up. Shahnaz, my uncle's wife, liked to throw big parties to outplay our mothers in a game between them known as "The Best Hostess." Her dinner table would always be colorful with various dishes, pickles, salads, and desserts.

After dinner, Shahnaz and the other women would move into the living room to sit on the sofa gossiping, waiting for Sakeen to serve them tea. My uncle and the other men changed into pajamas and moved into the guest room to sit on the silk Tabriz carpet and play trump. The boys — my cousin, Hossein and others — went to the storage room to play soccer. We girls — Shahnaz's daughter Naazi, my sister Shaadi, and I — moved to the kids' bedroom to play, hopeful that Sakeen would join us later.

The boys in the adjacent room set up their mini soccer goal nets and divided into two teams. Once their ball started thumping against the wall separating the two rooms, we knew their game had started.

On this particular night in the summer of 1978, Naazi insisted on playing Cinderella. We had told Sakeen Cinderella's story so often that, flipping through the pictures in the book, she could tell what happened in each scene. I tiptoed out of the kids' room and down the corridor leading to the living room to go get her. I stopped by the bathroom door where I could see women who, as usual, were immersed in a conversation about gold and jewelry. Then, while Shahnaz was bragging about a necklace she'd recently received as a gift from my uncle, I sneaked through the living room into the kitchen. Her sleeves rolled up, Sakeen was forcefully scrubbing the dishes.

Even though she was only three years older, Sakeen was much taller than me. Unlike Naazi and me, flabby girls from upper-middle-class Tehrani families, she was wiry and raggedy, overdressed for summer, wearing a headscarf and gray leggings under a long, thick skirt, like all maids. She was not beautiful, but with her black beady eyes and aquiline nose, she looked as powerful and intimidating as her mistress, Shahnaz, who had brought Sakeen from a village near Quchan, where her family owned land.

This was the time when women of well-to-do families could afford to bring in maids. As a result of the mass migration of villagers to Tehran, there were many women and girls from poor families living in the suburbs who were available to work as housemaids. Meanwhile, their husbands worked as day laborers for construction projects booming in north Tehran.

My father being a judge and my mother a legal secretary, we could have had a maid too. Actually, my mother wanted one badly. I also wanted someone Sakeen's age to play with me. If only my father was not a clandestine socialist, against both child labor and the shah. Every time I asked him for such a playmate, he would say, "How could you be so insensitive to ask me to separate a child from her family for your own interest? I thought I instilled good values in you." Every time my mother insisted that he should bring in at least an old woman to help her with housework, he remained firm, saying that he hated the culture of showing off that the regime promoted as modernity. It was not real modernity but "Westoxification." He felt that my mother, as a university-educated woman, should display higher values. In retaliation, my mother would go as far as to insult my father, saying, "You think you are progressive, wasting every weekend playing cards. And in such silly fashion, sitting cross-legged in pajamas on the floor but not removing your tie? No. You might be a judge, but you are still the same provincial man you were when you arrived in Tehran twenty years ago!"

I agreed with both my mother and my father: Papa and the other players certainly looked ridiculous rather than modern, and Maman was definitely jealous of Shahnaz. The year before, Shahnaz had returned her last maid, a very young girl who was the same age as my little sister at the time. Tala's dark complexion and scruffy appearance contradicted the meaning of her name—"gold." Her family had lied about her skills. She was too young to clean the mess Naazi and Hossein and their father left, and she couldn't cook properly either. Worst of all, she would break into tears whenever Shahnaz scolded her. Once Shahnaz had dumped Tala back in her village, she got into her car to go to the next village to find another family willing to send a daughter to work at her house. But a village woman approached her and begged her to take her daughter. The crying mother guaranteed that her girl, who was much older than Tala, wouldn't be a disappointment.

Naazi told me that Sakeen's mother had taken Shahnaz to a chicken coop where Sakeen's father had locked her up. The woman begged Shahnaz, saying that if she took Sakeen, she would be saving the girl's life and the family's reputation. There would be no monthly payment; Shahnaz could have Sakeen for free. When I asked why, Naazi told me a story that left me both impressed with and fearful of Sakeen, for, as my mother put it, she could "open my eyes and ears" to secrets beyond my age. Sakeen had run away from home with a truck driver; her father found her at dawn with the man in his truck on a dirt road close to a village. He dragged her home, locked her in, and threatened to kill her the next day. I wouldn't have believed Naazi had I not seen the whip marks on Sakeen's back and bruises all over her body the first time I met her in Naazi's room, stripped shamelessly, flaunting her injuries. The marks Shahnaz left on her body later were nothing compared to those she brought with her from her father's home. She was certainly tough. It was this toughness, which she displayed defiantly, that attracted me the most.

As I approached Sakeen from behind, I couldn't take my eyes from her hands, like those of a grown man, under the flow of hot water. When she turned and glanced at me, I reported to her why I was there, as I would report to my mother. "Leave the scrubbing. Just rinse the dishes and let's go before Naazi changes her mind!" My words didn't get her to speed up, so I pulled her sleeve and added, "You know Naazi has brought her mother's makeup?" At this, she finally turned her head. "I'll tell her you should get made up too," I whispered. Sakeen showed no enthusiasm; she just shoved me out of the way to refill the samovar. Then I noticed something different about her. She was shuffling awkwardly, her skirt trailing in a zigzag path behind her. What was this strange movement about? She had always been swift and nimble; at the religious ceremonies Shahnaz held, Sakeen carried a tray full of glasses brimming with hot tea on only one hand.

When Sakeen opened the fridge and bent to remove some trays of fruit, I noticed something more: she was not as flat-bottomed as before. Her butt bulged with something beneath. I lingered, trying to figure out what she was wearing under her leggings. "Get out of my way or I can't do a thing," she grumbled.

Yet I was too concerned with what was in her skirt to leave.

"Go!" she commanded, noticing my gaze focused on her bottom, "or I won't come to play at all."

FIFTEEN MINUTES LATER, there were four of us in the bedroom. Sakeen had her sleeves rolled down and her scarf knotted under her chin. Now we could put on the Cinderella play.

"So, what do you think, Naazi? Can Sakeen use your mother's makeup too?" I had made the suggestion before Sakeen joined us.

"Okay, but she can't be Cinderella," Naazi answered. Of course, Naazi saw herself as the most eligible candidate for the leading role; she was pretty enough.

"Sakeen is ugly and she doesn't know how to play a maid," Naazi asserted.

Shaadi and I scoffed. Sakeen was a *real* maid. Look at the way she was dressed. Her skirt was coarse wool, she wore Shahnaz's old blouse that was too big for her, and she was the only female in this party who wore a headscarf. Naazi had a point. She wasn't the best candidate for Cinderella. In fact, she looked more like Cinderella's stepmother.

Shaadi declared that Naazi was the prettiest and voted for her to be Cinderella. It was true: Naazi's hair, stylishly cut, was as black as a raven's feathers. She had a dimpled square chin and full lips, just like her handsome father, and her beautiful almond eyes had nothing in common with her mother's narrow Tatar eyes. My mother said that the whole time Shahnaz was pregnant with Naazi, she did not look at her own reflection because she feared the superstition that her child would turn out like her.

I gave in. "Okay, Naazi will be Cinderella."

Shaadi opted for the role of fairy godmother. This time, I agreed with a grin. I knew Naazi had a blue satin dress that was too small for her, so I suggested she give it to Shaadi. Before Naazi could disagree, I went to her walk-in closet, took it out, and held it in front of my beautiful sister, whose innocent eyes gave her the aura of a fairy godmother. Naazi gave her a nod of approval.

The roles of stepmother and stepsister remained for Sakeen and me. Sakeen broke her silence, rubbing her hands on the sides of her rough skirt as if wiping off dust. "Whatever you say, girls, but Cinderella should wear maid's clothes before she turns pretty."

She was right, though I feared what making the play so authentic would mean: Naazi had to swap clothes with Sakeen.

As the truth behind Sakeen's words dawned on Naazi, her face went sullen. To ease her feelings, I put a lilt in my voice as I spoke to her. "Naazi, if you want to be a *real* Cinderella, you should *definitely* look like a maid at first."

Naazi glanced at Sakeen's outfit and winced. Her eyes narrowed like her mother's, emphasizing how painful it would be for her to wear crude clothes with pants underneath. Her black irises displayed outrage. "I don't want to play Cinderella anymore," Naazi rasped. Once again she was ruining a night for us. I stifled a sigh.

Naazi seemed to read my thoughts, and attempted to justify herself. "None of us can be Cinderella. Cinderella is blond, and we all have black hair." She said this as if it were a major discovery.

But Shaadi was already changing into Naazi's blue dress. She looked up at me, puzzled. I shook my head, an indication that she should take off the dress. In anger, she trampled on it and shuffled toward me, naked. I kicked the dress out of the way, tugged her by the hand, and made her sit at the edge of Hussein's bed. I tried to pull on her shirt. She didn't resist at first, but when I tried to tuck her feet into her skirt, she kicked madly and burst into tears.

"Hush," I said. "Auntie Shahnaz can hear you."

Her tears stopped. When Shaadi tried to kick, Sakeen tickled her feet. Her giggle was delightful, changing the mood in the room and encouraging Sakeen to tickle her all over. I managed to pull up Shaadi's skirt as she fell into Sakeen's embrace. They rolled on the bed, tickling each other. I joined in their fun until I heard Naazi calling to us. On her third yell, the three of us finally stopped and collapsed in a heap, Shaadi gently pinned below Sakeen. Shaadi squeaked, as she did when she discovered something shocking. "What is this you're hiding under your leggings?" she asked, sitting up. "Look, she's bleeding."

Sakeen quickly shook Shaadi away and sat up. Naazi dashed across the room to inspect her. In haste, Sakeen got up, pulled her skirt over her trousers, and hurried toward the door in short clumsy steps. "I need to serve fruit."

Our bewildered gazes followed her. She turned around midway and pointed to Naazi and me, standing shoulder to shoulder, mouths gaping. "This is what I told you about that night. The thing that happens to girls when they grow up. You'll get it too." We looked at each other in shock.

JUST WEEKS AGO, during Ramadan, when our families had stayed at another uncle's house for the night, Sakeen had told us about menstruation. We girls all slept on the second-floor balcony. Shahnaz had brought along a pillow and two dirty bedsheets for Sakeen. Shaadi fell asleep, but Naazi and I stayed up and waited for Sakeen to finish her work. We moved our mattresses apart and made room for Sakeen's in between, giving her our clean sheets in return for things she would tell us about adult life. That night's story was a sickening surprise. "You know what's going to happen to you in a few years?" Sakeen asked. "You're going to bleed for a week once a month from there." Our eyes widened as, with no shame, she pointed to her vagina.

"This is a camel that one day lies by the door of every girl's house," she continued. "I am telling you, you can't escape it."

It was still hard to believe. We sat up together, looked at each other, and rolled our eyes.

Sakeen said that our mothers, too, bleed every month.

This news made Naazi as angry as I'd ever seen her. "Watch your mouth, liar!" she yelled. "My mother never bleeds, okay?"

Sakeen snickered. "Yes, she does. A lot."

"How do you know?" Naazi demanded, leaning over her in fury.

"I know."

"How?" I asked.

Before Sakeen could answer, I fired off a second question. "How then do they hide their bleeding?"

"How did they hide your peeing and pooping when you were a baby?"

"No way!" I squeaked.

"Yes, a pad down there. In their pants, between their legs." All Naazi could do was make a puking gesture.

"You'd better get used to the idea." Sakeen emphasized her words with a malicious laugh.

Still, I was sure she was a big liar.

AFTER SAKEEN LEFT the room, my sister asked me several questions: What was that bulging from Sakeen's behind? Did she cut herself? Was she sick?

I didn't know. If this bleeding happened to every woman, including my mother, how come I never saw a bulge in her dress around her bottom? Perhaps her pads were different than a maid's—smaller and thinner so that they couldn't be seen.

Pretending I knew more than I did, I told Shaadi that I would tell her later. My sister was too innocent to understand anyway, I reasoned. But she continued to demand answers, so I pressed my hand over her mouth to shut her up. More stubborn than Naazi and me together, she shouted even louder.

"You're too young to know!" Naazi said, finally coming to my aid. "We'll tell you in a few years." I knew she was referring to the time when we would start this awful thing Sakeen had told us about, a time when we'd know all about it. But Shaadi wanted to know right away. She burst into tears and started kicking the edge of the bed.

"I'll tell your maman you stole her makeup," Shaadi told Naazi, "unless you tell me why Sakeen's behind is bleeding." Shaadi's screams became louder.

Frustrated with my stubborn little sister, I hid my head between my hands and covered my ears, leaving Naazi to save the day. Naazi grabbed the blue dress off the floor and shoved it toward her. "If you'll stop crying, I'll wear Sakeen's clothes and we'll play Cinderella, okay?"

That idea was enough to appease Shaadi. It amazed me, how easily she could switch from one mood to another. Now her vengeful-sister personality appeared, and she asked Naazi—not me—to do up her zipper. And once done, she sat beside Naazi as if Naazi were her older sister. I couldn't tolerate this alliance, so I started chanting "Shaadi's a shaazy." *Shaazy* means "monkey" in Arabic. Naazi knew this because she had lived in Baghdad for a few years, but my sister didn't know.

"What is a *shaazy?*" my sister asked Naazi.

Naazi hugged her to stop her curiosity. "It doesn't mean anything. She's crazy."

I turned my face from my heartless sister who had chosen Naazi over me and lay alone on Hussein's bed, spreading myself across the soccer field printed on his blanket.

Sakeen was really taking her time with the tea service. I wondered whether she'd even come back. If she didn't, there would be no play that night; my sister would quickly get bored and go to sit on our father's lap and watch the men play cards.

From time to time I looked to see what Naazi and Shaadi were up to. I wished it were me flattening the frills of Cinderella's dress. For sure, I could do a better job than careless Naazi.

"Shaazy" was a traitor, so I decided I was not going to join the play if she was the fairy godmother. Ignoring her, I slipped under the blanket and closed my eyes, listening to noises from other rooms. Shahnaz was the loudest of the women, giving orders to Sakeen in frigid tones that intermittently broke through the soft flow of our mothers' chattering. Our fathers were the next noisiest, accusing each other of cheating. Third was the cheering from the boys every time they scored a goal.

Obviously, everyone was busy doing something. Only I was left out. And worse, if Sakeen came back, my absence in the Cinderella show would make no difference. Having a Cinderella, a fairy godmother, and Sakeen as a stepsister was enough for the play to go on. They didn't need a stepmother.

I was already imagining ways to ruin their play to take revenge. Naazi should have told Shaadi to apologize to me for her tantrum.

TO MY SURPRISE, Sakeen returned, with a tray of cut fruit and three glasses of cherry sherbet. She placed the tray of after-meal snacks on Naazi's nightstand for us to have later. Shaadi seemed to have forgotten about the blood on Sakeen's bottom, but Naazi hadn't. How could she? She had to trade clothes with Sakeen.

"Give me your shirt and skirt," Naazi ordered her maid. "I don't want your filthy leggings. I'll wear my own stockings."

Sakeen accepted the deal under one condition: "Give me a dress to wear instead."

"First give me your shirt," Naazi replied. "I'll get your skirt later, but not your headscarf. No way I'll be wearing that."

Sakeen retied her scarf back behind her neck, letting a tassel fall on her long brow. Then, with no shame, she stripped off Shahnaz's old blouse. She wasn't wearing a bra, and her breasts looked bigger than the last time we saw them.

Naazi took the shirt, wrinkled her nose, and went into her closet. She reappeared two minutes later in Sakeen's blouse, which reached down to her knees, and her own black stockings underneath. I volunteered to roll her sleeves up for her, and with that done, she turned into a perfect Cinderella. My little sister roared with laughter at our cousin's miserable appearance — laughter I hoped would break the new bond between the two of them. I forced myself to laugh too, even though to me Naazi looked more pathetic than funny.

Sakeen guffawed, drawing Naazi's attention to her nakedness, and reminded her that she had forgotten to bring her a dress. Naazi walked back to the closet to find Sakeen a party dress for the role of the mean stepmother. She pressed it against Sakeen's chest. Sakeen took it with a smirk and disappeared into the closet. When she reappeared, she flaunted Naazi's velvet dress, obviously too tight for her. Naazi flinched at Sakeen's appearance, and at the rough skirt Sakeen held out to her.

Putting it on, Naazi turned to Shaadi in anger. "See what you made me agree to with your stupid crying." She then turned to Sakeen, who looked like her mistress and not her maid, and chided, "Be careful not to make my dress bloody. Once the show is over, you're my maid again."

I cringed, wishing that for once Naazi had been able to leave well enough alone. Now my sister was curious again. Turning to Sakeen, she asked, "Have you cut yourself on your behind?"

To steer Shaadi's attention away, Sakeen said, "What about makeup?"

"Yes, we need that," I said, and went to open the makeup kit on the desk beside Naazi's bed. I pulled out a chair and nodded at Shaadi. "Come. The fairy godmother should go first."

When she took the seat, I said to Naazi, "I think Sakeen should do the makeup. You know she is good at it." I nodded toward the wall clock with my head to indicate time was ticking away, so Naazi wouldn't waste time objecting to my idea.

Sakeen asked Shaadi to sit still and keep her eyes shut as she powdered her face, applying blush to her cheeks and reddening her tiny mouth. She applied blue eye shadow and curled her lashes with mascara. Shaadi trembled occasionally with excitement as Naazi and I watched her transformation. When Sakeen was done she gently kissed Shaadi's eyelids, making her small face blossom with a beautiful smile.

I told Sakeen I didn't need makeup and put on lipstick myself. As Cinderella only turns pretty in the second act, Sakeen went about her own makeup next. It transformed her in an unbelievable way. The makeup brought out her sharp black eyes, emphasized her high cheekbones, and made her lips thicker and her nose smaller with just a few quick strokes of the brush. She became more beautiful than me.

Sakeen was an artist who had become an intimidating beauty, yet it did not rob her of her grit. Naazi, though, just looked hopeless. No matter how hard she tried to hold Sakeen's skirt away from her waist, it nevertheless touched her tights.

Shaadi waved a pencil with stars on it, pretending it was her fairy-godmother's wand, prompting us to begin. I sat on Hussein's bed as the stepsister. Excited, I watched stepmother Sakeen give tasks to Naazi, our Cinderella.

Anger shadowed Naazi's dark eyes as she ignored Sakeen, busying herself in the "kitchen" that was her bed while still trying to hold Sakeen's skirt away from her leggings. I decided I should come up with my own plans for tormenting Naazi, as I was still mad at her for turning my little sister against me, but I knew I could never best Sakeen when it came to tortures.

"Take your hands off your skirt" was Sakeen's first command. Why couldn't I have come up with such a great order first?

Naazi refused. "I'm still setting up the stage. Save your yapping for when the play starts."

We waited for Naazi to set up the toy dishes, and

then we all counted down from three to zero and the play officially began.

This time, Sakeen made me deliver the order for Naazi to let go of her skirt. When she hesitated, I smacked her on the back of her hand. Avoiding the skirt, she stood with her arms crossed on her chest.

Now it was my turn to initiate an order. I stood by the bed, arms akimbo, and called her over to make it. Sakeen reminded her that she was not allowed to touch her skirt. So Naazi dropped her hands and walked with a clumsy, awkward shuffling.

Once my bed was made, I messed it again. She'd done a poor job, I told her, and must do it again. As Naazi began re-spreading the blanket and straightening the ripples that creased the soccer field, Sakeen murmured into my ear. "Press her legs against the edge of the bed while she bends down." Naazi twisted in pain. But the ultimate torment, I thought, should have something to do with the skirt. It came to me immediately. "Cinderella, I want you to lie face down on the floor and roll across the carpet."

As Naazi lowered herself to the floor, I squatted over her and rolled her on the floor to the other end of the room. Once my hands were free, I rubbed them on her skirt and then touched her face with my itchy fingers. Naazi's feet started shaking, as if someone were choking her.

"You're not getting it," Shaadi said, chiming in for the first time. "The stepsister must be meaner!"

To my surprise, Sakeen agreed. "She's right. You're too soft for Cinderella's stepsister."

"And you're too dumb to be the stepmother," I proclaimed.

Sakeen started pacing the room, something I knew she did when she was furious. Meanwhile, Naazi retreated to "the kitchen."

Thinking she knew more than I did, my naive sister gave me instructions. "Like in the movies, you should give Cinderella orders to sweep the floor, to wash and iron your clothes."

Her simple idea gave Sakeen her next mischievous plan. She called Naazi over. "You're filthy," she said, and ordered her to take off the dirty skirt and wash it. Berating myself for not coming up with this demand, I watched Naazi handle this new task.

Our poor Cinderella spread the skirt on the study-desk laundry area. Her hands shook as she rubbed the fabric. I held my breath. Her silence was extraordinary. Perhaps she was not as spoiled as I imagined.

Sakeen yanked the skirt out of Naazi's hand and held it up to the light, only to shove it into Naazi's face again. "It's still dirty. It smells!"

She made Naazi sniff the fabric, but even this didn't break Naazi's resolve. So Sakeen motioned for me to get up and rub the fabric against Naazi's face. I hesitated, but fearing that she would punish me too, I carried out her order.

Naazi jerked away as I pressed the skirt to the flushed skin of her face, but Sakeen held her in place. Dropping the skirt on the desk, I quickly retreated to the bed. "Your little sister's right. You're not much of a stepsister. You take too much pity on maids."

Trying to stay as resolute as my role model, I shrugged, wishing that this play would end soon. Our tortures no longer made sense. No matter what we did, Naazi's eyes remained dry. Inwardly, I cheered for her. If I had been playing Cinderella, I would have yielded under the pressure. My body was already tense. Looking over at my little sister, I noticed that she seemed to be in the same state. Perhaps that's why she suddenly announced that the first act was over. "It's my turn now. Let's put on her makeup," she insisted, her shoulders shaking.

This was also what I wanted. Cinderella turning into a princess was Sakeen's ultimate defeat. "Keep your wriggling ass there on your seat, you little rascal. I am not done yet." The look Sakeen threw at Shaadi before disappearing into the closet stopped her from climbing out of the chair. Shaadi turned her face away from Sakeen and squinted at the clock on the wall, which seemed to be ticking slower now, as if it, too, were afraid of Sakeen.

I had to come up with a way to end this act as soon as possible. Not because my sister wanted to enter the play in the next act or because I cared about Naazi being further tortured. I wanted to win Sakeen as my own maid, as my playmate. There was no way Naazi would be able to bear her presence at their house after this play. And given that Sakeen's family would never want her back, I was sure my father would harbor her in our home, if I asked him.

I was still racking my brain to come up with a master plan to end the first act when Sakeen emerged from the closet with something in her hand. I pushed Naazi aside to see that Sakeen was holding her folded gray leggings. The arc of her raised eyebrows and the mischievous twinkle in her eyes revealed that she had the most wicked plan, one that Satan himself could not have concocted. A shudder ran down my spine as I imagined the cruelty of her ruse. In anticipation and fear, I held my breath and pushed my fingers into my palms.

Sakeen flung the leggings at Naazi and ordered her to wash them. "Stop staring and do the laundry. My daughter and I are going to a party. This must be washed before we come back."

I stared at Sakeen, confused. Was this her ultimate torture plan? What was the difference between touching her scratchy skirt and touching her coarse leggings?

On the face of it, this trick was no different than the last one.

Perhaps it was, though, because Naazi began to show signs of distress. She must have seen something in Sakeen's plan that I couldn't. Her flushed face looked like a spider web ready to be punched by the wind. She curled her fingers into fists to stop her hands from shaking before opening them again to collect the leggings. Standing up, she moved back to the laundry area. I followed, ignoring the sound of Shaadi's feet banging against the legs of the chair.

"You little brat," Sakeen barked at my sister. "Can't you sit quiet for five minutes?"

Once Naazi spread the folded leggings on the desk, Sakeen's underwear emerged from inside them. I turned around to see if Shaadi was looking in our direction and moved to block her view of the dirty panties with patches of dried blood. Approaching us from behind, Sakeen yelled at Naazi. "Rub them hard until the stains come out!" Even though I was repulsed, I couldn't resist watching Naazi's hands. They pushed Sakeen's underwear aside and then started to quiver before shaking uncontrollably while rubbing Sakeen's leggings.

"You also need to wash my panties." Sakeen's eyes gleamed devilishly.

As convulsions took hold of Naazi's whole body, she

shouted with a voice as brittle as a cracked glass, "Even Cinderella didn't do this filthy job."

I agreed completely, but I kept my mouth shut so as not to gag. My stomach turned at the sight of Sakeen's panties. The filthy maid had gone too far, asking my cousin to do something so disgusting. Who did she think she was to act like a real mistress? This was more than a role-play. Her treatment of Naazi was outrageous, meant to offend our whole family. I also felt humiliated and was about to cry.

Sakeen spoke steadily. "Oh, yeah? So how come I have to do this filthy job for your *nahne* every month?"

"Watch your mouth, village girl," I screamed. "It is your mother who's called *nahne.*"

This was the last straw. Naazi broke into a contagious wail that soon spread to Shaadi and me. Before I could move forward to hug my shaky little sister, her face a canvas of running colors, Shahnaz, our mother, and the other women burst in, behind them a troop including our fathers, Hossein, and his football gang— all come to rescue a fairy godmother, a Cinderella, and her ugly stepsister from an evil stepmother.

WE DID NOT see Sakeen after that night. Naazi said that when she woke up the next morning, Sakeen was gone. She didn't dare ask her mother anything. We never heard about Sakeen again, and we didn't play with the next maid or the succession of others who replaced her—all of them old women—until the revolution.

Butterflies on the Bus

For years my heart inquired of me
Where Jamshid's sacred mirror might be,

And what was in its own possession
It asked from strangers, constantly;

Was unaware that God was there
and called His name out ceaselessly.

—Hafiz

PARVAANEH WAKES WITH A start from her dream when
the bus driver slams on the brakes. She opens her eyes to
the activity, braces herself as the bus continues a series of
halts, still a hundred yards from the stop on Revolution
Street at Saadi Street. Two drivers lean on their horns.
Ahead, an orange taxi swerves to the shoulder to avoid
hitting a young man crossing the street to catch the
bus. A few men and women in chador walking down
the sidewalk turn and look. The taxi driver yells at the
man for almost causing an accident. Parvaaneh groans,
grips the handrail in front of her, closes her eyes again,
and tries for a few more seconds to hold onto the dream
in which her brother Navid is crossing a river.

It's impossible. She can't see if Navid has made it to
the other side. There is only the roar of the bus engine,
the horns, the shouts, and a continuous, murky current
behind her eyelids.

When she hears people bustle past her to take their seats, Parvaaneh sighs, gives up, and opens her eyes. She stares into a long line of people by the bus stop. They push against each other to get on the bus. The young man who was almost run over crossing the street is the final one to enter, and he stumbles on the last step. There is something about him that reminds her of her brother—his thick black hair. Three days ago, Navid stumbled in the river that traces the border between Iran and the Soviet Union as he crossed it to escape from fighting in the war. She jumps up from her seat, a few rows from the front, ready to go and help the man. But she sits back down when he steadies himself on the low-hanging iron bar.

The man hands his ticket to the driver. His back is toward her. Parvaaneh leans forward and squints into the driver's rearview mirror, trying to see the man's face through the reflected light. But he turns, walks past her to the middle of the bus, and slides into a seat a few rows behind her. He is the same height as Navid and just as slim.

Parvaaneh's eyes are heavy again. She has barely slept in three days. She is on her way to her friend Sima's place. It is Sima Navid will call to say he is safe.

WHEN PARVAANEH AND Navid first hit the road, they went from Tehran to Ardebil. She hired an Azeri acquaintance to drive them there. They departed before dawn. To give her brother the look of a sick person, Parvaaneh had wrapped his head in one of her scarves and yellowed his face with turmeric. Navid was excellent in the role. He lay down as soon as they slid into the back seat and put his head on her lap. She covered him with an old chador she'd brought as a prop for their show. Navid stayed in the same position the entire journey. It was wonderful to have him attached to her and to stroke his hair or pat his shoulder as they traveled farther away from their home and closer to Azarbaijan, where they would have to say good-bye for good.

The driver took the Khalkhal–Zanjan Road. Convinced by Navid's performance that he really was ill, the driver sped up and got them to their destination one hour early. They spent the following night with a distant relative — her mother's great-aunt, a placid old lady they'd met only once in their entire lives. This was the address they had given to the smuggler's contact, who'd told them someone would come for them in the morning. Parvaaneh was still awake when she heard him arrive at seven, and she stumbled with fatigue on the way to his car. She'd spent the night watching an alarmed Navid tossing and turning on the mattress and talking loudly from time to time about hating the war.

The smuggler, a lanky, bearded young man, had driven them along the winding and bumpy route

toward Astara. He told them it would be safer if they
traveled during the day, for they would draw less attention to themselves. The Revolutionary Guards thought
that people looking to escape would choose to make
their trip during the night, and on dirt roads. This time,
Parvaaneh sat in the back and the two men in front. It
was a configuration that would not arouse suspicion;
women and children always sat in the back. The man
smoked the whole way, which made Parvaaneh feel
nauseated. She remained silent, but moved close to the
window and put her head out for a while. The cool,
fresh morning air blew onto her face. The road was
wet from the night's rain, and more gray clouds were
gathering in the sky above the mountains.

Navid seemed lost in his thoughts; his head bobbed
and nodded. When Parvaaneh touched his shoulder
from behind, he shook suddenly.

The driver turned to him. "Are you all right, man?"

"I'm fine," Navid said, looking up. "Give me a
cigarette."

Then both men blew smoke at the windshield.
Parvaaneh fanned her hand back and forth, breaking
through the cloud of smoke that wafted to the back.
She didn't complain.

When they reached the road to the mountains, a fog
formed around them. Parvaaneh could barely see the
aspens lining the road.

"Another half hour," the driver said, "and we're there." He threw a cigarette butt out the window, where it disappeared into the fog. Parvaaneh slid to the side as the car turned right and headed into the valley, somewhere beneath the mist. A few more turns, Parvaaneh thought, and it would be time to say good-bye to Navid.

When the car came out of the fog into the valley, she couldn't resist holding onto her brother's shoulder from behind. How could she go home without him? As she asked herself this, she felt nausea rise within.

Navid's shoulder jolted under her hand every time the car turned or dipped. He glanced back, smiling at her. "Don't worry," he said.

"I'm not worried." She forced herself to smile.

SITTING ON THE bus that drives her through the Tehran streets toward Sima's apartment, Parvaaneh hears a voice, repeating the same words: "Don't worry."

She raises her head and looks around. She's been dozing, and the seats around her are vacant now. The voice is in her head. It is her own. All the other passengers have taken seats in the shade, on the other side of the bus. An old man sits at the front. He hits the floor with his cane as he repeats in a high voice: *"Allah-o-ma sale ala Mohammad va ale Mohammad"* —My greetings to Prophet Mohammad and his household. A woman in a black chador and her son in a school uniform sit behind him. The boy is about six or seven years old. His mother is feeding him rice with beans from a container sitting on her lap. Watching the mother and the son, Parvaaneh remembers how Navid hadn't eaten much in the few weeks before the trip.

"You have to eat," Parvaaneh had said, spooning rice and *ghormeh sabzi* stew from the plate he wouldn't touch. "Eat. You're no longer a child."

Navid hadn't listened. He sat still, hugged his knees, and remained silent. She brought the spoon up close to his mouth the way she used to do when he was a little boy and she just a teenager. Their mother had died giving birth to Navid, leaving Parvaaneh, at the age of ten, as the sole female in the family. Her father had enrolled her in night school so she could take care of her younger brother during the day when he, a high school math teacher, was at work. Navid grew up calling her *Ana* with the sweet Azeri accent of their mother, who was from Azerbaijan.

Navid pushed the spoon back. "Don't do this," he said morosely. "You embarrass me by playing my mother. I am a grown man, for God's sake."

"I'm sorry," Parvaaneh said. "I am not myself these days." She brought her trembling hand down to her lap and sighed.

Navid looked into her eyes. "You understand why I don't want to go to war?" he asked. His head—covered with his thick, straight, shining black hair, so like hers—bobbed as he spoke. "It is not because I'm afraid. I don't believe the war is just. I don't want to participate in it."

"Of course. I know you better than anyone—even better than myself." Her brother's charcoal eyes glowed as if they were on fire. The corner of his lips, which were tightly pressed against one another, twitched. She didn't want him to die in a war, whether it was just or not.

"Now, eat."

And again, automatically, she brought the spoon up to his mouth. Noticing her mistake, she was about to lower her hand when Navid stuck his tongue out at her and cracked up—a familiar gesture from his childhood. Parvaaneh laughed out loud for the first time in weeks.

Parvaaneh herself hasn't been able to touch food for the past three days. She is starving. Her mouth is dry and her stomach burns, but she doesn't want to think about herself until she learns of Navid's whereabouts. To ward off her hunger she concentrates on images from the street outside the window. The bus is moving at a snail's pace. It passes a mural depicting a group of soldiers lying in a trench and shooting at an approaching tank. One of the soldiers appears to have been shot dead. Blood blossoms out of his chest like a red rose. Unlike Tehran's smoky sky, the sky above the soldiers' heads is blue. There is a banner across the sky with a slogan: *God has promised heaven to martyrs.*

It is hotter than usual today, and Parvaaneh is sweating in her headscarf and her long black coat. The seats in front of her that are exposed to the sun are still empty. Watching the light bouncing off them, she winces as an image of Navid crossing the river fills her mind. He is caught up in a whirling vortex of rising, foamy water. The image makes her feel dizzy, so she turns back to watch the busy streets again. People cluster by bakeries and meat shops. There are beggars, soldiers in military uniform, and a few young girls in light gray coats entering a boutique across the street. The bus stops by a bank at the corner of Lalehzar Street, where a middle-aged bald man with a Samsonite waits. A woman holding one screaming child while dragging two others after her also gets on, following the bald man. She holds the hem of her chador between her teeth so that it does not slip back. Parvaaneh leans her brow on the hot iron bar in front of her and feels the burning between her legs that she had forgotten about for a while.

If it were up to Parvaaneh, she would just call Sima to inquire about Navid. But Nasser, her older brother who lives in Germany, had warned her not to call Sima from home because her calls might be monitored. Parvaaneh thought Nasser was too timid and careful. Years ago, he had been a clandestine member of the communist Tudeh Party, back when the party was illegal. But that was before the revolution. He had left the country to study abroad and had never come back; he sent letters from time to time. These days, in 1982, the Tudeh Party supported the regime and its holy war; nobody in the government was after its members. Nevertheless, Parvaaneh promised her older brother that she'd go to Sima's apartment downtown, and that she'd call him from a long-distance call center afterward to inform him about their younger brother.

Parvaaneh has only vague memories of Nasser. The things she knows best about him are his handwriting and his voice. If there were no Nasser, Parvaaneh has often thought, Navid, as the only male in the family, would be exempt from military service, and she wouldn't have had to go through the horrible things she'd experienced over the last three days. But she does have an older brother, and because of that she is now trying to fight the fatigue and the severe burning deep down inside her, where the sergeant entered her. The bleeding hasn't stopped since the police station, and she feels as if she is filled with fire. Still, it's not as bad as this nauseated feeling in the pit of her stomach that from time to time surges up her throat and suffocates her.

· · ·

SUFFOCATED. THAT WAS how Parvaaneh felt when, packed in the smuggler's car, they had reached the bottom of the valley and finally come out of the fog. She clutched Navid's drooped shoulders with both hands to protect him from jolting forward as their driver pushed on the gas and the car soared on a dirt road that was suddenly visible. When Navid straightened himself and leaned back, Parvaaneh put her head out the window. Namin, the village the man had told them about, could be seen in the distance. She also saw the river for the first time, down the embankment. A guard post loomed over it.

"Look over there," she said, bringing her head inside. "Are you sure it is safe here?" she asked the driver.

"I know this area like the back of my hand," the man growled under his breath. "The river goes for miles. I know places that are not protected."

No sooner had the smuggler finished his sentence than a car appeared behind them in the distance. Parvaaneh couldn't see clearly enough in the rearview mirror to tell whether it was a military patrol or not.

"Calm down, woman," the driver said, seeing her worried reflection in the mirror. "One look at your face and they'll know what we're up to."

Navid looked back. His face was also pale.

"You have the cash, yes?" the driver asked.

"Yes," Navid said, turning back. "Do you want it now?"

The driver extended his hand. "Give it to me. I'll use it only if it's necessary."

"My sister has it. Give him the cash, Parvaaneh."

At her brother's command, Parvaaneh bent over to hide herself from the man's gaze in the rearview mirror, furtively opened one of the buttons of her coat, inserted her hand, and pulled out a bag she wore around her neck, inside which she'd hidden a bundle of bills.

"Here." She tapped on the driver's shoulder with the bag.

"I hope it's not the Revolutionary Guards," the driver said. "They are difficult to bribe."

He slowed the car to a stop by the side of the road, got out, and opened the hood.

"Get out." He came to the window and spoke to Navid. "We must pretend the car is broken."

"You stay there," the driver said when Parvaaneh opened her door to get out too.

The car was not a military patrol but a beat-up Paykan driven by an old man. A villager. He had animals—a sheep and a few chickens—in the back of his car. Navid and the driver waved him on and closed the hood when the old man slowed down to help.

They got back in when the car was gone, the dust rising in the air after it, sending Navid into a coughing fit.

• • •

PARVAANEH STILL FEELS the same agitation she felt on that trip a few days ago. The bus she took at Imam Hossein Square near her house crawls forward, closer to Revolution Square, but as on that day, she finds she cannot do anything about the anxiety boiling inside her. She cannot even put her head out the window and breathe. The only thing she can do is press her face against the windowpane, endure the pain, and watch the activity out in Ferdowsi Square. Today, there is no currency-exchange dealer waiting for customers on the south side by Ferdowsi Street. The intersection is blocked by a military patrol, which stops young men to check if they've been drafted. Parvaaneh wishes the driver could speed up and pass the patrols; they take her back to a time and place she'd just as soon forget. But the bus is stuck, and Parvaaneh surrenders to memories of the past year, when Navid had to stay in hiding at home as the Revolutionary Guards roved the streets, hunting for young men who hadn't yet turned themselves in for military service. They would send those they arrested directly to the war zone and the front line. But how long could Navid stay at home? He got grumpier every day as he slept away the hours or sat silent in front of the television watching the news.

Parvaaneh had snapped at him one day when she got home, tired from long hours of standing in a line to buy meat. Navid hadn't even lifted his gaze from the TV screen when she entered. She took the bags of groceries, beef, and two fresh *barbari* breads to the kitchen. She cut the beef, placed everything in the fridge, and came back to the living room only to find her brother in the same fixed position, his eyes still glued to the screen. He was watching a show about young girls who married war casualties — men who had lost feet, hands, or another part of their body.

This time, the show's guests were a young woman clad in a black chador and a man in a wheelchair whose feet had been amputated. The woman said she was proud of her act because it was driven by a noble cause. She thought that God approved of her action; it was out of God's love that she had married this man. The show host nodded his agreement, asserting that her action was equivalent to jihad. Even though she was living, he said, she had achieved the rank of martyr for her sacrifice of the self for a higher good.

"What is this crap you're watching all day?" Parvaaneh grumbled.

"What do you want me to do? Wear a skirt and dance for you?" Navid snorted.

"You could help me." Parvaaneh sat down on the floor. "I am tired of doing all the work."

Navid leaned back against a pillow and extended his feet. "I'm a man. I can't do housework. It's women's work."

"I don't know," Parvaaneh said. "Do something else besides watching TV."

"Like what?"

"Anything other than watching this crap."

"How do you know this is crap?" Navid said jokingly. "It's actually very entertaining. Listen to the stupid things this woman is saying. She's nuts."

Now the woman on the show was saying that she had learned to be a lover from butterflies — *parvaaneha* — as they are described in Sufi poetry. A *parvaaneh* is drawn to the flame and lets it burn her. This is the metaphor for love, for sacrificing the self for a greater cause.

"See, she is talking about you, Butterfly." Navid nudged his sister.

Parvaaneh pushed Navid's elbow back. "Stop it."

But Navid didn't stop. "Imagine I wasn't your brother. And imagine I lost my feet like this man. Would you marry me then?" Navid's eyes glowed with the same spark they'd emitted when he was a child and had done something forbidden.

"I told you to stop it."

"I asked you a question. You answer. Imagine I am a casualty. Since you're a *parvaaneh*, would you marry me?"

Looking at the man on TV and imagining Navid like him, in a wheelchair, Parvaaneh suddenly burst into tears.

"Sorry." Navid hugged her. "I didn't mean to hurt you. It was a joke."

He got up and walked across the room to their old TV and changed the channel. "Don't cry! See, I am going to switch to your favorite program." He winked and flicked the channel to the one showing a children's program. A group of children, three and four years old, were leaping in butterfly costumes after an old man, fluttering their arms up and down and singing, *"Par par par par parak."*

"Oops. This one's about you too," Navid said apologetically. "All programs are about you."

Parvaaneh laughed out loud. As her brother turned off the television, she told him to let it be. "I like kids."

After that day, Navid always switched off the TV as soon as Parvaaneh returned home from shopping. He got up and helped her carry the bags to the kitchen. Then, if Parvaaneh was in the mood, they would watch something together. She'd bring the vegetables she wanted to prepare for dinner and spread them on a rag on the floor so she could work on them. Sometimes Navid would help. He'd separate the fava beans from their skins and throw them in a bowl by her feet or cut parsley on a board.

"See, the damn war has turned me into a housewife," he joked.

During Navid's home incarceration, as he called it, they kept the curtains shut all the time. Navid also stayed away from the windows, as neighbors were always a threat. Parvaaneh had told everyone that Navid was exempted from military service due to an old disease, and that he'd left the country and joined their Nasser in Germany. Nevertheless, she always feared that someone devoted to the revolution and the regime would spot him at home and report that there was a young man at their house. Early one Saturday morning, when Parvaaneh was waiting in line behind the poultry shop, Mrs. Monir, who had known their family for a long time, asked Parvaaneh about her brothers. Parvaaneh had heard that when Nasser was a first-year student at the Iranian Military Academy, before he had quit and gone abroad, he'd had eyes for Mrs. Monir, who, like him, had a thick Azeri accent when she spoke Farsi. Parvaaneh had no idea how much the young Mrs. Monir had resembled this fat, middle-aged woman wearing heavy makeup and a floral chador who was so curious about her brothers. Fortunately, at that exact moment the butcher put his head out and shouted that he was out of chicken for the day. Even though Parvaaneh's poultry coupon, for which she'd registered as a family of one, would expire the very next day, she didn't go back; she feared running into the nosy woman again.

Parvaaneh had searched around for possible ways to get Navid out of the country. And for that they needed money. Nasser was already helping them with their daily expenses, and Parvaaneh did not want to ask him for more. So, she put their deceased father's house up for sale. The deposit she'd receive from the potential buyer was enough to pay a smuggler. The money that would come upon the completion of the sale was sufficient to lease a small place for herself, close to Sima. Navid insisted that they should include a cancellation clause in the contract in case something went wrong and Parvaaneh wanted to stop the sale.

They staged the house, and Navid hid in the shower and let the water run every time someone showed up to view it.

"I'm sorry I can't show you the bathroom," she'd say. "My aunt is visiting and she is in there." She couldn't believe how many people walked away just because they couldn't see the bathroom.

Parvaaneh waited for months for someone to make an offer. It was from a family with five children, two of them intellectually disabled. The father, who had come to see the house, didn't mind that he couldn't see the bathroom. He also didn't mind the cancellation clause.

They started planning Navid's trip as soon as the offer was made. First they thought of traveling west to find someone who would take Navid to Turkey through the mountains. But that was the route that everybody took, including those affiliated with outlawed political groups. There were rumors that every day more and more of those who did take it were arrested. Also, the route itself was dangerous and difficult. The journey took several days on horseback, by mule, or on foot through the mountains. And even when the fugitives made it to the other side, the Turkish police were a threat. They could send the runaways back to rot in jail or be executed.

Later, Parvaaneh found out about smugglers in the south who took people by boat to Dubai from Bandar Abbas or other coastal places. She paid the first instalment to a smuggler's contact in Tehran with the money she'd saved for her dowry. But when the departure date arrived, she didn't let Navid go. News was spreading about those who had drowned in the Persian Gulf when their boats overturned, or when they were pushed into the dark ocean in the middle of the night by the smugglers themselves when they heard the roaring of the Revolutionary Guards' boat engines in the distance, or when they were shot dead by the United Arab Emirates Coast Guard.

The Aras River, which separated Iran and Azerbaijan, was the last route of escape. With luck, the Soviets would not turn Navid back. Nasser told Navid that he should give his name to the police when he made it to Soviet soil and ask them to send him to East Germany. From there, he would be able to sneak into West Germany, where Nasser lived, and claim refugee status. Parvaaneh used the deposit on the sale to pay for another smuggler who promised to drive Navid to an unguarded shore of the Aras where he could safely cross to the other side. To ease her feelings about having to move out of their childhood home, she thought about herself as a *parvaaneh*, as a metaphor for self-sacrifice. It was surprising how much she resembled the woman on that awful TV program.

THINKING ABOUT THE bride of the wheelchair man featured in the TV show, Parvaaneh recalls the woman's recitation of the Koran: "God created for you wives from among yourselves, that you many find repose in them, and He has put between you affection and mercy. Verily, in that are indeed signs for a people who reflect." Bowing her head to the amputee, the woman had concluded that, following the teaching in this verse, she believed her only purpose in life was to submit to and serve her husband, and try as best as she could to create a home that would give him repose. As a result, God had created affection between her and this man. Love before marriage was not necessary, she said. Women needed only to obey God's order and love would follow.

The recollection makes Parvaaneh re-examine her own idea of self-sacrifice. Were women created to take care of men's needs and give them peace of mind? Yes, she had devoted herself for the last little while to saving her brother's life. And she was known for her legendary, Job-like patience with her little brother. But none of that meant she must forget about her own life or continue to devote herself to the same task for the rest of it. She also had a place in creation.

Parvaaneh turns away from watching the patrols along Revolution Street. The bus has filled with new passengers and is now packed on both sides. A fat woman donned in black from head to toe is standing by Parvaaneh's seat and holds the bar above her. Her sleeve has slipped back, and a small portion of her forearm is exposed to sight. She is wearing several gold bracelets that knock against one another and jingle as the bus moves along.

Good for her, Parvaaneh thinks. She has her marriage gold to sell when worse comes to worst, which is what is happening to Parvaaneh now. She has to move out of the house by the end of this month, when the new owner takes possession. Even though the money she will receive from the buyer in two weeks is enough to lease a room near Sima, most families do not accept single women as renters. What is she going to do if nobody accepts her? She cannot live with her uncle Reza and his family all her life. Nor can she live with Sima and her husband for longer than a short time. The only solution will be to rent a place north of Tehran, where people are more open-minded. But they'll want monthly rent in addition to a large sum as the lease. Still, with her father's pension that she receives every month and the small allowance Nasser sends her, she'll at least be able to afford to pay the rent and her monthly expenses.

Parvaaneh drops her eyes from the fat woman's bracelets. As difficult as the situation is, selling the house is not the worst thing that has happened to her. And thanks to Navid, who'd insisted on the cancellation clause, there is still a chance to stop the sale and keep the house. No, the worst was losing her virginity to the sergeant. There is no way to cancel that. She can feel the scar between her legs as she restlessly shuffles in her seat. The fat woman moves aside and asks if she wants to get off at the next stop.

"No," Parvaaneh says with a raspy voice. She turns to the window and closes her eyes as the light bouncing off the woman's wrist reflects on her face. Maybe it is shame that has made this lump in her throat. Having lost her virginity to the sergeant, she is no longer able to have a good long-term marriage in the future. No decent man wants to marry the *sigheh* of another man. A *sigheh*'s usefulness expires after she fulfils her role of providing pleasure during the short-term marital contract. This is especially unfortunate because now that she no longer needs to worry about Navid, she has been looking forward to being able to work on her own life and possibly settling down with a good man. At least she hopes that will be the case. In her mind, she constructs the scene that she hopes is about to be realized: Sima opens the door, embraces Parvaaneh at the threshold, her face wet with the tears of joy, and murmurs in her ear that her brother has already called, that he's safely made it to the other shore of the Aras. This could happen in just a few minutes—if only the bus would move, for God's sake!

And what if when she gets there Sima shakes her head and says Navid has not called yet? What if he never calls? This last question pops Parvaaneh's eyes open again. The bus is still stuck in traffic and she is stuck in it, feeling even more anxious than the day she and Navid were in the smuggler's car, moving down the curvy road toward Namin.

THE SMUGGLER HAD said they were close to the Aras, but the short drive seemed to drag on forever. The mountains on the Soviet side were gray with a purplish hue around their peaks. Parvaaneh took her purse and slung it across her body.

"We're getting there," the smuggler said when he noticed her restlessness.

She was the first one out of the car when they finally arrived.

"You see that trail?" The man pointed to a clearing on the left side of the road. "It takes you down to the river." He stared straight ahead and kept the engine running.

"Okay." Navid nodded his head. "Thank you."

"Good luck," the driver replied. "I'll take your sister back to the town."

But Parvaaneh didn't get back into the car. Instead, she stayed with her brother. Navid was pale. Parvaaneh embraced him, pursing her lips, holding back a cry that was welling up in her throat.

"Call Sima, okay?" she gasped.

"I will." Navid rubbed his forehead against hers.

"Get back in the car, lady," the smuggler shouted impatiently. "I need to get some cigarettes."

She didn't budge.

"Hey, you! Didn't I tell you it's dangerous to stay here?" the man shouted again.

"You should leave now," Parvaaneh told Navid.

She embraced him once more before dropping her arms.

As she was about to turn, Navid grabbed her arm. "Promise me you'll go and stay with Uncle Reza or with Sima after you've turned the house over to the buyer," Navid murmured into her ears, "at least until you find a place to lease. Okay?"

"Tell your sister to get in or I'll go," the man shouted. "Like you, I also don't want to die."

"Okay, we heard you," Navid yelled toward the driver and then hugged his sister one last time. "I'll bring you to the other side when I am settled. You know that, don't you? Yes?"

Parvaaneh was silent.

"It won't take long. I promise."

Parvaaneh shook her head. "Don't worry about me. I am a woman, I'll survive."

She straightened the collar of the brown waterproof jacket she'd bought for him. "Take care of yourself, and don't forget to call," she said before returning to the car and closing the passenger door.

Parvaaneh looked back as soon as the car started moving away. Navid ran up an embankment toward the woods and disappeared into the trees.

She hesitated, then turned around and looked at the road ahead. The driver was going full speed, taking her farther and farther from her brother. She suddenly started shivering and bent over to ease a sharp pain in her stomach.

"Are you all right?" The driver stopped the car.

It was as if a million butterflies, all black, were beating their wings in her head, smothering her. She could hardly breathe. And deep inside, a voice was telling her that something bad was going to happen to Navid; that he was in danger; that she should immediately go back and help him. She held her head between her hands.

The driver got out and opened the passenger door for her. "What's wrong, lady?" he said. *"Lanat bar Sheytaan."*

She only regained her composure when the driver pulled her out of the car. He went around to his side of the vehicle, brought out a thermos he kept under the driver's seat, and offered her a sip. Parvaaneh took a gulp. The water was stale and hot.

"Now say God's name and get back inside."

Instead, she turned and ran back the way they had come. Her feet carried her along the road; her body flew as if her previous panic had doubled her strength.

"Wait!" the man shouted after her. "What are you doing? Are you crazy? I am not going to wait here for you."

She could not have cared less about the man's shouting, or the sound of the car starting and then driving away.

The cool air refreshed her. She inhaled deeply as her arms swung by her side and her feet propelled her forward at full steam. She veered off the road and along the short trail through the woods. With each breath, she felt the nasty black butterflies fly free, turn to colored ones, and fly with her out toward the Aras.

When Parvaaneh, out of breath, reached the riverbank, she saw that Navid had made it only to the middle of the river. His black head bobbing on the water was all she could see from that distance. She made her way to the river's edge to watch his progress, but the sound of traffic from the road drew her attention: it was an engine, one that sounded as if it belonged to a vehicle much bigger than the smuggler's worn-out car.

When she heard the car come to a stop, she turned back and scrambled up the muddy rise. If she could intercept whoever was approaching, maybe she could keep them busy long enough for Navid to make his way to safety. Before stepping out toward the road, she stopped and glanced through the trees one more time to see if Navid had made any more progress.

Stepping out of the woods, she saw—too late—two armed men in khaki desert military fatigues. They ran toward Parvaaneh, their guns trained on her. Fortunately, as the color of their uniforms indicated, they belonged to the army. The Revolutionary Guards' fatigues were green.

"What were you up to down there by the river, lady?" one of them, a bearded corporal, asked in a thick Azeri accent. The private, a lanky, pimple-faced man, stood some steps behind him, still aiming his gun at her. He looked down at the hem of Parvaaneh's black coat, dirty with mud.

She answered in Azeri, her mother's tongue, in an effort to appear as a local, to look less suspicious. She was aware of her Farsi accent. "I went down to see the river, I was on my way—"

"Really?" The corporal didn't let Parvaaneh finish. He turned to the private. "Go and check down there. I'll take her to the station."

"I...you know..."—Parvaaneh blocked the private's way and continued—"wanted to go to the village. I paid a driver to take me there but..." She left her sentence unfinished and looked up the road, as if after a departing car. "Didn't you see it?"

"No," the private said, sizing her up. "What kind of car was it?"

"I don't know about the brand, but it wasn't a Paykan."

"Maybe he went that way. We came from Astara," the private said, trying to push his way past Parvaaneh to reach the trail.

Parvaaneh stopped him again. "It was my fault. I told him I wanted to see the river. I didn't think he would be so impatient." She forced herself to cry. "He left without me. Who is going to take me to the village now?"

"Which village?"

"Namin. I came to buy free-range eggs and dairy from local farmers." She sat on her knees and started wailing, knowing that her answer was so bizarre that even a child would know she was lying.

The private shouted at her to compose herself, and then shook his head. Lowering his tone, as if talking to himself, he added, "Only Tehrani people would do such a strange thing." Even though her story made no sense, the private seemed to believe it.

The corporal did not look convinced; his expression, however, indicated confusion. Good! Parvaaneh continued to moan, rocking her body back and forth. "What should I do now? Can you take me to the village? Please."

"We'll take you to Astara and you can get the bus home from there," the private said.

"But I want to go to the village! My aunt won't accept me if I don't have what she sent me to get. Last night, the old woman craved free-run eggs and local butter and cheese badly. She said, 'Don't come back before you get them.' Now what can I tell her?" Parvaaneh was amazed at herself, instantly making up an entire story this way. Her great-aunt, who could hardly hear a thing, would probably just shake her head in amazement if asked to confirm Parvaaneh's story.

"You can find a new driver in Astara."

"But I don't have any money left. I already gave it to the other driver. Couldn't you take me to the village? Please!" she said in a theatrical way.

The private turned to his superior for an answer.

"Leave the woman to me—she's lying," the corporal

shouted. "I told you to go and see if anyone is down by the river."

"Yes, sir." This time, the private passed Parvaaneh before she could get in his way.

"I'll send somebody to pick you up," the corporal shouted after the private. Then he turned to Parvaaneh. "Pull yourself together and get in."

She got up and climbed into the Jeep, beside the corporal. The private had just reached the aspens marking the edge of the trail. The corporal shouted after him. "If you see anyone swimming, shoot him before he reaches the other side. Shoot the bastard." Then he sat back and cranked up the engine.

PARVAANEH SAT ALONE in an office. With its almost empty walls and minimal furniture, including a rusty metal table and one chair with a black vinyl seat, the space looked like a teenage boy's room. Like Nasser's room before he left Iran. "I can't let you go until you've answered some questions," the corporal had said before he left. "Wait here. The sergeant will be with you soon."

The police station was outside Astara in a protected area fenced by barbed wire, overlooking the mountains. At each corner, a guard post stood over the yard. As Parvaaneh had gotten out of the car, a military convoy passed by. The corporal waved at the soldiers crammed inside before guiding Parvaaneh into the building. He took Parvaaneh to the main office, to the left of the corridor. Parvaaneh sat herself on the only chair, wondering where the sergeant was going to sit. The paint on the walls was dirty and already peeling. Pictures of Imam Khomeini and his future heir, Ayatollah Montazeri, hung side by side above the desk. They loomed over Parvaaneh.

There was a smaller room just off of this one, separated by a half-open sliding door. As soon as the corporal left, Parvaaneh crossed the room and peeked through. There was a foldable aluminium bed set by the wall, with a thin gray blanket on top. On a coat rack facing the bed hung some men's clothing—pajamas and a sleeveless sweatshirt. A small window on the wall to the left overlooked the back of the building. It was closed. After this quick inspection, Parvaaneh returned to her chair and sat straight and still, waiting for the sergeant to show up.

After a while, Parvaaneh laid her head on the metal table. Its cool surface gave her a chill. The minutes passed and again she felt a surge of anxiety in her stomach with every breath. The black butterflies were back in her head, and they'd brought with them a throbbing urge to get out, to go back to the river and make sure Navid wasn't dead. It was silent outside except for the occasional sound of a car passing by. She got up again and paced the room. Had they arrested Navid? If so, would they bring him here or send him somewhere else? If she stayed here, she might be able to find out. She decided she shouldn't leave.

Parvaaneh went back and sat down, her gaze fixed on the door. The imaginary butterflies had made their way from her head to her breast, flapping their wings with the same rhythm as the corporal's words when he'd ordered the private to "shoot the poor bastard."

The good thing was that Parvaaneh was still dealing with men from the military, and not the Revolutionary Guards. The lower-rank army men, like the private, were ordinary soldiers doing their military service. Navid could have been one of them if he'd been conscripted and sent to a safe place like Astara, far from the war zones in the south and west. The higher-rank army men were officers who had completed their training and started their service during the shah's time. They were not known for their revolutionary sentiments and could be more lenient toward men like Navid who escaped the military service. The sergeant Parvaaneh was about to meet belonged to this group.

The sergeant arrived an hour later in a wheelchair. In his lap sat a police radio, its antenna pointing at Parvaaneh. Both his legs had been amputated above the knees. Landmines, probably, she thought as she jumped to her feet. Navid could have ended up like this, had he not just escaped. Perhaps this sergeant was one of the army officers sent to the front line in the early days of war. Perhaps his position as the head of this remote station was his reward for defending the country and pushing back the Iraqi army that had invaded Iran and captured a few cities. Parvaaneh had both pity and respect for the sergeant. If not for men like him, the Iraqis would have reached Tehran a week after they invaded, as they'd planned. God knows how many women would have been raped and how many children and civilians would have been killed.

"Sit down," the sergeant said.

Parvaaneh sat down as the sergeant wheeled himself behind the desk and placed the radio receiver on it. Like so many members of the military from the shah's time, the sergeant sported a mustache instead of a beard, which made Parvaaneh feel comfortable. She expected he would let her go very soon.

"What were you doing down by the river?" the sergeant asked. He spoke with the accent of people from northern Iran. Men from there were known for their liberal attitude toward women.

"Well, I was . . . you know . . . how to put it," Parvaaneh stammered, trying to remember the story she'd made up earlier. As it came back to her, she continued in the even tone she'd always used to calm Navid down. "I was at Ardebil to see my aunt, Mr. Sergeant. She sent me to the village to get her fresh, local food for breakfast. She is originally from Namin, but now lives in the city. Last night, she woke in the middle of the night to tell me she craved eggs and dairy from her village. Next morning, the first thing she did was to send me to fetch them for her. I paid a driver to take me there. He took the money and left me in the middle of the road. I wanted to see the river. He said he would wait for me, but he didn't. Thanks to God, your men came by. I have no idea what I would have done if they hadn't shown up."

Catching her breath after the long speech, Parvaaneh hoped the sergeant wouldn't send anyone to interrogate her great-aunt, although she was quite confident that the old woman wouldn't understand a word.

The sergeant gazed suspiciously at her face. He had piercing eyes Parvaaneh could not bear to look at. She lowered her head. Even so, she could feel him investigating her features. Maybe it was because they had arrested Navid. Their resemblance was unmistakable.

"Are you from Turkmen Sahra?" the man asked. Parvaaneh's narrow, slanted black eyes, thin lips, and small nose often led people to take her for somebody from that region.

"No, I am from Tehran. But my mother is originally from Ardebil."

"Do you have your ID?"

Parvaaneh handed the sergeant her birth certificate.

It was good she had listened to the smuggler's advice and brought it; at the time, his suggestion had seemed counterintuitive to her and Navid. She tried not to cower, and looked away. There were dents on the wall that seemed to have been made by a sharp object. A table? This table, perhaps? Parvaaneh's skin crawled as she touched the cold metal surface.

"Tell me the truth. We know why people come here, especially nowadays," the sergeant said. "We catch runaway soldiers every day. The river gave up two of them just yesterday. The Aras makes our job easy; it kills them off even if we can't catch them."

The sergeant chuckled at his macabre joke, and Parvaaneh's heart lurched. The butterflies in her chest flew up her throat, beating their wings at full speed. She almost gagged as she lowered her head to prevent the sergeant from seeing the concern in her eyes.

"Tell the truth and make your life easier."

"I don't know what you're talking about." Parvaaneh scratched her head through her scarf. "I told you, I wanted to go to the village to buy —"

"Was it your husband or your son?" he asked as he opened her birth certificate. Parvaaneh went blank as the man checked the second page, where the names of one's spouse and children are recorded. She gasped as she remembered Navid calling her *Ana*. It took her a minute to get over her confusion and realize her mistake: Navid was only her brother, and unlike the names of one's children, those of one's brothers and sisters are not recorded.

Actually, nothing was recorded on the second page of her birth certificate; she did not even have a husband.

The only way the sergeant could tell that she and Navid were related was to see her brother. Even though they were many years apart in age, they looked so alike it was as if they were twins.

Glancing up from the birth certificate, the sergeant looked even more confused than she did. "You never married?"

"No."

"You're not ugly!" the man's eyes roved over her.

"I took care of my old father. He is ill," she lied.

"Where is your mother?"

"She died many years ago, when I was very young."

"Do you have brothers or sisters?"

"No. All of the children after me were stillborn."

"Strange stories you make up, lady. Do you really expect me to believe them?"

"I'm not lying. You can check things on me."

"I will surely do that." The sergeant put her birth certificate on the table but continued looking intensely at Parvaaneh, sizing her up.

"Who do you live with?"

"I already told you. With my father."

"Is he paying for you?"

"Yes, *Al hamd-o-Allah*. We live on his retirement money," Parvaaneh mumbled.

"Is it enough?"

"Sir, I don't understand why you arrested me." She stood up. "Can I go now?"

"Maybe later. When I am convinced you're not lying." The sergeant motioned with his head, suggesting that she should sit back down. She did, feeling choked under his gaze as he constantly stroked his mustache with two fingers. He did not ask any more questions.

Parvaaneh released her breath only when a knock on the door drew the sergeant's attention.

"Come in."

A soldier Parvaaneh hadn't seen before entered, carrying two large glasses of tea on a tray. He placed the first glass in front of the sergeant. His left hand was wrapped in a bandage, and fresh blood oozed out onto the white cloth. The sergeant wrinkled his nose and turned his face away from the soldier's hand and back to Parvaaneh.

"Put down the tea for the lady and leave."

The soldier placed the second glass in front of Parvaaneh without casting a single glance at her. "Do you need anything else, sir?"

"No. Just leave." He waved his hand at the soldier.

The sergeant started drinking his tea as soon as the man left, scrutinizing Parvaaneh the entire time. The silence was unbearable. Parvaaneh's finger burned as she touched her glass, and yet the man was gulping his tea down. His lips, framed by his bushy mustache, were wet like those of a wild dog that had just ripped the first bite from its living prey.

"This war has left many women husbandless or without a male guardian," he said, speaking as if to himself. "There are not enough men for every woman. Someone should take care of them."

Parvaaneh put her glass down. The man's rambling was directed at her, and she felt the danger in his words. Her immediate thought was to to get up and ask the man to let her go, but the sergeant's radio receiver crackled before she could move. Parvaaneh sat alert, listening to what he was telling the person on the other end of the line.

"Stay there. I am coming over," he said, his tone signaling that an important event was happening out there at that very second. Out there somewhere. Could it be about Navid's capture or death?

A shiver ran down Parvaaneh's spine. How could she find out? As she looked over at the man preparing to leave, she came up with a plan. She would stay in the police station—at any price—and get her answer out of the sergeant. She had heard that the killed escapees were either buried in some unknown grave or thrown back into the river. Their families would never receive news of their fate. She couldn't be one of them; she couldn't go home waiting for the news of her brother's death that might never arrive. A life in waiting was no life. If Navid had been killed, she wanted to know right now. There was even a possibility she could get the body, given that this man looked like somebody she could negotiate with.

The sergeant put the radio back in his lap and wheeled himself out from behind the table. "You can go, lady. Don't forget to take your birth certificate. Also, next time remember not to hop in a private car. "

She didn't stand up. "You know, sir, the truth is that... I lied. That driver dumped me there on the road after he ... after he finished his thing. He didn't even pay me."

She broke into tears and started trembling, knowing how much she had degraded herself with this lie that suggested she was a prostitute. But the words had already poured out of her mouth, leaving her shuddering as hard as if an earthquake had just happened.

The sergeant had already reached the door, but he paused now. Parvaaneh saw his hands press on the wheels in order to turn his chair around. She wailed loudly to further capture his attention; it was too late to change her humiliating plan now.

The sergeant turned around and wheeled himself over to her. "So I was correct?" he asked, his face close to hers.

"Yes!" Parvaaneh cried. "I am so miserable, but I have to pay for my sick father!"

"But why come here? So far from Tehran? Do you really live there, or did you lie about that too?"

"I live in Tehran, but if anyone finds out what I'm doing, my father will lose face." Parvaaneh dropped her head. "I go with bus drivers who travel between cities. My father and neighbors think I work at some rich people's villa in a northern city by the Caspian Sea."

"I see." The sergeant rubbed his mustache with two fingers again. "I wish I could help you, but my wife already has a housemaid—a poor local widow who has three children—but let me..."

The crackling of the radio receiver cut the sergeant off. He picked it up and held it to his ear. "I said I'm coming."

"You stay here." He turned to Parvaaneh as he hung up. "Maybe I can find some other way to help you. I'll be back soon." He paused before leaving. "Hand me your birth certificate from the desk." She did as he requested.

So Parvaaneh was left alone for a second time in the same room—this time without an ID and feeling more desperate than she had when she'd first been brought in. For a few seconds, she was unable to make sense of what she had done. What would happen to her now that she'd pretended she was a prostitute? She pushed the thought from her mind, telling herself that she should be concerned only about what had happened to Navid, and not about what might happen to her. She paced the room again to the smaller room at the back. There was nothing going on there. It appeared to be sleeping quarters. She turned, went back to the exit door, put her ear against the door, and listened. The corridor was silent. She walked back to the chair and sat, still alert and listening, but she did not hear any footsteps for the next hour. After a while, her body went completely numb. It was late afternoon and the room was hot.

Sometime later, Parvaaneh heard a convoy drive up, followed by the sound of men talking. She ran into the yard, only to find the corporal and some other men climbing into a patrol van, which sped off. The soldier with the bandaged hand appeared. He nodded at the purse hanging from Parvaaneh's shoulder and asked her why she was there.

"I was looking for the washroom."

"It's inside. Come with me. I'll show you."

When Parvaaneh stepped out of the washroom, the soldier was gone and the corridor was empty again. She thought of sneaking out and finding a way back to Tehran, but she remembered the reason for her lie and chose to go back to the room and wait again.

. . .

IT WAS GETTING dark when the sergeant finally opened the door. He looked at her and his face lit up. Parvaaneh's first impulse was to knock his wheelchair over and run away, but she stayed frozen. She fixed her gaze on her shaking legs as the man approached, thinking that he was a decent man with a chivalric attitude. Maybe she could tell him the truth and ask him if he knew anything about her brother. Hopefully, he would know nothing about Navid, which would mean that her brother had safely crossed to the other side.

"Listen," the sergeant said, "I've figured out a way to help you and your father. I want you to stay with me. You know what I mean — but it should be done in the proper way. Temporary marriage is for times like this."

Parvaaneh could not have been more shocked if she'd heard Nasser make such a proposal to a widowed Mrs. Monir. So much for the high principles she'd stupidly thought this man had! At least members of the Revolutionary Guards stood on high moral ground. Her voice trembled as she finally answered. "But I can't stay here for a long time, sir. I should go back to Tehran to my father. He is sick."

"I am not intending to keep you here permanently. As I told you earlier, I have my own family. I am doing this for God's sake. You stay with me for one or two nights and I'll pay your marriage portion. It is enough for you to go back and take care of your father for three months and ten days until you're allowed to remarry. You don't need to worry about getting pregnant. I'll be careful because I don't want to pay alimony for another child. After this period, I recommend that you to go to the Foundation of Martyrs and War Casualties. You show them the temporary marriage certificate as a proof that you were my *sigheh*. They can help you find your next temporary husband. In this way you won't sin and you'll be safe. You are still young. You can continue like this for a while. God willing, one day a good man will marry you permenantly."

The sergeant's words washed over Parvaaneh like the waves of a swelling river and drowned her heart. She had made a huge mistake, and now it was too late to change anything or escape. Her knees were only an inch away from his wheelchair.

"Should I take your silence as a yes?" the sergeant asked after a while.

Ready to burst into tears, Parvaaneh could not open her mouth. But no, this wasn't the time for self-pity. She clenched her jaw and put her hand on the stump of the sergeant's right leg, and immediately felt disgusted with herself. But what else she could do at this point? Her body was her bargaining tool. She had come on this journey for Navid, and she would see it through.

The sergeant pulled himself back, letting her hand drop. "I want it clean," he said. "I'll take you to a clergyman, and he can perform the ritual." He wheeled himself to the door. "I'll make the necessary arrangements."

Parvaaneh felt completely numb after the sergeant left. Not being able to make sense of the events of the day, she sat there, wishing that what had just happened was not real. She didn't know how much time had passed when the soldier with the bandaged hand came in and brought her a dish of rice and kebab with a Coke for dinner. He also had a black plastic bag, which he placed beside the tray of food. Even though she was hungry, she was too anxious to touch the food. She opened the bag and found a long and loose cotton dress with a flower pattern and a white chador. So the sergeant and his shameless proposal were real. And he could reappear at any minute.

Parvaaneh felt nothing as she went to the small room with the bed at the back of the office, closed the sliding door, and changed into her new clothes. It was as if her body was empty inside, and a ghost who had somehow sneaked in was moving it around. The ghost was thoughtful, like a caring sister. In order not to have her clothes on display, it folded and hid them in the black bag and slid it under the bed. After a while, however, it left Parvaaneh by herself and vanished through the closed door.

Some time later, the private she had met in the morning came to let her know that the sergeant was waiting for her in front of the station. She followed the man outside to where a black suv was parked. The sergeant was already buckled in on the front seat, his folded wheelchair placed behind him on the back seat. Parvaaneh sat beside it and listened closely, hoping she would be able to find out something about Navid by eavesdropping on any conversation the sergeant and the private might have along the way.

The car passed the town's main square, where an abandoned tank rested on a flowerbed, its gun pointing skyward. It was already dusk, and the sky streaked with red resembled the bandage on the hand of the soldier who'd brought her the tea and food. Neither the sergeant nor the private said a word. The private parked at the end of a narrow alley that the suv could not enter. Parvaaneh waited inside until he removed the wheelchair, unfolded it, and placed the sergeant in it. It was obvious that the sergeant was too heavy for the lanky private. Parvaaneh glanced at his sweaty forehead with compassion as she got out of the vehicle. Ordinary soldiers like him, who were doing their military service, had to put up with all kinds of things. But at least this private had not been sent to the front line; his mother must be very happy. The young man threw Parvaaneh a look of pity in return. Her new look—covered in a white chador but wearing her old shoes, brown and flat—was no doubt the look of a destitute prostitute.

The private wheeled the sergeant up the middle of the alley. The mullah lived in a large, renovated building that sat among dilapidated two-storey houses. The narrow street with a gutter running through the middle was lit by the lights on a *hejleh*—a metal frame in the shape of a house, decorated with several mirrors and lights, among which the picture of a recent martyr hung. The *hejleh* stood by the house of the mullah's neighbor. Parvaaneh couldn't help but think that *hejleh* was also the name for a decorated nuptial chamber meant for newlywed couples, the place where a groom took his bride on the first night of the marriage.

Parvaaneh had no idea where the sergeant was going to take her for the night. Hopefully to a room with no lights, so she wouldn't be able to see him. If she wasn't able to find out what had happened to Navid by the time she was alone with the sergeant, her plan was to knock the man down and run away. After all, she still had her legs. She would cross Aras and flee the country. Given that the sergeant had her birth certificate and could find her, she had no other way.

The mullah was a short man who limped; his turban tilted to the right as he leaned forward to greet the sergeant in his wheelchair. They kissed each other on the cheek. "How are your kids and your wife, Sergeant?"

"Fine, thank you."

Parvaaneh hoped that the sergeant wouldn't take her to his home, where his wife and children lived.

The mullah invited them to a small room separated by a curtain from the living room. The floor was covered by a red Kashan carpet. A folded blanket sat by the front wall for guests to sit on, and three pillows rested against the wall. Parvaaneh sat on the blanket and leaned against one of the pillows. The mullah sat on his knees, facing her, and the sergeant wheeled himself to a spot beside the blanket. A Koran lay beside the mullah. Next to it were a pen, a piece of paper, and her birth certificate.

A few frames hung on the wall with sayings from religious texts. After a while, a woman appeared, keeping her black chador very tight, covering her chin and mouth. She pulled back the curtain, pushed in a tray of tea, and then left without a word.

"Everything under control in the area?" the mullah asked.

The sergeant nodded. He suspended a sugar cube in his mouth and gulped his tea. "I am here for the God-willed action," he said, nodding in Parvaaneh's direction.

"Yes. Men of God should take care of widows and women during war. That's what the Prophet Mohammad—our blessings to him and his household—ordered them to do," the Mullah said, looking straight into Parvaaneh's eyes. "Otherwise, Muslim women deviate from God's path." The mullah poured his tea onto his saucer and dropped a sugar cube in it. He brought the saucer to his lips and sucked the tea from the edge. "You are doing the right thing, Sergeant. You are a man of God."

Next, the mullah turned to her. "I hear you are taking care of your old father?"

"Yes," Parvaaneh said under her breath.

"That is good. Taking care of the parents is one of a Muslim's main responsibilities. God bless you for doing so. But you should also think about your own life, your future. There are many good men who are casualties of the war and are in need of the care of good Muslim women like yourself. Keep up the good deeds."

Parvaaneh's tea cooled as the mullah performed the wedding ceremony. He began by reading verses from the Koran and then lifted her birth certificate, opened it, and turned to Parvaaneh. "Khanoom Parvaaneh Ehya, do you give me your consent to make you the wife of this good man of God for one week?"

Parvaaneh had a hard time to find her voice. "I have to go back to Tehran tomorrow. My old father is waiting for me." She made sure to keep her head low.

"The lady doesn't consent for one week, Sergeant. What would you like to do?" the mullah asked.

"One night is fine," the sergeant answered.

"Khanoom Parvaaneh Ehya, do you give me your consent to turn you into the wife of this sergeant for tonight, this good man who gave his legs fighting the enemies of God?"

Before Parvaaneh could answer, the sergeant said, "Excuse me, you didn't mention the wedding money, *Haj agha*?"

The mullah asked Parvaaneh the same question again, but this time he added that the contract was under the condition that the sergeant would pay her ten thousand tomans as her wedding money.

The sergeant took a bundle of bills from a small brown bag he had hidden beside him on the wheelchair and passed it to the mullah to place in front of Parvaaneh. He then started rubbing his mustache with two fingers.

She stared at the bundle for a brief moment, and yet the image before her eyes was that of Navid caught in the foamy water. She knew the two men were waiting for her answer, but her mouth was clogged, as if she were underwater. She gathered all of her strength to overcome the stream of disturbing thoughts surging through her mind and breathed out, "Yes. I'll give my consent."

"And so, I pronounce you man and wife for one night. Congratulations, and may God bless both of you." The mullah then took the pen and paper to add new information to what was already written there. "I write here that the marital contract is valid for one night only," he proclaimed. He slid the paper inside her birth certificate and passed Parvaaneh's ID to her. "You'll need to take the certificate with you to the Foundation of Martyrs and War Casualties to prove your marriage. As you know, temporary marriages are not recorded in birth certificates."

The sergeant wheeled himself to the door as soon as Parvaaneh put the document and the marriage money in her purse. "Stay longer," the mullah said.

"No, thank you. We have to go."

"At least let the lady have her tea," the mullah said, straightening his turban.

Parvaaneh pushed the cup back and got up. "It's okay, *Haj agha*." The private was waiting for them out in the alley, and she wanted to be back in the suv as soon as possible. She still hoped something of what had happened that day might come up in conversation between the sergeant and the private during the ride.

"My door is always open to you, Sergeant. I am at your service any time you need me." The mullah knelt and kissed the sergeant on both cheeks. Parvaaneh saw the sergeant pass a few bills to the man.

The private drove them without a word, leaving Parvaaneh alone with her thoughts. Was she really a temporary wife to this man, and did she have to spend the night with him? The butterflies that had been sitting silently for a while in the pit of her stomach began to swirl around again. "Oh no, for God's sake, please calm down," she spoke to them in her mind. When they didn't stop, she thought of opening the car door and throwing herself out. She was certain now that she wouldn't get any information out of this man. So wasn't it better to let herself die under the wheels of a car than die from fear? Without Navid, her life had no meaning. But who knew if Navid was dead? He'd promised that they would be reunited as soon as he got settled in Germany, or any other country that would accept him. "Only one or two years," he'd told her. "I'll get you out of this hell and take care of you."

The private pulled into the police station once again. Parvaaneh had no desire to get out. She held onto the edge of her seat with both hands as the private unbuckled the sergeant and lifted him into his wheelchair. He was weary from moving the heavy man, and sweat beaded on his forehead. He wiped it with the back of his hand and stood up to catch his breath. Noticing Parvaaneh still sitting in the car, he stuck his head through the passenger door and chided her. "Why are you still there? Move yourself, lady. I have to go."

Parvaaneh got out and reluctantly followed them. The guards looked away as the three of them passed through the yard, as if they didn't recognize them. She paused at the entrance to the building, unwilling to move farther. She had led herself into a trap and now had no idea how to escape.

"What are you waiting for?" the sergeant asked. Parvaaneh shuffled forward and followed the man down the main hall.

The sergeant entered the same room on the left where Parvaaneh had spent the afternoon. He wheeled himself to the end of the office and into the small room at the back. With his back to Parvaaneh, he asked her to come and turn on the light.

As Parvaaneh stepped into the dingy room, the noxious smell of mold overwhelmed her. She flicked the light switch on the wall to her right and turned to watch the man pushing the gray blanket back and heaving himself from his wheelchair onto the bed. He lay on his back.

"Take off your chador. We are *mahram* now." He stressed the word *mahram*," which indicated that since he was her husband he could see her without hijab.

"Can I open the window?" Parvaaneh asked while hanging her purse on the coat stand over top of the pajamas hanging there.

"Yes, but shut the door."

She opened the window slightly and trudged to the bed. She took off her shoes and dropped her chador on the bed where the man's legs would have reached, if he'd had any. She sat on the edge, the farthest place from his reach, and looked down at her dress, which bore a flower pattern similar to the one on the sheets that covered the bed. "It is still early to sleep. Let's talk first. We do not know each other yet."

"What do you like to talk about?" The man had already unbuttoned his uniform. Soon, the part of his chest that was not covered by his white undershirt was revealed. It was covered by thick black hair.

"I'd like to know a little more about you, if you'd allow me. You said we are *mahram* now."

He leaned on his side. "What do you want to know?"

"Well..." Parvaaneh's mind was blank.

"Help me take this off," the man ordered as he struggled with his undershirt.

Parvaaneh hiked the garment up over his head and removed it. The man breathed out and turned to Parvaaneh, an expression of relief on his face. "I am this man you see—with no legs. But don't worry, I can make you happy." He rubbed his mustache against her side, which gave her goosebumps.

She lay down and, turning to the sergeant, asked, "You left me alone for a long time this afternoon. Where did you go?"

Instead of answering her, the man pushed up her dress and shoved his hand under it.

"Did you hear my question?"

The sergeant screwed up his face. "After some business."

"By business, you mean—"

The sergeant did not let her complete her question. He yanked at the side of her dress. "Take this off."

She did not obey. Instead, she pulled her dress back down. The man grabbed her thigh and started rubbing it vigorously. The movement sent a chill through her body, but she continued talking. "I want to know about your job. I am very impressed, very proud that you accepted me as your wife. You should be set as an example. Even though you're a casualty, you still fight enemies, like the ones you went after today." The words poured out of Parvaaneh's mouth—words she could scarely believe she was speaking.

"What is this you are talking about? My job has nothing to do with you." The sergeant looked at her in the way a wise man stares at an idiot.

Parvaaneh had no answer for him.

"Now let's go about our business and see what I have to show you here." He opened his fly and took out his penis, his revolver still attached to his waist. "Look at this. Is this what you want? Yes? Hold it." He reached out and clutched Parvaaneh's hand, pulling it toward his genitals, a half-erect brownish lump. Her hand brushed against the revolver case as the man pushed her hand down toward his ugly organ.

Parvaaneh felt vomit rise in her throat. Even though she had opened the window, the rotten smell filling the room filled her nostrils. She yanked her hand out of the sergeant's grasp and jumped out of the bed.

"Where are you going?" he yelled after her. "Come back here! I order you! I am your husband now."

She had already reached the sliding door. Her fingers were on the handle when she remembered she was wearing only a dress. She turned back for her white chador and shoes, but it was the sergeant who grabbed her attention. He had already pulled himself to the edge of the bed and was now reaching for the wheelchair that she had pushed away from the bed in her escape. Parvaaneh immediately turned around, reached for the light switch on the wall, and turned it off.

"I can't do it in the light," she said, stepping toward her shoes, which were on the floor by the wheelchair.

"Damn Satan," he grunted. "You women are so tricky. Now come back here. You cannot refuse me. You said yes before the clergy and collected your wedding money."

As the man shuffled and jabbered, Parvaaneh spotted the white chador in the dark. Partly stuck under the sergeant, it hung from the edge of the bed.

"I am coming. Move over a bit," she said.

As Parvaaneh approached the bed, her knees began to shake. But she didn't stop. She told herself that she was much stronger than this cripple, and that she should not be afraid. She could put the filthy pillow on the sergeant's face and sit on it until every movement in him receded. Then she could run to the road, to the village, and up to the river. She could cross it and join Navid.

But she had underestimated the man. As soon as she bent over and reached to grab the chador, he clutched her arm with one hand. Using the other, he pulled her to the bed and slid her hips underneath him. Parvaaneh had no voice to scream, no power left in her arms and legs as the man nailed her down by pressing his chest against hers. He was as heavy as a tree stump and his revolver poked into her side. She turned her face and felt his mustache prickle against her cheek. Even if she yelled, what good it would do? She was in a police station guarded by men under the sergeant's command. She resigned herself to death, and let her mind go completely blank.

Parvaaneh came to as the call to prayer played from the speakers in the station. She realized where she was when she sensed the sergeant wriggling beside her. He gave her several hard nudges on the side, indicating that she should get up, turn on the light, and help him back into his clothes and onto the wheelchair.

Feeling sore, she sat up only to notice blood on her dress and the sheets.

"Dirty woman. You should have told me you had your period," the sergeant grumbled. "Now help me. I've got to clean myself."

She pulled his shirt over his head and helped him to his wheelchair without looking at him. She was afraid she might hit him if their eyes met. The sergeant was also furious. He kept swearing at her: "You dirty bitch. Why didn't you say anything about having your period?"

As soon as the man wheeled himself out, Parvaaneh closed the sliding door and took off the dress. She cleaned the blood from her thighs and between them using the white chador she found crumpled on the floor. Next, she pulled out the bag of clothes that she'd hidden under bed. Then, she ripped a piece of fabric from the sheets to use as a pad. Finally, she grabbed her purse off the coat rack and removed the temporary marriage certificate and the bundle of money the sergeant had given her. After tearing the shameful document into pieces, she felt a bit better and could put on her clothes. Before leaving, though, she dumped the blood-soaked chador, the sheets, the white dress, and the dirty money inside the black plastic bag, and slid the bag under the bed.

She left the small room, and then the office itself,

only to be shocked by the presence of a man in the semi-dark hallway on the other side of the door. It was the grave-looking and bearded corporal. "Come with me. The sergeant has ordered me to take you to the bus station in Astara to catch the seven-thirty bus to Tehran."

AS PARVAANEH BLINKS herself out of the horrible memory, the bus she is on slowly passes the bookstores across from the University of Tehran, which has been closed for two years since the cultural revolution. People stand in front of the bookstore windows, browsing. After a few seconds, her attention returns inside the bus. While her thoughts were transporting her to other places, the woman with the bracelets left. Parvaaneh remains positioned in her seat a few rows behind the driver. The driver's mirror shows that the back of the bus, like the front, is still packed, and that, like her, everybody else is feeling impatient to get out. She stands up to scout the traffic ahead. The street is crammed with cars and motorcycles. The sidewalk is bursting with a crowd of soldiers, women in black coats and chadors, and many people shopping at busy doughnut shops, juice shops, street vendors, and food coupon dealers. Farther ahead, she can see the monument in the middle of Revolution Square. If only the bus would move, it would get to its destination very soon. Parvaaneh sits down, thinking that, from there, she needs only to walk two blocks. In no time at all, she'll arrive at Sima's. Are other passengers also like her, eager to get out and rush to a place where an important message might be waiting for them?

In the front, new passengers are on board, their bodies pressed against one another. It's a good opportunity for men to grope women, which is just what a skinny man wearing blue jeans, a flashy T-shirt, and trendy black leather shoes is doing by rubbing himself against a young woman sandwiched between him and another woman in a navy-blue coat. The girl moves forward slightly and leans over Parvaaneh. Her heavy breathing makes Parvaaneh squeeze herself toward the window to make more room. Parvaaneh can tell she is bleeding again. Her body is soaked in sweat, and she feels trapped — the same way she did in the small room in the police station. She wishes the bus would get to the last stop as soon as possible. But the bus is stuck, and so are Parvaaneh and the young girl above her. Parvaaneh can see a chain of sweat forming on her forehead. The old man in front who, like Parvaaneh, has been on board from the start, again bids the passengers to send their blessing to the Prophet Mohammad and his family, as if it will make the bus grow wings and fly over the traffic.

"*Allah-o-ma sale ala Mohammad va ale Mohammad.*"
Several people, including the woman in the navy-blue coat and a man in green military pants, chant after him.

Parvaaneh and the girl stay silent, one choking because of what is being inflicted on her in the present by the young man who again presses his crotch against her behind, and one choking because of what happened to her two days ago, the memory of which she is unable to push out of her mind. The black butterflies are back in her throat, flapping their wings against the knot in her scarf from inside. Soon they start to multiply and swarm her entire body.

AT THE BUS station in Astara, where Parvaaneh had waited to be shuttled back to Tehran, she'd considered slipping away to the village closest to the Aras; she could ask the locals whether they had found anyone who had drowned. But the corporal hadn't left her alone long enough to try. She'd even thought of getting off the bus midway through the journey and going back, but it was too risky. What if she were arrested again and sent back to the sergeant?

Lacking any concrete knowledge about what had happened to Navid, she'd decided to ask her heart for an answer. When her mother was still alive, she had always said, "Mothers know in their heart how their children are doing. They don't need to see with their eyes." And Parvaaneh was like a mother to her brother. She'd gazed down toward her heart and asked if Navid was alive. She waited for an answer.

But her heart had been silent, just like the Aras. She'd caught a glimpse of it from the bus window where she leaned her head. It was calm and muddy that morning, nothing like the churning she'd witnessed the previous day.

Unlike her heart, her mind spoke—loudly and outrageously. And it gave her orders: *Get off the bus, go down to the river, drown yourself. You are nothing but that piece of dirty sheet between your legs. And Navid is dead. Without him, you are nothing. You sacrificed yourself for him last night. Get out, go down to the river, and throw your corpse into it.*

For the eight hours of that bus ride, which had felt like a lifelong incarceration, Parvaaneh clenched her teeth against the orders issued by her commanding mind. To others, she must have looked like she was asleep, or maybe unconscious. The bus had stopped three times to give its passengers a chance to stretch their legs, but she did not get out even once. The feeling between her legs was damp and sticky, but she didn't budge from her seat, not even when the driver himself came to check on her. "She is breathing," he'd announced to her concerned bus-mates. "The corporal who bought her ticket said she was sick. Perhaps she took some medicine that has knocked her out. I'll shut the door and let her sleep."

. . .

"LAST STOP! EVERYBODY OFF!"

Parvaaneh opens her eyes to the yelling of the driver and the bustling of passengers toward the exits. It takes her a few seconds to realize which bus she is on. It's the one in Tehran, the one taking her to Sima. Still disoriented, she watches the sweaty girl move down the aisle, keeping a safe distance between herself and the young man in the jeans and T-shirt.

Soon, however, she tires of watching her fellow passengers file out. Her mind drifts back to her journey to the Aras with her brother, and her own journey back to Tehran, alone. She had gotten off the bus feeling as if she'd woken from a deadly sleep, sick with the knowledge that she'd returned to the city without the information she had sacrificed so much to discover. On the bus she took from the terminal to go home, she'd pulled her scarf down over her eyes and cried quietly as she turned yet again to her heart for an answer about Navid's survival and did not hear a thing.

The memory makes Parvaaneh anxious again. How is it possible to feel nothing, to know nothing? What about the saying that goes: "A mother's heart is said to be working like a magic mirror, like Jamshid's sacred mirror, revealing how her children are doing wherever they are at the moment." Was this just nonsense? Hadn't she mothered Navid? Why was her heart silent?

Fighting the feeling of being smothered from within, Parvaaneh takes a deep breath and slowly lifts her head from its inclined position, forcing herself to look away from her heart. She is about to slide out of her seat when she sees Navid's face reflected beside the driver's in the rearview mirror. Shocked, she immediately sits upright and stares. Navid's hair falls outside the frame, but the face is surely his, especially those black Tatar eyes and that certain childish innocence.

Parvaaneh grips the handrail and shudders as Navid looks back at her, patiently, without even blinking. From time to time he presses his lips together, stressing the line of his cheekbones. She doesn't take her eyes off her brother until she sees the driver turn around, looking at her and beyond her. Does this image belong to the man who got on the bus after the Saadi Street intersection—where it had almost collided with the taxi—and who now sits a few rows behind her? The young man who stumbled on the steps?

As Parvaaneh squints, trying to test her speculation, the Navid in the mirror imitates her gesture. His stare is so intense that, for just a moment, Parvaaneh looks away, turning her attention toward the empty seats on the right side of the bus, which are fully bathed in sunlight. The blinding light shining off the iron bar hung above them illuminates a floating river of dust and particles. Parvaaneh's gaze crosses this river and returns to the mirror. Transfixed, it lingers there until it finally dawns on Parvaaneh that she has been looking at her own reflection; it is her own face that she took for Navid's.

Instantly, the recognition brings total relief from the suffering caused by the question that has occupied her mind ever since she left Navid at the bank of the Aras and ran up the trail to meet the soldiers. Her heart has finally answered. It has shown Parvaaneh her own face as a confirmation: like her, Navid is alive.

Parvaaneh shakes her head, and a small smile turns up the corners of her mouth. The answer has been here, right before her eyes, from the moment she got on the bus. Had she seen it earlier, she would have known she did not need to hear any news from Sima. She exhales a sigh of relief, which releases the black butterflies inside her. They fly out and exit the bus via the front door. Now, only Parvaaneh and the driver remain on board.

"Last station!" he yells again. "I am turning around."

"I am coming with you," Parvaaneh announces with the new power she has found inside. "I am going back home."

The driver shrugs and closes the automatic doors. In a second, the bus is rolling again. I still have two weeks to cancel the sale of the house, Parvaaneh thinks, if I can pay back the deposit I received plus the 5 percent penalty. She decides that upon arriving home, the first thing she must do is to reach out to Nasser. If he cannot help, she will ask Sima. She is determined to start a new life for herself, and her childhood house is where she will do it.

With this fresh thought, she takes another look out of the window. The monument in the middle of Revolution Square rises amid the yellowish grass as the bus turns around.

Yellow Light

I HAVE COME TO see Arman's girlfriend, Aazin. I am half an hour early. She and Arman finish work at five. I heard from her former boyfriend that Aazin recently got Arman a job at her office. He has given me the address. I wait in an alley.

It is one of Tehran's windy nights; if I were filming, the shadows would be playing havoc with my camera's exposure. I have disguised myself in the same black chador — one that fixes tight around my face with an elastic band and that I used to wear during the ten years I spent visiting Arman in prison. This morning I had to rummage in my storage closet to find it crumpled in a plastic bag under an old shoebox containing my childhood photographs. I am wearing my green headscarf underneath so that the chador, never washed and still holding the filth of those years, will not touch my hair.

People pass by as I shuffle along a brick wall, await-
ing Arman and Aazin. Most of them seem to be rushing
home to have dinner with their families. I am in no
hurry. My family used to be Arman. I catch a glimpse
of him walking past the alley, so I move and follow
him down the sidewalk. He is with Aazin, the woman
whose name means "bundle of lights," as in a bundle of
lights used for celebrating, for showcasing, for illuminating something else. That something else is Arman,
a political hero in many people's eyes, whom she high-
lights with her youthfulness and naïveté. Otherwise —
as Mehrdaad, Aazin's ex-boyfriend and Arman's ex–best
friend put it — there is nothing special about her. Not
like me, he told me. He also told me to come and discover this for myself.

I follow Arman's every step like a camerawoman
on a movie set following an actor, except he doesn't
know I'm there. He strides along, with Aazin at his
side but slightly behind, walking briskly to avoid falling
behind. So this is the woman he started dating when
he was still living with me, the woman he talked to on
the phone for hours, the woman whose name I had to
learn from Mehrdaad. Aazin, a bundle of lights who
adorns Arman's life.

A couple with their children turns onto the sidewalk in front of me and joins the line by a bus stop. I
wait until they pass, keeping an eye on Arman as he

moves farther away and listening to my racing heart thump in my ears. Gripping the strap of my shoulder bag with one shaking hand and holding the chador under my chin with the other, I quickly cut through the crowd and run up the street. "Idiot," someone shouts after me.

I arrive at the intersection of Valiasr and Revolution Streets almost out of breath. They are heading to Tehran's City Theater, perhaps to see a show. A crowd is waiting for the traffic light to change. Searching for Arman, I stand on tiptoe and finally spot his bald head. He and Aazin are standing at the front of the pack. I push myself into the crowd and close the gap separating me from him. Now I am near enough to keep his profile in view but not near enough to be noticed. As soon as I start marveling at Arman's new goatee, he lowers his head toward his girl, which makes me venture even closer. For a moment, I think of ripping the filthy chador from my body, pushing Aazin aside, and taking her place. Instead, I stop beside a tall man with a peaked cap and hide myself behind him. From here I can safely watch Arman without having to see Aazin. He looks different, even behaves differently, like a typecast actor who's found himself in a new role alongside a star.

The red reflection of the traffic light shines on Arman's face. It reminds me of how I fell in love with

him when I saw him onstage at the University of Tehran's Performance Hall, bathed in a red light. It was our
class's final production. We were both theater majors in
the Department of Dramatic Arts in the class of 1978,
and lucky to graduate before the first waves of the revolution rolled through the city. I'd been afraid that they
wouldn't let Arman graduate, as he'd devoted himself
entirely to bringing down the shah. Even before the
demonstrations, he was being watched by SAVAK for
his open opposition to the regime. When the Islamists
took over in early 1980, they attacked leftist and Muja-
hedeen students on university campuses and expelled
many. That was in April. In June, they closed down
the university; it stayed shut for three years. If I hadn't
graduated in 1978, they wouldn't have readmitted me
until after their so-called cultural revolution was over
and the universities reopened.

By then, I had become the wife of a political prisoner. My former classmates thought I was the lucki-
est woman alive for marrying him. Arman was the
Prince Charming of our class, desired by many girls.
Since he always got the lead male role, they would
compete to win the lead female role. I heard from my
close friends that Arman's mother had died when he
was a boy, and that he was an only child. His father
never remarried and dedicated himself to raising him.
According to Arman, his father had showered him with

so much attention and love that Arman had never felt the absence of a mother in his life.

Arman's allure was not strictly due to his looks. He was a good speaker, too. Women were attracted to his progressive ideas and the leadership role he always seemed to take. And all of our classmates found him willing to take time away from his political activities as a Fadai-ye-Khalg—a devotee of the people and the working class—to listen to their stories. They would find reasons to bring these stories to him frequently, enjoying his advice and empathy.

Unlike many of my female classmates, I did my best to hide myself from Arman, afraid that he would see the flame of desire in my eyes. But in our final class production, in which I played his lover, he saw what I was trying to conceal. My gaze wasn't that of the legendary Shirin (played by me) for Farhad (played by him), but the burning gaze of a woman in awe of her hero—a man she believed capable of doing things much greater and more significant than carving a way through Mount Bisotoun, as Farhad had done. That night, wearing a green dress he later said he found very attractive, I stood face to face with him, watching his lips move. He whispered in my ear that he, Arman, was in love with me, Sedighe.

Now his lips are whispering something in the ear of the woman leaning on his shoulder.

I peek over the shoulder of the man beside me to get a glimpse of Aazin's face, but she's too close to Arman for me to see. My fists curl on their own; they want to punch Arman in the face. But that's not the real me. I still desire Arman. I still hope to be able to gather my strength, shove this woman aside, draw my husband to me, and inhale his breath instead of this cold wind that is gusting in my face.

He is right there, not behind bars. Only a few steps away. Alive. My fists are still clenched. The day he left me I promised myself that the next time I saw him, I'd raise my hand and slap him right across his face. In my imagination I assumed he'd be standing with Aazin, and that I wouldn't let that stop me. If I couldn't take revenge, I could at least humiliate him in front of his girlfriend. Mehrdaad, however, says that Arman did not walk out on me, that I was the one who threw him out. He is right: I did tell Arman to leave. But he made me do it. I didn't mean anything I said that night, and he knew that very well.

When I first contacted Mehrdaad, he told me, "Sedighe, you should have given Arman more time. He would have gotten tired of Aazin soon enough and dumped her. This infatuation he has with young and inexperienced girls ends quickly. You know this, don't you?" Mehrdaad makes me angry, saying such strange things to the woman who spent years visiting Arman in prison! I know how old and bitter I have become, thanks to all I have gone through. Unlike me, Aazin is young. She is, after all, a bundle of lights. Every time I say this, Mehrdaad laughs. "Even if she is," he says, "those lights are cheap; they will burn fast."

Mehrdaad tells me that Arman is a fool, a coward. I should forget him. I deserve someone who does not take me for granted, someone who sees me as the real deal. "Arman cannot see that you are the real light, the real delight." He wants me to replace Arman with him, not realizing that even if I were attracted to him, my infatuation would soon fade. He is too dumb to ask himself why I would ever want to be with Aazin's ex. I am not as simple as my name suggests. Nevertheless, I did want the information about Arman's new job and the address of their office, so I promised Mehrdaad I would go to his place tonight after seeing Aazin.

I do not regret the promise, even though I hate degrading myself like this. I feel small for deceiving a young man to get something out of him, and I'm embarrassed to be debasing myself by chasing my former lover and his new sweetheart down the street. I can't help it, though. I need to see Aazin for myself, to assess whether Arman is going to stay with her or not. If I decide he will, I might go to Mehrdaad's and sleep with him. I am stubborn. I am still the same woman who decided to marry Arman on the night of our graduation performance when he confessed his love. If I can't have my Arman back, I'll slide to the end of this slippery slope and into Mehrdaad's bed!

The accumulating force of this grudge jolts me back to the present. I am still waiting at the Valiasr intersection facing the City Theater. The man in the peaked cap is still hiding my view of Aazin; all I can see is Arman. He has gained weight, and his clean-shaven cheeks, which used to seem hollow even under his beard, are fuller. The red reflection from the traffic light still illuminates his long forehead, summoning once again my memory of him onstage years ago. As on that night, I have a sudden urge to be seen by him. If I move just a few steps to the left, and his gaze slants to the right, just slightly, I can catch his attention.

And then what? My fingers clench again, and I wish I had my stress ball in my pocket so I could squeeze it forcefully, the way I've done every night for months. It was Mehrdaad who suggested I try practicing with the stress ball, after I told him that my boss at the video production company—where I work as a camerawoman in addition to being the daytime secretary—had warned me he wouldn't tolerate any more blurry shots. But the camera continued to shake in my unsteady fingers, and my heart raced every time I remembered the day Arman left. I dislike my job and would let it go if I had a better option, but the Islamic Republic of Iran

Broadcasting Company would not hire me, given my association with a political prisoner. I wasn't allowed to apply to a government office to become a civil servant either. My theater degree was not useful. Filming weddings and parties was the best job I could get.

A familiar unsteady feeling is coming upon me now. I hide behind the tall man with the hat and try to calm down as I continue to watch the couple from behind. Aazin is still holding Arman's arm, but she lets it go and starts rummaging in her bag. At the same time, the light turns green and I move along with the crowd. When I glance back, I notice that Arman and Aazin have remained in place. I try to resist the flow of people pushing against me and driving me forward, and I end up close behind them. Holding the chador tightly around me, I shut my eyes and listen to the rustling of clothes and the stamping of feet. It is as if I am standing on an ancient battlefield, refusing to take action amid the clash of swords and shields around me. Trying to stand straight, I open and close my fists every time somebody bumps into me. Then I let my hands go slack. I remove my armor and bare my breast to be stabbed. Dying on that battlefield, my life plays out before me.

YOU, ARMAN, WERE on the phone with the woman whose name you would not reveal. Yes, for hours you'd talk on the phone with her. For seven months. Early every morning when I left for work, you were in a deep sleep, tired from being up late on the phone. All day at work I could think of nothing but the woman on the other end of the line. When I could not bear it any longer, I started calling in sick so that I could stay home and watch you on the phone, giving advice to Mehrdaad's girlfriend.

"She needs my help," you said. I knew that her relationship with your best friend was on the verge of ending.

"But this is not your business," I said.

"It is," you answered. "The suffering of people has always been my business. Prison didn't change that. I am still a Fadai-ye-Khalgh. You know well that I always stood up for what I thought was right. Can't you remember who you are married to?"

How could I not remember? I was the one who prayed every day for you to survive, the one who waited ten years for you to be released, waited for the man you'd changed into. During the first two years of your imprisonment, when you were held in Evin Prison, every time I came to visit I expected to hear that you had been executed. We women waited in the cold in a long line along the prison's wall.

One time, a woman in the line received news of a death and began crying loudly. We begged her to keep quiet and to cry under her chador. They would cancel visits if we didn't keep order in the line. When she didn't stop, a few women circled tightly around her, holding onto her hands while she clawed at her face. They fixed her chador over her disheveled hair, covered her face with the edge of their own black chadors, and held her up so she would not collapse. When it was clear that she couldn't remain standing, the women took her and her children out of the line.

I had taken the arm of many women and walked them away from that high cement wall with the barbed wire on top. I thought that a day would arrive when the others would escort me out of the line and, if I tried to bang my head against the wall, would fix my hijab and tell me that I should go home. I knew that you wouldn't get a proper burial, and that they'd force me to keep quiet about your death. I feared I would be forbidden to receive your belongings: your clothes, toothbrush, watch, wedding ring, or any other small thing you'd left behind. You see what I had to endure, not only the fear of your death but also not knowing where you would be buried?

Throughout the years — the years during which they moved you from one notorious prison to another, first from Evin to Ghezel Hesar, and later from Ghezel Hesar to Gohardasht in Karaj, farther from Tehran — I stayed up the night before every visit and prayed to God to keep you alive. I never told you about my prayers. I knew you would scold me for trying to believe in God. You said God was the product of the imagination of the oppressed, those desperate ones who rely on super-natural powers to save them.

"You and I depend only on ourselves for our libera-tion. Remember?" You would look me straight in the eye and I would nod my head.

One day when you still were in Evin, a man from the prison called and told me to show up at the southeast parking lot of Luna Park. I knew that several families had been told to go to the amusement park to receive news about their loved ones; since most of the "news" was about executions, the authorities didn't want a commotion in front of Evin. I thought they wanted to give me your belongings. That's it, I told myself as I hung up. My prayers were all useless. God does not exist: my Arman is gone, shot dead, like the others.

The amusement park was closed for the winter. As instructed, I arrived at the gate next to the control tower at noon. A crowd of families had lined up before me. When it was my turn, a man with sleepy eyes, sitting in the booth, asked my name and checked in a book. He told me to go to the barracks, a short distance behind the booth in a protected area, to get the news.

"What news?" I asked.

The man shrugged.

My hands started trembling; I was sure I would soon receive a bag holding your belongings.

A few others who entered the gates before me rushed forward to the barracks, but I was too dizzy to move fast. I stayed in the cold for a while, gazing at the empty green, yellow, and red seats of a roller coaster in the distance. I had ridden on those seats as a child. My father used to take us to Luna Park every summer when we came to Tehran for holidays. I always chose a green seat; my brothers, red seats; and my sisters, yellow. As I started walking again, I imagined children on the seats, their joyful screams echoing in the forlorn and chilly chamber of my mind. The colors blurred together and my head started to spin. To prevent myself from falling, I mustered all the energy left in me and quickened my pace toward the building a hundred yards in front of me. It was crazy to be thinking, exactly at that moment, how much I wanted to have a child of my own. Crazy because I was already old, and here I was about to find out you were dead. I laughed out loud.

I was still laughing as I opened the door to the building and entered a waiting hall. Immediately many heads turned toward me. Distressed and concerned eyes — eyes that belonged to people like me, who were filling up the room — glared at me in surprise and terror. I am sure they all thought I was crazy. A few were sitting on the benches set on the two sides of the large room, a few were standing, and a few were gathered around a heater on the right side. Like me, each woman was clad in the only hijab permissible, which was a black chador. At the end of the room, opposite me, was a small office. Its door opened and I heard a hoarse male voice shouting, "Shut up or I'll have you lashed." The owner of the voice emerged, charging at me like a wild animal. The man was full-bearded and looked like guards I had seen at Evin. He raised something that looked like a motorcycle's brake cables in the air. Later, I found out his name was Haji Karbalayi; he was a warden famous for his cruelty. His furrowed brow and bloodcurdling shout sent a shiver running through my body. He stopped halfway, turned, and went back into the small room.

As he left the scene, a few voices came alive and bid me to come in. "Close the door, the warm air is drifting out."

As I stepped in, a teenage girl with dark circles under her eyes standing next to the heater waved at me. "Come here." She gave me her place to warm myself and then started pacing the room impatiently. I stopped following her movements when I began to feel dizzy again.

Just as I began to warm up, the door of the small room opened again. An old man with a navy-blue woolen hat stepped out, hugging a black bag and trembling as badly as I had been a few minutes before. He reminded me of your father, who passed away suddenly soon after you were arrested. The room went quiet and everybody turned to the old man. The woman who had given me her place by the heater ran to him, her arms outstretched. "Baba...Baba." Her feet tangled in the hem of her chador and she stumbled a few times over the short distance. She wrapped her arms around her father, who cradled the bag as if it were a dead child. He burst into tears. "They killed him. May God take revenge on them on behalf of us. May God restore justice in this country."

"Shut up, you jackass. Take your cries and curses outside." The bearded man came out of the small room, holding the same cable with which he'd threatened me. He raised it and brought it down toward the old man and his daughter, lashing the air. The blow was hard enough to make the old man's hat fall off. "Your son was an infidel, a *kaafar*. We cleanse our Islamic society of garbage like him."

He then called another name. An old woman came forward, her face as white as a shroud. I jumped at the sound of the bearded man's marching steps as he walked her into the room he was using as an office and slammed the door behind him. The father and daughter left in shock.

A chilling silence settled on the hall, enveloping those of us who remained. It was as if all the warm air had drifted out of the room with the old man and his daughter. We all shuddered for a while, even those of us who stood by the heater and held our hands over it. I was dead sure all of us were rehearsing the same tragic scene in our minds: coming out of the small room embracing a black bag. I was right. People started chatting under their breath again. "Murderers. They've brought us here to throw in our face the news of the death of our sons, daughters, brothers, and sisters. If we dared to protest, they'd kill us too and nobody would know it." I trembled the whole time I stood there waiting while other visitors were called into the small room and came out with black bags and ashen faces like leaves that had survived on autumn trees until winter.

When my name was called, to my surprise, my body felt numb. I didn't want to cry or laugh. I sat across the desk from the bearded man, who was obviously indifferent to the news he was about to deliver. He glanced down at my wedding ring.

I was a corpse. No news—even news of a death—could shake a corpse.

I came back to life only when I heard the man say that there had been a mistake. He told me I should go back to Evin to visit you. But not today. Next week.

This was a miracle, I thought. You were alive, and my own death was not real; it was just a near-death experience. Laughter poured not only from my open mouth but from every pore of my body. The man threw me out; he shouted something about fixing my chador, about me being a whore, about sending me to the same place as you, Arman, where we could be finished off together. But no matter what he said, or how many times he hit the back of my chador with his cable, he couldn't scare me anymore. As I walked out of the building, the joyful children in my head screamed with excitement, like children do when a roller coaster pauses at the summit before suddenly plunging toward the earth. I even saw a girl on a green seat, eyes aglow.

My heart made a spontaneous prayer of thanks. If Khoda could save you, He could also bless us with a child after you were released. For the next week, while I was waiting to come to see you, I did the New Year spring cleaning ahead of time. I brought the old stereo back from the storage. I sang along with your favorite music and danced. I was over the moon.

My happiness lasted only until my first visit. You had lost a lot of hair and had become so thin I could barely recognize you on the other side of the glass. As I sat down, the phone almost fell from my hand. You didn't even pick up yours. You clenched your teeth and grabbed your knees, rocking your body back and forth. A bulky prison guard stood over you. I avoided his pestering stare. I didn't want him to see in my eyes that I pitied you. You looked nothing like the capable actor who had always played our lead, the compassionate man in whom women confided, or the political Fadai hero you'd once been.

Even though seeing you this way was hard, and even though you rarely talked to me during the visits, I kept returning to Evin to be carried through its dingy corridors filled with stuffy air to sit face to face with you and give you hope to stay alive and sane. I couldn't abandon you. You had no one in the world other than me, and the rumors were that many prisoners, especially the deserted ones, committed suicide or went mad. My parents asked me to go back to Shiraz and stay with them, but I refused. I stayed alone in Tehran so I could visit you. Rent cost me almost everything I had. I became thinner each time I saw you until I was nothing but skin and bone. Just like you.

I had to bite my lip to keep from crying. Like a man on a cross, your body was diminished and your head drooped, projecting your receding hairline. Sweat oozed from your full-grown beard and shone on the long brow that rubbed against the glass between us. Your skin was jaundiced. Your bones shook as you tried to utter names I didn't know but assumed to be executed inmates. The guard told you to shut up. Many times, the phone slipped from my hand as I cowered in pain on my side of the glass. I held my breath to prevent the screams echoing in my head from escaping.

Later on, in August 1988, they cancelled all visits for more than a month. It was around the time the war with Iraq ended. People in the streets were happy because their worries had finally come to an end. I, however, grew more worried every day. Why was I not allowed a visit? I took the bus and went to Gohardasht Prison in Karaj, where they had moved you six months earlier. They told me to go back home and not to worry. "We are doing renovations in the prison," they said. "When they are done, you can come for a visit." I did not trust them. I came home and searched for the phone number of the wife of one of your friends, Ahmad. I knew Ahmad was also in Gohardasht. What she told me was horrifying. News about what was happening inside the prisons had already spread among the families. I was the only one who did not have a clue; I was the only one who was out the loop for so long.

Since the war with Iraq was over, Ahmad's wife told me, the regime wanted to clean the prisons of their remaining opponents before starting fresh—a new era. She began to cry as she shared the details: they asked the prisoners if they believed in God and the Prophet Mohammad, if they still had faith in Islam. If a prisoner said no, he was finished, even if he was serving a previous sentence. Her constant sobbing made it difficult for her to speak: "For a month now, huge meat trucks have been brought to carry the bodies to Khavaraan." It was the first time I heard the name of the deserted place several miles outside of Tehran where they dumped the bodies of dozens of hanged prisoners into mass graves.

After I hung up, I went straight to the closet to pull out a prayer rug I'd brought back with me from Shiraz when I went for my father's funeral. Shuddering under my white chador, I prayed all night that you would not be as stubborn as those who continued to deny Khoda's existence—that you had faith in something bigger than yourself or your ideas, something that would keep you alive. Maybe even something like my love. Maybe you wouldn't mock the goddess of love the same way you mocked God.

While you were incarcerated, I avoided everybody's calls, even those from my own parents. I cut ties with my brothers and sisters. I could not answer their questions, could not tell them what was happening to you. Then came the news of my father's death and I had to reconnect. I saw my siblings at the funeral in Shiraz. They gazed at me as if it were my fault that our father had died so soon and unexpectedly. They were waiting for me to apologize to them for marrying you; only divorcing you would count as a proper atonement. When I remained silent, they gazed at me as if it were I, not father, who was dead. Recently, I heard from Auntie Mahin that they told everyone I had behaved boldly at Papa's funeral, wearing a green headscarf as if I were at a wedding. I did not explain that Baba had asked me, years ago, to wear green at his funeral. He had told me that green was my color. Arman shared his opinion. My siblings also said that I was the only one who had not shed tears. I could not remember if this was true.

I came back home lonelier than ever, but still I did not lose faith. I hoped that you would survive for me, showing, after all, that God exists. I wanted you and I wanted a child with you. I believed that Khoda would save you. And he did. Not you, but the man they turned you into. Your body was half of what it had been; I could easily have lifted you up in my arms. But I was forbidden to even touch you. I had to wait until you came home.

The first few weeks after your release, you wanted to sleep alone. You had no strength to hold me, so I held you, silently. Your face, with that long forehead I used to adore, had shrunk to the size of a baby's face — the baby I desired to have with you. You resisted my embrace. You said that your body hurt. You could not sleep.

I soon gave up the thought of having a child with you. Instead, I decided to film you, to have all of you on camera, the same as I had my whole family — my parents and five siblings. Then I could look at you even if they arrested you again, could have what was left of you all for myself, could have all of the man you'd become, taut skin hanging on bone, rolling over in our bed.

It could have been a perfect movie, my artistic masterpiece, but then you saw the camera's shadow when you moved out of one of your nightmares toward me. You took the camera for a gun aimed at you and shouted. You took me for a warden and shouted again, louder than I'd ever heard someone scream, even those women lined up along the Evin prison wall.

You yelled so loud that I was afraid your bones would shatter into splinters on the bed. You thought they'd come to take you back to "the coffin," to one of those boxes in which they made prisoners at Ghezel Hesar sit for months, crouched. To one of those boxes that smelled of urine, blood, and rotting flesh. To one of those boxes from which most prisoners were sent straight to the psychiatric ward at Amin-Abaad. During those long stretches in the coffin, you would lose track of everything, even your own name.

During your long imprisonment, I had also lost track. Within the walls of my room, I lost track of life. I was suspended between heaven and earth, hanging on to anything, to a thin rope of faith I knew could give way at any moment. I had also forgotten who I was, until one day, when I came back from visiting you, clad in black from head to toe, I opened the door to our apartment and caught a glimpse of myself in our wedding mirror. Only then did I know that I was a widow, an old wretched widow who would never give birth to a child.

After the night when you almost destroyed my camera, you did not come back to our bed. You slept one time on the roof, another time on the balcony, even once in a hole in our yard, burying yourself in the ground. I slept at your side between the cold sheets, shivering and feeling like an orphan. It seemed to me that you were suffering from something immense. Was it what they had done to you and other inmates in the prison or some kind of guilt? I had heard about prisoners who became what was known as *tavvab*, repentant. They gave in under the pressure and renounced their beliefs on camera in the presence of fellow inmates. Some even went as far as to spy on their comrades for the interrogators or collaborate with wardens to torture others.

I could never bring myself to ask how you survived. I didn't care if you were one of the snitches. I didn't want to know anything about what you had done while you were in prison. That's why I stopped communicating with Ahmad's wife. You didn't contact anyone either. I knew this much: they had made you sign a letter stating that you wouldn't involve yourself in political activities and would not get in touch with any of your former inmates or their families. You had to go to the Islamic Revolution Committee in our neighborhood every month for two years and report your whereabouts. I thought once you were recovered, you'd be entirely mine.

One night, a few weeks later, you unexpectedly slipped back into my embrace. I kissed your body when you were sleeping deeply. Was it due to a newfound faith in the goddess of love, manifested in me, that your health and appetite improved? You started going out, doing errands and shopping. I left extra money on the table so you could buy yourself whatever you liked. I had saved that money for this day, for the day you would once again live under one roof with me. The more you became the Arman I knew, the more I became myself, a Sedighe who fell asleep easily, had pleasant dreams, and woke up refreshed and motivated to go to work and make a living for us. I had a recurring dream that made me think things would be sunny again in my life. I was a child on a carousel, holding the bar with one hand while clutching in the other a banana-flavored ice cream. My eyes were glowing with excitement, my mouth open.

This dream's sweet sensation lasted throughout the work day and kept me going despite my dislike of my job as a secretary. The worst were the nights I had to go out to film weddings or birthday parties. But whenever I said I was going to ask a colleague to fill in for me, you said, "Don't." Stupid me. How could I be so naive? You were not concerned about me losing my job but about having enough time alone to talk to another woman on the phone. I should have sensed that something was going wrong in my life when one night in my dream I fell off the carousel.

I might never have known about your relationship if that rainy-night wedding hadn't been cancelled unexpectedly. That night, I came home early and heard your voice from the hallway. You didn't realize I was back. Engrossed in talking to another woman, in romancing her, you noticed my presence only when my shadow fell over the phone.

After that, I once again became the miserable woman I'd been during your absence. You didn't care. You insisted that I was mistaken, that there was nothing immoral about giving advice to your friend's girlfriend. Every time I implored you to stop interfering with Mehrdaad's relationship you told me I was being hysterical.

"I must save her," you would repeat with indifference. "She is oppressed."

"Forget her! I want you to save *our* love," I cried.

"What do you want from us?"

"Us? What do you mean, 'us'?"

"She and I," you said, your voice calm, composed.

I jumped up and started beating you with my fist. "I want you to save our love!"

You pushed me back. "I don't love you."

I stared.

"Do you hear me? I don't love you anymore. It's over."

Finally, one night, I gave voice to the suspicion I'd held inside for a long time. "You were one of those *tavvabs*, weren't you? You sold out your friends to the wardens to save your own skin. You made a false oath that you believed in Khoda and whipped Islam into the inmates. You are not a hero but a betrayer, a cheater." Still in shock from the hurt I had just inflicted, I barely registered the scream that emerged from my mouth, followed by even more devastating words: "I hate you. I wish you hadn't survived!"

You should know I did not mean what I said. I didn't mean any of the things I did to you next, either. I asked the telephone company to disconnect the phone. I stopped giving you money. I ate my food at work, hoping you were tortured by the sight of an empty fridge. I called Mehrdaad and told him you were involved with his girlfriend. Then came my last blow. When you came home late — yet again — I stood in the doorway and screamed, "Go back to where you were!" You took one step forward but stopped when I said, "Tell her, whatever her name is, that she can provide for you from now on."

You looked into the room behind me, pointing at our wedding mirror on the wall.

"Look at yourself. Jealousy has gotten the better of you."

I refused to turn my head, and instead kept my gaze on you.

"You look like a monster."

"Save me from the monster, Arman. Kill the beast and save the beauty." I laughed nervously to keep myself from falling on my knees in humiliation.

"How?"

The words poured from my mouth on their own. "Make love to me before leaving. I want a child with you."

You looked away from the mirror and straight at me. "You are beyond saving." This time it was you who laughed out loud.

IN MY HEAD, Arman continues laughing as the scene in which he is leaving our home is replaced with another: the final scene of our graduation production back in 1978. Farhad has finished digging a canal through Mount Bisotoun, the epic task his rival King Khosro of Persia has assigned him, thinking no man would be able to accomplish it. Farhad can now go to Khosro and claim Shirin. But unexpectedly, a messenger arrives to tell him Shirin is dead. Unaware that the news is false, Farhad instantly drops dead. This was King Khosro's ploy to discourage Farhad from finishing the task and cause him to forget about Shirin, the woman Khosro wanted for himself. As Shirin, the Armenian princess, I am positioned at a far corner of the stage on the top balcony of my palace, looking down at Arman, who is lying flat at the center of the stage under the red light. Playing the dead Farhad, his arms are spread and his open eyes are fixed on the ceiling. Tears start trickling down my face. But why is Arman laughing? His laughter has a strange echo, similar to the times I heard it coming from the other room while he talked on the phone with Aazin.

With tears filling my eyes, I look around. I am back on Valiasr Street, wearing a black chador, standing among pedestrians waiting for the light to change. How long have I been standing here? How many red lights? And why am I here? I check to see if Arman is still there. I remember that the light had turned green but the couple hadn't moved forward. I had planted my feet and tried to remain in place against the crowd rushing to cross the intersection to Revolution Street.

In a sea of strangers, I spot them: Arman and his new woman, the one I came to see. The entire time I was remembering my past with Arman — the time that felt like the span of a life to me — has been only a few seconds, not even enough for the light to change. And apparently they've been so focused on each other that they didn't realize I was standing only a few steps away from them.

Six months ago, Arman turned his back on me and left. Six months ago, I went inside and smashed our wedding mirror. And here we are today, among a new crowd of people waiting for the light to turn green. As the tide pushes me away, I cast a last look at him. Even though he stands there, alive, with the red light illuminating his long brow, he looks like the dead Farhad lying on the stage. It dawns on me that the war inside me has finally ended. All of those clashes I've remembered while standing at this intersection have ended, and the children inside my head have stopped their screaming. Like Farhad, Arman made a mistake, taking something fake as real — and, as a result, he dropped dead. Like Princess Shirin of Armenia who waited for Farhad, I waited for Arman to finish his struggle and come back to me. When he didn't, I lamented for him. My face is still a bit wet, but it is starting to dry. I need to leave the past behind now and move forward, continuing with a life in which Arman no longer has a place.

The streetlight turns green. My feet, still charged with my past intention to chase Arman, automatically carry me forward; my eyes, still wanting to assess Aazin, inadvertently seek her form. Yet I can no longer summon the image of my fingerprints on Arman's face, left after slapping him on the cheek in front of my replacement — something I'd been imagining for months and was going to do today. Even Mehrdaad's voice in my head begins to fade, the voice that insisted I should go and see with my own eyes that Aazin is nothing special: "Arman is a fool. He does not deserve you. You need a real man who knows your worth, a man who knows you are a rare diamond." It is not only Mehrdaad's beguiling voice that is fading but also my own, the brooding one that is trying to convince me to give in to Mehrdaad's talk and stay with him for the night. My fists have unclenched and my heart is no longer beating hard for Arman. He is officially dead in the drama that is my life. So what's the point in chasing him now, in showing myself to Aazin, the woman who is there to complement him with her decorative light?

I feel like someone newly released from prison. I am ready to go straight home, which is in the opposite direction from the flow of the crowd. I command my feet to stop in the middle of the intersection. Then, paying no attention to the angry faces and grumbles of people who call me crazy, I release the rubber band that fixes the black chador around my head, remove the garment from my body, and drop it at my feet on the asphalt. I still have on my green scarf and my long gray coat. I stamp on the chador when the wind tries to lift it up and drag it along with the crowd.

The light turns yellow. Most people have already made it to the other side of Valiasr Street. Some move left toward Student Park, and some, like Arman and Aazin, continue to the right. They walk hand in hand toward the City Theater, with its distinct circular shape and monochromatic gem facade that always reminds me of a wedding ring. As I turn to make my way back to the sidewalk before the yellow light turns red, their figures, captured in my eyes as they recede into the distance, fade like images on undeveloped film left out in the sun.

The Gordian Knot

The worst is the situation of that captive [*aseer*]
whose captor has left him for good.
                    —from a poem by Hazin Lahiji

TODAY IS THURSDAY, the last work day of the week,
and the clock at Pari's office at the Telecommunication
Company of Iran reads 11:45 a.m. Pari leafs through
the file in her hand for the tenth time, but pays no
attention to what she is reading. Since she arrived
at work today, her mind has been busy with something else. She is thinking about her former husband,
Anoosh.

She'd heard the news on the radio while she was getting dressed to go to work exactly one week ago. There
would be an exchange of the first group of prisoners
of war at the Iran–Iraq border city of Qasr-e Shirin at
noon the following day, Friday, August 17, the day of
mass prayer. Standing naked, Pari paused to listen to
her heart, which had suddenly woken up and was throbbing with love for Anoosh, who had been captured
while they were still married.

The war had ended almost two years ago, in July 1988, when Khomeini was shown on TV—his head slightly lowered, his gaze slanted, and his piercing eyes half-hidden under bushy eyebrows—saying in a grim voice that he approved the United Nations resolution, even though accepting a proposed ceasefire with Iraq was more deadly than taking poison. "Having submitted myself to God's will, I now drink this hemlock," he asserted. Nonetheless, Saddam Hussein had not allowed the exchange to happen until this hot August.

Pari continues to pretend that she is studying the file in her hand until her colleague, Mrs. Hekmati, asks from across the room, "You're still working on that contract? Aren't you supposed to leave at noon?" Mrs. Maleki, an older colleague who is sitting at the other end of the room, joins the conversation. "You should go prepare yourself and help your mother. If it were me, I would have taken the whole day off, not only the last two hours."

"Yes, it's almost time for me to go," Pari mumbles. "But no one is going to show up until six. And I dropped in at my mother's last night, but there was nothing left for me to do. She'd already prepared everything."

Mrs. Hekmati laughs sarcastically. "She seems more excited than you are. She's called four times this morning."

Her humor triggers another comment from Mrs. Maleki. "I'll be the same. On the day a girl is born, her mother begins counting the days to her wedding. Pari, you never had a child, so you can't fully understand. I've already told my daughter that after she graduates from university, she has one month to get married."

Pari is the only one who doesn't laugh at Mrs. Maleki's impatience. "It's too early to talk about a wedding," she says. "They come tonight to propose. I still have time to say no."

"Why ever would you say no?" Mrs. Maleki gives a short shriek. She fans herself with one of the files. "Don't do this to your poor mother!"

"I agree — don't!" Mrs. Hekmati speaks as if she were advising her younger sister. Perhaps she thinks that being a mother gives her seniority over Pari. She is no longer laughing and has put on a stern face. Her tone changes from humorous and playful to serious and reprimanding. "Pari, be wise. You are already thirty-six; the clock has started ticking. This is a once-in-a-lifetime opportunity. He is not like your other suitors, who were old or wanted you as a second wife, or those you didn't know. We all know him."

"The chief engineer for one of our top contractors," Mrs. Maleki announces from the end of the room. She continues to fan herself frantically. "You're lucky. All of the young, single girls in the engineering department are dumbfounded as to why he's opted for a woman his own age from the contract department, a woman who is not an engineer. And they don't even know this woman has been married once before."

She stands up on her thick legs, drops the file on top of the others scattered on her desk, and shuffles forward to Pari. "Please don't get offended. I'm not trying to be mean." When she reaches Pari's desk, she shrieks again, this time louder than before. "You look unusually flushed." She takes the file from Pari's hand, bends over her, and reaches to pull up her wimple-like veil, remove it from around her face, and make it hang loose on her head. "Lean back and relax." She fans Pari's neck with a file as she addresses Mrs. Hekmati, who watches them like an inspector. "Please watch the door. Some contractors come even during lunch and prayer time. The Iranian ones are worse. They barge in without knocking."

Pari is annoyed by her concern. And she is annoyed by the pictures hanging on the wall over Mr. Maleki's desk, which she can't help but notice as she endures the tilted chair and fanning by the persistent Mrs. Hekmati. The faces of Supreme Leader Kahmenei and the former Supreme Leader Khomeini, who'd called the war "bliss," bring up memories Pari doesn't want to recall at this particular moment.

"You're too stressed out," Mrs. Maleki decides. "Like a girl who is getting married for the first time. It's not good to look too excited in front of the suitor and his family."

Offended by the remark, Pari sits up straight and gently pushes her arm away. "I already said I am not sure I'm going to say yes."

The anger in her voice drives the concerned Mrs. Maleki a step back. Pari looks over at Mrs. Hekmati's desk, which is as organized as the desk of an investigator. And exactly like an investigator, the woman is inspecting Pari's moves. "Maybe Pari is excited for somebody else. She is a secretive one. We should ask her mother."

Before Pari can respond, the phone on her desk rings. It must be her mother. "Please tell her I left the office and will be at her place soon." She grabs her purse and heads toward the door.

Leaving the building, Pari considers Mrs. Hekmati's last stinging remark. Mrs. Hekmati is good at reading people, and her suspicion that Pari is excited about someone other than her suitor is correct. Pari has many secrets. According to her mother, Dokhi, she is also unpredictable. She even surprises herself from time to time, like in the way she is currently feeling an almost overpowering excitement about Anoosh. No one, not even her mother, who knows all her secrets, would suspect she is thinking about him. Pari tells herself that before she gets to her mother's she must make up her mind about visiting Anoosh. She conceived the idea exactly one week ago, on the day she heard the radio broadcast about the prisoner-of-war exchange. Mothers can read their daughters' minds just by looking at them.

On that day, after turning off the radio and waiting for her heart to slow down, she'd immediately called in sick. Taking the risk that she might run into Anoosh's family, she'd gone to the office of the Foundation of Martyrs and Veterans Affairs to inquire about where Anoosh stood in the lineup for the prisoner exchange. She pretended to be his wife. "Haven't you been informed?" asked the man behind the counter, who, like authorities in other government offices, sported a beard. "We have already called the families."

"We have a problem with our phone. Our line has been down for a week." She kept her head down as she spoke, something she was not used to doing. Nor was she used to wearing a chador. The female security guard had given it to her to don so that she could enter the building. It helped complete the guise of a wife who'd been waiting several years for her husband's return. Not that she needed to pretend too much; she really did want to see Anoosh again, even though her excitement was mixed with embarrassment. There she stood, wishing to see the man she'd insisted on divorcing without ever telling him why. She had let him simmer with questions during his captivity, assuming things she'd known would make her look awful and jeopardize her family's honor.

The bearded man was clearly only half-convinced, but he agreed to give her the information. Anoosh would be among the second group; they would be released and repatriated on Friday, August 24. Along with other captives originally from Tehran, he'd be flown to the capital. The chartered aircraft was scheduled to land at noon.

After she dropped off the chador at security and exited the Foundation of Martyrs and Veterans Affairs building, she made a promise to herself as she walked to the bus stop: she would go back home to visit Anoosh after his return. She needed to look him straight in the eye and tell him the truth about the terrible act she'd commited in 1985 when he was missing, back before she found out he'd been captured by the enemy. It was an act she'd regretted even before doing it, and it had weighed on her conscience ever since.

Pari had divorced Anoosh because she wasn't able to confess to this act in the letters that she'd written, delivered to him in Iraq by the Red Cross. She divorced him to punish herself. Certainly, she didn't deserve Anoosh. Unlike other women whose husbands were missing, husbands they hoped would be found one day; unlike women whose husbands were martyred, women who remained unmarried and raised their children; unlike women who married war casualties, men without limbs; unlike women whose husbands were captured by the enemy, women who remained faithful to their marriages, she was a disgrace to society. This knowledge created a scar, a knot in her heart, in his heart, in their relationship. Pari's promise to herself is to see him face to face, to tell him the truth, and to apologize. She hopes that if Anoosh learns why she divorced him, he will help her undo the knot.

But, Pari asks herself, how soon should she go? Anoosh will arrive tomorrow, on Friday. She knows she should not be at his parents' house when he arrives; she has no right to be there. Should she go at night, when all the guests there to celebrate his return are gone? No, perhaps she should go much later. But she can't wait. If she waits until Saturday morning, the guilt might choke her. And if she somehow escapes that fate, she knows that the desire to see the flesh-and-blood, free Anoosh will kill her. The last time she saw him it was only his moving image, a resemblance of him; he was an *aseer*, a captive — one in a lineup of many, footage projected on a large screen for family members whose loved ones had gone missing in the war.

OTHER PEDESTRIANS WALK fast, purposefully, but Pari tramps along the sidewalk toward the rundown International Hotel, which has been occupied by refugees from southern cities since the start of war. Cars pass, men on motorcycles zigzagging among them. Old buses are crammed with people. They pollute the street with their loud engine noise and the heavy fumes pouring out of their exhausts.

It takes her twice the usual time to make it to where Shariati Street meets the Seyed Khandan bridge. She crosses the street and, as usual, stops at a newspaper stand at the corner. The headlines of *Kayhan* and all the major newspapers are about the POW exchange. Seventy thousand were repatriated last week, and more will be arriving up to the end of August. Two thousand a day, including wounded and sick prisoners. The papers feature pictures of the Iranian *aseers* who came back last week. They wear flower wreaths over the Palestinian scarves around their necks and cry in the embrace of their families at the airport. Other pictures show their celebration on their streets, where the whole neighborhood has gathered. *Aseers* are carried on the shoulders of the crowd to the entrance of their homes, which are decorated with colorful lights and flowers. There, a butcher and a few other men hold down a sheep to slaughter the moment the returned prisoner's feet touch the ground.

Pari's gaze settles on the picture of one particular *aseer* who is holding prayer beads identical to the ones Anoosh was attached to before going to the war. Anoosh's were ruby red. Pari can't tell the color of those the *aseer* in the black-and-white picture has in his hand. Even the color of the stream of sheep's blood he is stepping over to enter his home is black. So are the inquisitive eyes of the teenage newspaper seller, watching the people browsing the newspapers and magazines on display. "Do you want to buy this *Kayhan*?" he asks.

Pari nods, although she doesn't need it. She thinks how lucky this boy is that the war is over; otherwise, he would be conscripted soon. She takes five tomans from her wallet and puts the money beside the paper on the ledge in front of him.

"This is everything for you, Khanoom?"

"Yes."

"Are you sure you do not want *Today's Woman*?"

"I am sure. Just the *Kayhan*."

"Is your husband one of those *aseers*?" The boy points his finger at the man with the prayer beads.

Pari nods. "He arrives tomorrow."

The boy raises his eyebrows. "Does he also like prayer beads? I do."

"Yes, he loved his. But the string broke...before he went to the war."

"Did you repair it?"

"We did, but then the beads couldn't turn because of the knot."

"Where are they now?"

"At my home."

"The knot must be too big." The boy wrinkled his nose. "It happened once to mine but I fixed it. Let me show you."

He disappears briefly and then reappears with his prayer beads in hand. "I made this small knot. It moves inside and outside the beads. Watch." The boy proudly turns the large black beads on the string.

"I see," Pari replies, "but the thing is, many times in the past my parents have tried to undo the knot by hand and couldn't. It is impossible."

"Your parents are old. You are young. You can do it. You still have time before your husband comes back tomorrow. God willing!"

"I'll do my best," Pari remarks. "And thanks for the tip."

Pari turns and walks in the opposite direction of her mother's house up on Khajeh Abdollah Ansari Street. What is the point of hosting her suitor and his family if she doesn't want to marry? For her, the last chapter of her life with Anoosh is still open; divorce did not put an end to it. And who knows, Anoosh might have a change of heart once he sees her. These things happen. Some day in the future, he might give them a chance to mend the thread of their broken relationship. On that day, Pari will say yes to him, she is certain.

Pari crosses Shariati Street under the bridge and waits at the beginning of Resalat Boulevard for a taxi.

There are two other people waiting under the scorching sun to get a ride from some passing vehicle going close to their destination. At two o'clock, when the telecommunication offices close on Thursdays, there will be a larger crowd here competing to get a ride. Mrs. Maleki will be one of them. Pari needs to leave before she arrives, otherwise the woman will get suspicious and ask why she is not already at her mother's. A few cars and orange taxis slow down as they pass. Pari and the two men, one skinny and the other burly, bend and shout their destinations into their open windows: Majidieh, Tehran Pars, Narmak. Finally, a beat-up Hillman stops at a distance, its tires scratching the asphalt and sending up a puff of smoke. The brawny man and Pari run to the car. As the back seat is full, they both cram into the front, Pari leaning her side against the passenger door. She places the paper on her lap.

As the Hillman takes off, the hot air blows through the car. She turns her face from the window and looks down. Once again, the image on the front page of the newspaper grabs her attention — the man holding his prayer beads dearly against his chest. Anoosh must have felt very lonely without his. In the first two years of their marriage, Anoosh carried his beads everywhere he went: to the dinner table during meals, to the love-seat where they lounged after dinner to watch TV. Often, while the Japanese series they liked to watch played on the screen, Anoosh would hold Pari's hand with one hand as he turned his beads in the other. The black-and-white *Years Away from Home* opened with a man's voice, so serious he could have been reading a war declaration: "Life is a rotating prism..."

Always, as soon as the show ended, Anoosh would abandon the beads and hold Pari with both hands, pulling her toward him. Then, he'd lift her up and carry her to bed, as if she were living prayer beads.

By 1984, when the four-year-old war had become a stalemate and Anoosh had decided to sign up, he and the prayer beads were inseparable. "Turning the beads helps me clear my head," he'd say. He even brought them to their bed. One night, seeking her husband's embrace, Pari grabbed at his favorite object, trying to pull it from his grasp that was as firm as that of a soldier holding onto his rifle. As Pari let go, the string broke and the ruby-red beads spilled onto the white comforter.

Feeling a shiver run down her spine, Pari sat up. It felt like a bad omen. "I do not want you to go to the war," she told him.

"I didn't know you were superstitious," Anoosh replied as he gathered the loose beads. Holding them all in one cupped hand, he used his free hand to hold one of Pari's and cup it as well. He poured the beads into it. "Let's fix it together."

Anoosh twisted together the broken threads that still held one large bead. Pari passed the other beads one by one to her husband, who strung them together while holding one end of the broken thread between his teeth. Pari took it once her hands were free. She brought her end close to the one in Anoosh's hand.

As they knotted the loose ends together, Anoosh recited a poem: "I broke the long thread of love binding us together so that I will mend it again and grow closer to you, my beloved."

Pari knew of another verse about a broken thread, a verse her father, Jalal, used to recount: "If the string connecting us together is torn, sure, you can fix it. But then there will always be a knot between us." She didn't recite it.

SIX YEARS LATER, Pari knows that that knot is in her heart. She can feel the weight of it, heavier than this burly, rugged man sitting beside her, who leans closer every time the driver changes gears. She doesn't have even an inch to move farther to the right; she can't even stir. Why is everybody in her world—her mother, her colleagues Mrs. Maleki and Mrs. Hekmati, and others—pressuring her, not leaving any room for her to live her life as a single woman and make decisions for herself, not letting her breathe? Pressed against the Hillman's door, she senses heat, distress, and agitation rising inside her. She wants to open the door and throw herself out, exactly like the night four years ago when she'd come so close to getting out of her father's car and running away from the gynecologist's office they'd come to visit.

The doctor was a longtime friend of her father's, and he'd agreed to do the illegal operation to abort the fetus that was growing inside her.

Looking out the window of her father's car, Pari had seen that the building was already closed and the lights in the offices overlooking the street were off. To prevent herself from running in the opposite direction, she'd held onto the car door after getting out.

"Let's go home," she'd said when her father motioned for her to close the door. "Please. I don't want this."

"My poor child." Dokhi walked to her daughter with heavy steps, panting from being overweight. She put her hand on Pari's shoulder, resting it on the black chador she was wearing for the occasion. Then she turned toward Jalal, who was locking the car on his side. "We can't force her to do this if she doesn't want to."

"It's for the best," Jalal said, joining them. "And it is best for the baby. God knows how long this war is going to last." Jalal placed his hand on Pari's, which was still holding onto the door, as Dokhi wiped her tears.

"I can't be a father to your child, Pari, you know that. I am like the sunlight at dusk. I'll die soon," Jalal whispered. Then he raised his voice a bit. "And the real father is dead."

"Not dead," Pari wailed. "Missing!"

"Like his comrades, he is dead. Only his body is missing." Jalal tried to gently release her grip on the edge of the car's door by caressing her hand. "Don't fool yourself into thinking Anoosh will reappear one day."

But Pari hadn't let go until Dokhi's trembling voice came to her husband's aid, revealing a secret she had kept until that very moment. "I never told you this, but one day, after Anoosh had gone missing, I ran into the mother of Anoosh's friend Ali. You know him, the only one who survived the Iraqi attack that night. His mother told me that Ali was at a mental hospital. She said his comrades had exploded into pieces in front of his eyes. All of them—including the ones the authorities say are missing."

Now, Pari wishes her father were alive to see Anoosh reappear, to see that he was mistaken about her husband being dead and wrong to force her to make her child with Anoosh disappear. Jalal had said she needed a future, that no single young man was going to marry a woman with a child. Pari knew he had forced the awful act upon her out of fatherly love, but it was devastating nonetheless, to both of them. He hadn't lived more than a few months after Anoosh was found to be an *aseer* in Iraq. Confining himself to his room for most of the day, he would try to avoid seeing Pari drowning in pain. Even so, he continued to wane until the guilt and the shame devoured him behind the closed doors of the master bedroom.

Pari cannot forgive herself for listening to Jalal. Will Anoosh forgive her, tomorrow night or later, when she tells him that she didn't try hard enough to resist her father? Even if it was because she loved him so, and couldn't bear to see his growing distress once he'd found out she was pregnant? Anoosh knew well how much Pari loved Jalal, but was love for your father a good enough reason to sacrifice your own child?

"Stop." Pari's loud voice echoes in the taxi. "I'll get out here."

The driver pulls in and stops until he is paid the fare he requests, which is more than the ride should have cost. Pari doesn't care; she just wants to go home. From there she will call her mother to let her know she'd better cancel the visit from her suitor, because Pari is not going to show up. She'd agreed to meet the suitor only because it would allow her to reject him more easily later, by pretending to have found a character flaw in him, something as ridiculous as smacking his lips after taking a sip of his hot tea. But now Pari thinks that giving in to her mother's arrangements was a stupid idea. If Anoosh finds out about it later, whatever slight chance she has of reuniting with him will be ruined.

His imaginary accusing voice rings in Pari's mind: *You say you want to give us another chance and mend our marriage. You say you still love me. Why then did you invite a suitor to your house the day before my return?* Pari is spellbound. The voice continues, turning scornful. *Don't tell me that your mother invited him and you sheepishly went there to please her, as if you were a child.*

No, Pari cannot afford to let her mother or anyone else talk her into something she doesn't want to do. Especially now that Anoosh is coming home. At this moment, Pari should be concerned only about how to face him, about how to explain why she'd insisted on a divorce. She had aborted their child. She'd believed her father when he said that Anoosh was not alive. She'd believed him when, with tears in his glossy old eyes, he said, "Believe me daughter, had I thought Anoosh knew you were pregnant, I would have wanted you to keep his child so that his soul could live in peace." When Pari had found out that Anoosh was an *aseer* and they'd started exchanging letters, she'd felt a responsibility to tell him the truth. But the truth—the whole truth that the abortion was her parents' idea—would ruin her family's reputation. She hadn't been able to do that to her father, and she cannot do it now to her mother.

The scandal that ensued after Pari divorced her *aseer* husband had worsened her father's depression. Once the news leaked out, Jalal lost his credibility as an elder who had always worked as a mediator to resolve disputes, mend broken relationships, and bring couples or family members back together. Neighbors would cross to the other side of the street and pass him by without saying hello. Even in their extended family, everybody stopped trusting Jalal, blaming him for letting Pari dump a war hero. Pari's brothers came one night, without their wives, to express their anger. After that, they stopped visiting their parents altogether until Pari agreed to move back to the apartment she had shared with Anoosh, which Jalal had given them as a wedding gift. She would have preferred to continue living with her parents, and they would have preferred to have her in their home, but she wanted peace in the family. Pari's departure was the last blow to Jalal. He died soon after and left Dokhi a widow at only fifty-five.

It would not be fair to cause her mother any more pain, Pari thinks. When she sees Anoosh, she'll tell him she found a doctor and went by herself. She will tell him that her parents, like him, never knew what she did. They were innocent.

Reviewing her speech in her mind and holding the newspaper to her chest, Pari turns quickly in the direction of home. She can't stop herself from running down the busy 16 Metri Street as fast as if she were a mother and her baby's life were at stake. A family of four coming from the opposite direction moves to the left to avoid a collision, and Pari almost crashes into a young girl walking beside her. The father of the family turns around and yells at Pari. "What is wrong with you, woman? Slow down!" His wife joins him, shouting after her, "You are not a child playing hide-and-seek with other kids in the street, you know?"

Pari does not slow down. She runs faster, and in no time reaches her apartment building on Bayat Street, panting and soaked in sweat. After taking a moment to get her breath back, she places the paper under her arm to fish the keys from her purse. As she lifts her head to unlock the door, she feels the weight of somebody's gaze looking down on her from above. It is her upstairs neighbor, Mrs. Shamsi, who is a friend of her mother's from a Koran reading group they both attend. The woman is leaning out from her green-framed window and fanning herself with the hem of a white chador decorated with small red roses. "Your mother called. She is worried to death, thinking you had an accident," she shouts.

Before Pari can even open her mouth, she continues. "Why are you here? Did you forget about the suitor?" Mrs. Shamsi's sons appear in the window on either side of their mother and, holding onto her shoulders, crane their necks and sing in chorus, "Bride, bride." Afraid that in a moment all of the building's residents will stick their heads through their windows to watch the embarrassment on her face, Pari opens the door, throws herself into the foyer, and rushes up the stairs. She hears the boys running down the stairs toward her, singing "bride, bride" in tandem with their mother's tromping behind them.

The boys beat Pari to her floor by a second. She pushes them back by waving the paper in front of them and makes her way to her door. Their mother appears as Pari inserts her key in the lock. "Tell them to be silent, Mrs. Shamsi," Pari huffs.

"Boys, the bride says shush!" Shamsi scolds them and then turns to Pari. "Your suitor is coming at six. Why are you here?"

"You already asked this." Pari grimaces, whacking the two brats who are waiting as eagerly as their mother for her answer. "It's a long story, and if I stop to tell you, my mother will need to wait longer."

"Oh, a long story. I hope everything is fine and that you'll make it to your mother's before the suitor."

Pari turns toward the door, turning the key in the lock. "That's my problem, Shamsi Khanoom, not yours."

"I am just worried about your mother."

"Don't be," Pari snaps while pushing the door to her apartment open. "I am going to call her right away and talk to her." She slams the door on the boys, who are about to enter after her.

The heat locked in her living room jumps at her like an armed enemy. She drops the paper on the coffee table and rushes to the window to draw back the heavy curtains and open it. She sticks her head out and breathes. The air outside is muggy, but it's better than the air trapped inside. Pari surveys the wilted flowers in the neighboring building's yard, which droop their heads like a bunch of *aseers*. After a moment, she closes the curtain and turns back into the room to call her mother.

The phone barely rings before her mother answers. "Where are you? You were supposed to be here an hour ago." Dokhi's scream echoes in the receiver. "Why have you gone home?"

"To find Anoosh's prayer beads." The words jump out of Pari's mouth.

"To find *what?*" Dokhi's voice is so screechy that it hurts Pari's ears.

"Anoosh's prayer beads—the ones Baba gave to him the day after our wedding, when you came to visit." She tries to speak calmly.

Her mother's answer is silence. As it drags on, Pari feels panic begin to rise. She starts to shiver. Has her mother just had a stroke? "Maman...Maman?" The last thing she wants right now—at this critical moment in her life, when she needs all of the strength and courage she can find to reveal her injured heart to Anoosh—is to

have her mother's dead body on her hands. "Maman…
please answer me. I am dying from worry here."

"Are you?" Dokhi's anger breaks the silence. "If you
cared a bit for me, you'd have come here right after
work. You wouldn't have gone to home to find some
prayer beads. And for what? God knows what you're
cooking up in your head right now! You are my daughter, but I can never understand you."

"If you let me talk, I'll explain," Pari shouts back.

"Okay, explain. But be fast, because you need to get
here before your suitor arrives."

As Pari contemplates how to break the news to her
mother, Dokhi continues impatiently. "Listen, Mrs.
Maleki and Mrs. Hekmati have both vouched for him.
I just talked to them."

"You called them again?"

"Yes, when you didn't arrive by half past twelve.
You'd better call them. I am sure they are worried for
you too. Anyways, I was saying that this suitor is so
perfect. You have no reason to reject him. Do not spoil
this chance. Opportunity never knocks twice!"

Pari holds the receiver away from her ear for a
moment before speaking. "I am not going to reject him,
because I am not coming at all," she says, her voice
serious. "You either call them and cancel their visit or
tell them on my behalf that I've decided not to marry
at this time. I am going to keep my options open."

"What nonsense are you talking about? First prayer beads and now this: 'keep my options open.' This is more than your usual unpredictability. You have gone mad!"

"I am not mad." Pari takes a long breath before she delivers the speech she has prepared in her mind. "You must have heard in the news that the *aseers* are coming back. Anoosh is due tomorrow. I am going to see him and tell him about what I did to . . . "

"O imam of martyrs, Hossein! She is determined to cause my death as she caused her poor father's by insisting on divorce, and then by suddenly leaving us," Dokhi whimpers theatrically. Pari imagines her beating her chest as she continues. "God, please kill me. I have had enough with this daughter. Three sons have not made us so much trouble as she has!"

"Maman, you cannot make me feel guilty about this. I already feel guilty enough—for listening to Baba and you and . . . oh God, how could I do this to my—"

"Bite your tongue." The receiver crackles with Dokhi's shaken voice. "Confessing this will only destroy Anoosh's life forever. Have pity on him and on yourself."

"What, 'destroy'? We can still have another child."

"Pari, have you forgotten what he wrote in his letters when you wanted a divorce? He believes that you had a lover, that you wanted to be one of those women with no strings attached. How can you go back to someone who insulted you like this, let alone your father and me?

You need to wake up. Anoosh will never take you back, especially if you tell him about the abortion."

Pari is boiling with anger, but lets Dokhi continue. "I beg you to come here now. I want to see you happy again before I die. You're my only daughter."

Pari feels the heat rising up her neck. She can't continue this conversation. "No, this time I'll decide what I want to do with my life," she says, preparing to hang up. "And my decision is to not come tonight. I'll decide whether I'm going to see Anoosh or not; I'll decide whether to tell him about what I did or not."

A few moments after ending the call, Pari is still perspiring heavily. It takes a while for her heart, which had thumped in her ears during the entire conversation, to calm down and get back to normal. It is already four o'clock. She should have cancelled the visit from the suitor last Thursday, when she found out about Anoosh. It isn't fair to give the task to her mother at the last minute. But until this afternoon, she'd thought she could do it, that she could sit through another proposal visit. Had she cancelled it during the week, she would have had to explain her reasons to her colleagues. But Pari didn't want to confide in them, especially not to the "investigator," Mrs. Hekmati, who thinks she knows more about Pari's life than Pari.

The minute this thought crosses Pari's mind, the phone rings. Pari lets it go unanswered, her eyes darting around the living room, seeking an object to rest upon. Nothing of Anoosh is in the room. After the divorce, his family came and took all of his belongings. They even took the wedding album, which she knew they would later burn at their home. The room is furnished with Pari's dowry, old-fashioned and dusty: the loveseat she never lounged on after Anoosh left; the Rococo chair Anoosh used to sit in when he was distressed, rolling his prayer beads; the cabinet with the large open space in the middle for a Philips TV; and the clock, which ticks madly. This is all that is left behind.

The phone rings for a second time and Pari struggles to ignore it. She manages only by focusing her eyes on a framed picture that sits above the TV. Three-year-old Pari has her arms wrapped around the shoulders of Jalal, who is holding her up. Her head is turned toward who-ever took the picture. Pari doesn't remember when the photo was taken, but she has been told several stories about how inseparable she and her father were, right from her earliest days. She was always looking up to him, always seeking his approval, always wanting to be the woman he wanted her to be. But if Jalal were alive right now, Pari thinks, she would not have consulted with him about her decision to meet with Anoosh. And what about her other decision, to tell Anoosh about the fetus she didn't let grow into a baby? Maybe her mother is right and the truth, the whole truth, would only destroy her remote chance of reconciliation. She can tell Anoosh that she asked for a divorce because she was badly depressed, so bad that she contemplated suicide, so bad that she thought she would never get better. She could say she didn't want to let him see her like that, didn't want to fail him with her failure.

The story has a lot of truth in it. But things have changed since the end of the war, two years ago now. Pari has recovered, and the unborn fetus belongs to the time of war. Now it is time for peace, for rebuilding, for reconciliation. Pari closes her eyes, cutting off her view of the old picture with her father; that also belongs to the past. Behind her eyelids, a wish is nested. They say young people are allowed to have wishes, no matter how crazy they look to their elders. Pari's wish is that on Saturday, after she tells him the "white truth," Anoosh will say yes. She'll give him back his ruby-red prayer beads, and when she is accepted, she can ask for his hand!

The beads once belonged to Jalal, but on the day Anoosh came to propose to Pari, Jalal had given them to his future son-in-law. The beads remember the touch of all three of them; they can connect them to a happy time, long before the bloody years of war, death, and separation. But she cannot give them to Anoosh before undoing the old knot and making a new, delicate one, one that, as the newspaper boy put it, can be made only by young women. But where are the prayer beads?

They must be in the drawer in her bedroom, in the box Jalal gave her on the day she moved back to this apartment that she'd abandoned for a few years, to the apartment Jalal had purchased in her name, as his only daughter, when she was born after three sons. Pari is about to get up and find them when the phone rings for a third time. This time, she picks it up. "Maman, please don't call again. I'm not coming."

The sound of Mrs. Hekmati's voice surprises her. "Pari, it is too late to change your mind. Many people's reputations are at stake! I worked on your suitor's company file. He called me yesterday, looking for reassurance that you weren't going to refuse him like you did your other suitors. I didn't think you were as unpredictable as your mother says! Thinking of remarrying your ex-husband? Will he even accept? He has probably gone crazy under the Iraqis' tortures."

Pari interrupts the woman's spiteful speech. "I never said I wanted to remarry him. My mother has given you the wrong information. I said I am going to see him and apologize."

Mrs. Hekmati continues as if Pari had not spoken. "And I haven't yet talked about Mrs. Maleki's reputation. The old woman is the one who convinced your suitor's mother to tell him to propose to you tonight. If we are nobody to you, think of your poor mother."

Pari's patience finally boils over. "Enough is enough! You, Mrs. Maleki, my mother . . . why don't all you poor people leave this 'unpredictable' woman alone? Deal with whatever you have cooked up in your conspiracy. I am out, and I'm unplugging the phone."

She slams the receiver down and her rage turns to tears. She crumples onto the sofa, still in her sweaty work uniform and hijab. She is utterly exhausted, unable to clean her face and nose with a tissue, unable to get up, go to the bedroom, and change her clothes. It is as if she has turned into one of the three fairies in "Pari-ya," the poem her father used to recite when she was a little girl, lying beside him for her nap. She weeps ceaselessly, exactly like the three fairies who are captured, taken to a cold and dark place by a beast, and abandoned.

Although her name means "like a fairy," the poem was nevertheless a surprising one for her father to read to her as a child. Written by the political poet Ahmad Shamlu, it was intended for adults who had given up hope, as motivation to make them struggle to change their circumstances. Now, as Jalal's voice echoes in her mind, she feels like a hopeless *pari*, a desperate fairy who needs a nudge, a wake-up call, in order to stop whining, get her act together, and do something about her situation.

Just then, there is a firm knock at the front door. Pari knows it is Mrs. Shamsi because she can hear her sons' duet echoing in the hallway. "Bride, bride." She wipes her tears and moves to the door.

She opens it just wide enough to push the woman's rascals aside and shout at their mother. "Look at you! You're in such a hurry to come pester me that you're wearing your chador inside out." She slams the door in her face, but continues to yell through it. "You'd better go back to your place fast. If our male neighbors see you like this, they'll think you're available for temporary marriage, for becoming a *sigeh*!"

Mrs. Shamsi shouts back from behind the door. "I just came to give you a message from your mother. You are betting on the wrong horse—on a dead horse." Her voice fades as Pari retreats to the bathroom to cry without interruption.

As she splashes cold water on her face she thinks of the many hot showers she shared with Anoosh and lets him materialize before her wet eyes. But it's not the Anoosh who at times surprised her by unexpectedly opening the shower curtain and joining her under the water that she sees; instead, it's the ghost she'd picked out on the screen as the Red Cross film of new war captives played. A man from the Foundation of Martyrs and Veterans Affairs had called her office and told her to go to the screening. Pari sat in the middle of the movie theater while a queue of captured Iranian soldiers with dusty black hair and boots passed before her eyes. Their mud-spattered military fatigues still appeared khaki-colored. To Pari, however, the men all looked similar. She did not tell her father that she went to these screenings; he was sure Anoosh was dead. She did tell her mother, although she asked her not to say a word to her husband.

On that particular day, like the gray-haired man on her left, Pari held onto the armrests of her seat. Their hands were close, almost touching, but Pari was not concerned about this. She was concerned that she might have missed Anoosh stumping by on the screen. Her eyes were blurry with tears, making it difficult to distinguish between the captives in the line, all of whom kept their heads low. The image almost appeared to be of a single overexhausted *aseer* stretched across the screen, an *aseer* with drooped shoulders, so dirty it seemed as if he'd been dragged through muddy ground or stomped on by muddy shoes. Pari tried to concentrate on the captives' faces rather than their boots, but she was still unable to tell one man's face from another. Still, she continued to squint at the screen, trying to find the familiar face that used to rest beside her on a pillow, until suddenly a woman sitting on her right grabbed the armrest and pressed her hand over Pari's, causing Pari's eyes to open wide and, in that split second, capture

Anoosh's face. She heard herself screaming, "Stop the movie! Stop! It is him!"

She heard the voice of the man sitting on her left, also shouting, "Stop the movie." The woman on her right, who was still holding onto her hand, joined the chorus. "Stop. It is her...son." Her words startled Pari like the crack of a whip, reminding her of the child she'd aborted a year ago. Pari doubled over, a sudden pain pouncing at her from inside. "My poor child," she murmured.

The woman, who thought Pari was Anoosh's mother, shouted louder. "It is her son!" The certainty in her voice encouraged others to also speak up, demanding that the movie be stopped. All at once, the queue of prisoners on the screen stopped its march, covered by the silhouette of the man operating the projector at the front of the room. The shadow looked like a marshy ground in which the soldiers were trapped. Anoosh was no longer among them. But someone else's loved one was. From behind her, Pari heard a woman screaming. "It is him. It is him! My son. My Reza. Thank you, God! I found my *aseer*."

PARI EMERGES FROM the bathroom feeling elated. Her mind is finally made up, and she has sworn a new promise to herself: she will go to see Anoosh on Saturday, but she won't tell him about their unborn child. *Every woman has a secret and this is mine*, she thinks, *a secret I am going take to the grave*. She heads to the bedroom she once shared with Anoosh to find his prayer beads. But first she needs to change her clothes. She opts for something unusual: the scarlet lingerie she wore on their wedding night, with its crimson laces and ribbons decorating the edge. The last time she wore this was the last night she'd spent with her husband. The night she became pregnant. They had made love all night to kill the feeling of dread that was hanging in their bedroom.

Pari looks at her sunken face and her slim figure in the mirror. Although her body is much older than it was on that last night with Anoosh, she still looks young. She reaches behind the mirror where she has hidden a picture of herself and Anoosh together. It is their happiest photo. They are on their honeymoon by the Caspian Sea. Pari has dropped her white scarf. She has short hair and is wearing pearl earrings. They are leaning into one another, head resting on head, arms around shoulders, and are laughing wholeheartedly. Their hair, the same shade of black, looks so similar that it's hard to tell their heads apart. It is as if one person has leaned toward a mirror, touching her hair to that of her own image. As if a woman has grafted herself to her image with one breath.

From the bottom drawer of her dresser she pulls out the box she thinks holds the prayer beads. It is a small wooden box with a line of Hafiz's poetry carved on the top: "Any breath drawn seeking love and peace is a good breath / Good deeds do not require permission." Pari carries the box and the picture into the living room, where she sits down in the Rococo chair to open it. Yes, the prayer beads are there. "Seek and you shall find," her mother would have said if she were here.

But something else is also in the box, tucked under the beads: a piece of paper. She hangs the prayer beads from the arm of the chair and takes out the paper. When she unfolds it and reads what's written, in Jalal's handwriting, her heart squeezes in pain. It is the same pain she felt forty days after Jalal's funeral when she'd discovered a paper inside an old copy of Hafiz's book of *ghazels* that was very dear to him. On that day, the family, including her brothers, had gathered to sort through their father's belongings. The writing on the paper is a list of baby names: girls' names on the left and boys' on the right. The names her father had had in mind for her and Anoosh's baby. She'd refolded the paper, put it back inside the book, and taken the book as her only inheritance.

Pari clips the paper to the corner of the picture with Anoosh and puts them on the coffee table, on top of the newspaper. Then she returns to the chair to deal with the knot that prevents the prayer beads from rolling. The knot that they made, and that to this day nobody can open. One time, Pari had wanted to cut the string, but he wouldn't let her. Perhaps it was because he was a man who could never sever any of his ties or replace an old thing with a new one.

But that is exactly what needs to be done to this knot, Pari thinks, examining it. Her parents' attempts to undo it by hand and her own attempts to undo it with her teeth have just made things worse. The only way out of this predicament is to thread the beads along a new string. Pleased with her solution, Pari gets up, removes the prayer beads from the chair's arm, lays them on the coffee table beside the other objects, and returns to the bedroom to fetch her sewing box.

When she returns a moment later, she notices that the living room is getting dark. She draws back the curtain, allowing the remaining light of this long day to fall on the coffee table. She sits down on the Persian carpet close to the coffee table and, leaning against the lower part of the loveseat, pulls the table closer to herself. She has everything she needs for what she is going to do. First, she arranges the newspaper under her hand; next, she chooses a thread thick enough to not break easily; and finally, she picks up the scissors.

Holding the old thread taut in her hand, she cuts the Gordian knot, letting the beads fall and spread out over the images of the *aseers* — the first group, who arrived home last Friday, on the day of mass prayers. Pari guides the new thread through the eye of the needle and, once more, strings the beads together. When she is done, she leans back against the edge of the loveseat and looks up. The clock on the wall reads six o'clock, the time her suitor was supposed to arrive at her mother's house. It doesn't matter if he has or not. Unlike Anoosh, he is history now.

Let Go of My Hair, Sir!

THE FIRST THING I DO when I get up is listen to the message Victim Services left on my answering machine yesterday. I'm still hesitant about whether or not to follow up with the case I filed against Antonio. This morning, however, I feel certain I want to take back my complaint, but I want to remember all the thoughts that ran through my head during the night. That is why before doing anything else — even before fixing myself a drink (you heard me right, a drink, as I do almost every morning if I have the supply), before waking my daughter, Mojgan, and putting her into dry clothes (if she, yet again, wet herself in her sleep) and preparing her for kindergarten, before going grocery shopping with the money I have borrowed with much difficulty from my friend (I have already spent my welfare check and the fridge is almost empty except for a piece of bread, the remainder of the jam, and a cup of chocolate milk I have saved for Mojgan's breakfast)—I unplug my phone from the wall and stand in front of a mirror to give myself a pep talk. I have three good arguments as to why I, Gisou Ghafoorzadeh, am not a victim—a *ghorbaani*. Before presenting them, however, I look myself in the eye and say out loud: "Don't ever call yourself a *ghorbaani*. Do you hear me, Gisou? Not ever."

FIRST ARGUMENT

I am not a *ghorbaani*. *Ghorbaani* always reminds me of the sheep people sacrifice in Eid-e-Fetr, when Ramadan is over. Several folks from our neighborhood went to Mecca to take part in hajj, and on the day of their arrival, in order to welcome them, their families sacrificed a sheep.

This is how the sheep becomes a *ghorbaani*. The butcher lays her flat on her side on the hot tarmac with her neck placed on the edge of a gutter. To prevent the sheep from kicking him away, he kneels on her. Then, when the time comes—when the new haji approaches him, and his companions cheer in the name of Our Prophet Mohammad—the butcher cuts the sheep's head off with one quick swish of the knife. The headless sheep still kicks and tries to get on her feet as the blood gushes from her body, but then she goes into a tremulous fit, which recedes after a while. It is at this very moment that the sheep turns into a *ghorbaani* — when her body becomes still, when her large eyes are caught in disbelief and her tongue is partly sticking out.

As a *ghorbaani*, the sheep does not kick anymore. But I still kick. So I am not a victim — not even on that night when Antonio came over, nor on the next day, when I called the Vancouver police. I called because I needed their help to make Antonio leave me alone; it didn't mean that I was a *ghorbaani*.

That night, the Italian bastard kept calling. I had already told him that I didn't want to see him anymore, and that I'd already met a new guy through Lavalife — another Italian, but a different type — and that I was waiting for his call. No way did I want to see him again. I know: he liked to drink and I liked to drink. He was rich and could afford to pay for us to party every night. He could have been the perfect guy, if he hadn't become a snoring corpse after we downed the bottles of wine he brought over. Every time Antonio called I repeated that our relationship was over and then hung up, but he called again. The bastard rang so many fucking times that he finally woke up Mojgan and she went into one of her screaming fits. I tried to put her back to sleep as the phone rang and rang. It was impossible. So, after twenty rings, I finally picked up and screamed in Farsi, *"Vel kon zolfo!"* He said, "What?" and I gave him the literal translation: *Let go of my hair,* which is a common expression that is sometimes used in exasperation. This was a mistake. I should have shouted the English equivalent: "Get off my back." Or "fuck off." That would have served him even better. The idiot was so drunk that he wasn't listening to me, anyway.

It happened that while I was seeing Antonio I slept too long and failed to pick up Mojgan from the daycare on time. This wasn't my first time. Once I was an hour late. My poor baby was the only child left, and she'd cried so much that her face was swollen. Her teacher was totally pissed. She told me that she'd called me a million times but I didn't answer. After the third time, she called my social worker, and he called the Ministry of Children and Family Development and they threatened to take Mojgan away from me if I was late one more time. They wanted to know what my problem was.

Of course my problem was Antonio. He was no good for me. That's why that night I told him, *"Vel kon zolfo, agha"*—Let go of my hair, sir! But he didn't. He was at my building fifteen minutes after he'd hung up the phone. Meanwhile, I was trying to put Mojgan back to sleep, but she kept crying, clawing my face, and pulling at my hair. It was a recent development that she'd go crazy when her sleep was disturbed, and nothing could calm her down except chocolate milk, her favorite. It was fortunate that we had some left. Chocolate milk, though, was only a temporary solution. I knew I had to do something before Antonio called again and made her even crazier. I could think of no better way to calm her than to give her one of the pills the doctor had given me the year before to help me with my sleep. I warmed up her chocolate milk and dissolved a quarter of the sleeping pill in it. She stopped screaming when I gave her the glass. In a few gulps, she finished her chocolate milk. It worked very fast: she was out before Antonio got there.

A *ghorbaani*, I thought, when I looked at my drugged-out baby. Her innocent face resembled the face of the sheep when the last drops of blood had drained from her body and fallen onto the asphalt. I know I shouldn't have given Mojgan my medicine. But I had no other way, because now it was the buzzer instead of the phone that was ringing nonstop.

I wasn't going to let Antonio in.

But I did when he started yelling from downstairs and throwing things at my window. I should have called the police then, before the scandal happened, before I ran out onto the terrace with my Mojgan, looking more dead than asleep in my arms, before I shouted out for help so that the neighbors called the police for me.

The police told me I should call Victim Services in case Antonio called and harassed me again. They let him go the next morning because he hadn't hit me yet, and it was me who, *voluntarily*, as the police put it, opened the door for him. Antonio called me as soon as he was released. He said he wanted to come over and play with my hair, which meant: Let's have sex. Antonio was good with foreplay. He knew how much I loved the way he would passionately stroke my hair, lick my earlobes, and make me feel special all the way down my body. Of course this happened only on nights when he wasn't dead drunk.

After reporting his call to Victim Services, the next thing I did was to get a haircut. It was a painful experience. Very painful. I could hardly look at myself in the mirror for a few days. I hadn't cut my hair so short in years. All of my passport pictures were with long hair: the Iranian passport I'd left the country with to go to Turkey; my second passport that the Netherlands immigration officer confiscated when he noticed it was fake and sent me back to that shithole, Turkey, and to that asshole, Abbas the smuggler. Finally, a year after I left home in 1995, I arrived in Canada with the third passport that Abbas had forged for me.

After the Amsterdam police sent me back to Turkey, I had wanted to cut my hair short, but Abbas forbade me to do so. He said that with long hair I looked more like an Italian. Like Sofia Loren. I looked like shit when I arrived in Toronto. I hate the photo the immigration officer took at the airport, the one stapled to my refugee paper. With a yellow face and limp hair, I looked like someone who had just been released from the hospital. Mojgan, too, looked awful. She was only a year old then. Those large black eyes of hers which are her special feature, like my hair is mine, looked sickly and lifeless in that photo.

Perhaps it was a good thing that I cut my hair. When I came out of the hairdresser's I told myself, "You did it; you still kick; you're not a *ghorbaani*. Understand? Don't you ever say it to yourself, Gisou. Ever."

SECOND ARGUMENT

I am not a *ghorbaani*. *Ghorbaani* always reminds me of the story of Ibrahim and his son Ishmael in the Koran. Ibrahim would have certainly cut off his son's head if God hadn't blunted his knife and sent him a sheep to sacrifice instead of his son. Unlike crazy Ibrahim, I would never sacrifice my Mojgan; instead, I have made sacrifices for her. I have always fought for her life. That's why I told Antonio to get lost. I didn't want the ministry to take Mojgan away from me and put her in foster care.

The ministry people do not understand how much I care about my *cheshm siyah* — this is what I call Mojgan, "the black-eyed." My social worker says I shouldn't call my daughter belittling nicknames. He has never paused to look into her beautiful, dark eyes. Maybe he thinks *cheshm siyah* is the same as *cheshm sefid*, "the white-eyed," which is an expression for people who are bold and continue doing things their way even when they are told not to. But probably not, and I certainly don't care to explain the difference to him. He doesn't get such cultural subtleties. Like Antonio, he does not stop picking on me after I tell him to *"vel kon zolfo."* He doesn't understand that it is impossible to get a job when your social insurance number starts with nine, not with seven, showing that you are a refugee and not an immigrant. He doesn't understand that I have no love life as a single mother. I've lost at least three men—Kevin, Ali, and Ebi—over my *cheshm siyah*.

My social worker tells me that I should stop telling him about Ebi, the love of my life. He is not a family counselor or a psychologist, he says. He is there to make sure my welfare checks keep coming and to help me find a job. The psychologist I am seeing is no better. He also tells me I should forget Ebi.

But how can I forget him? He was the funniest, sexiest man I ever met. The problem was another woman, Firoozeh. He talked about that woman all the time. When I first met Ebi, Firoozeh had just broken up with him. I did everything to cheer him up. I became a new woman: got up early in the morning, cleaned my place, watered the flowers, went shopping, bought fresh vegetables for dinner, and made Persian food. Ebi loved my cooking. I let him talk as much as he wanted about that woman over dinner while he stuffed himself with homemade food. He was not a big eater but became one when I cooked. I lit the candles, put on nice music, and wished that it was me on his mind and not Firoozeh. But it didn't happen that way. All he could see in his head was that woman—the woman who never cooked for him, never did anything for him except tell him that she was too good for him. Iranians say that the more you avoid men, the more they become attracted to you, and the more you go after them, the more they escape you. Men are all *cheshm sefid*.

I could not escape my *cheshm sefid*, Ebi, no matter how much I told myself, *"Gisou, vel kon zolfo."* I was totally attracted to him, to the degree that even after dinner, when he had his head on my lap or on my breast, I let him talk about Firoozeh. I don't know how I tolerated all of this but I did, maybe because I knew that soon Ebi would reach into my dress or my panties and turn into a completely different man.

Nobody would tell by his appearance that Ebi could talk dirty in bed. He also was very funny, funny in a dirty way, when he forgot all about Firoozeh. Sometimes he fucked me three times during the night. I was all for it. In the morning when he left, I became depressed. My home suddenly became empty. I spent all day making myself ready for when he would come back at night. At least once a week, I went to a thrift store on Lonsdale, two streets up from my place, and bought a new dress to put on for Ebi. He was smart, though: no matter how new and clean the dresses were, he knew where I had bought them. He told me that Firoozeh never shopped at thrift stores; she was "high class," and used to be an architect in Iran. I never bought second-hand clothing in Iran either. I had also gone to university and studied Persian literature; I had a job too, working as a typist for a notary public. The difference between Firoozeh and me was that she was already an immigrant. And she didn't have kids.

Ebi says he broke up with me because Firoozeh started talking to him again. But I know this is not true. I think that he suddenly realized how involved he was with me and became scared that he would be stuck with a single mother. He was someone who had escaped commitment all his life. That's why he was still single at the age of forty-six. Still, I hoped that one day Ebi would eventually give up his own apartment, one street up from my home, move in with me, and become my husband and Mojgan's father. Since the first day of our relationship, I had wanted him for life. Ebi, however, never wanted a life with me.

After a while he started spending more and more time at his own place, where I wasn't allowed to go if

Mojgan was with me. He said the life he lived with me was not the life he wanted to live. He wanted to go to nightclubs, to do different things than staying at home every night and eating Persian food. He knew, because of my *cheshm siyah*, I couldn't go out to nightclubs with him. I had nobody to take care of Mojgan and I could not afford a babysitter.

I told him that we didn't have to stay at home all the time. I could go out with him to the beach or to other places on the weekend. Of course, with Mojgan. He agreed to give it a try. At that time I still lived in North Vancouver. One Saturday in June, I woke up and prepared sandwiches for our picnic. He said he would be at my place at ten. When he arrived in his convertible fifteen minutes late, Mojgan and I were waiting for him by the door. He said he had changed his mind and didn't want to go. He said that Ambleside Park was full of Iranians and he didn't want his acquaintances to see him with Mojgan and me.

I was so angry that I would have smacked him in the face if Mojgan had not been there with me. She ran to the car and shouted at me to open the door for her to climb in. Ebi said he could give us a ride to Lonsdale Quay. Mojgan and I could have our picnic there without him. I accepted, but only to make my *cheshm siyah* happy. She screamed with joy when we got into the car. Even though the quay was only two streets up from my place, I still wished that the police would appear and charge Ebi for driving with a child in the front seat. Neither Ebi nor I talked on the way. And then, just before we got out, after I undid the seat belt, Mojgan leaned forward toward Ebi, put her arms around him, planted a small kiss on his cheek, and said, "Thank you, Daddy." My *cheshm sefid* finally did her thing: she marked the end of my relationship with Ebi. What could I have done? Should I have brought a knife and chopped her head off to please Ebi, the same way Ibrahim wanted to make God happy?

Unlike Ebi, Ali wanted Mojgan to call him Dad. When we started to date, he asked me to force my *cheshm siyah* to do so. He didn't know that this *cheshm siyah* was also a *cheshm sefid*. Ali lived in the same building as I did. He moved in after Ebi was gone. He saw me in the hallway a few times and then one day when I went to take the garbage downstairs, he approached me and asked me to have tea with him at his place. I said I had my daughter upstairs. He said it was no problem; I could come over with my *cheshm siyah*.

Ali was everything Ebi wasn't. He was short and bald, had a mustache, a pot belly, and fair skin. He was neither a liar nor a joker. He didn't like nightclubs or sports cars, and was very homey. He told me that he had recently divorced his wife and was looking for a good, faithful Persian woman. He wanted a family life and he wanted commitment—as soon as possible—and he didn't have a problem with me having a child. But my child, my *cheshm sefid*, had a problem with him.

Mojgan simply didn't like Ali, and she showed it in all possible ways. She didn't greet him when he came up to our place or when we went downstairs to his apartment. Ali was big on educating children. He didn't stop picking on my *cheshm siyah*, no matter how much I told him, *"Vel kon zolfo, agha."* He grabbed Mojgan's shoulders, looked into her eyes, which by that time had turned charcoal black with defiance, and told her that she should greet him. Mojgan screamed and pushed him back, ran to her closet and started taking out her toys and clothes and flinging them across the floor. She was smart enough to know this would make Ali extremely mad. Ali was tidier than any woman—all his spice and herb bottles were labeled.

Ali was also a good cook. He cooked for us every time he invited us over. His food was delicious but Mojgan refused to eat it. She wanted to sit on my lap, and Ali thought she should sit on a separate chair. I was too afraid of Ali to lift Mojgan up onto my knees. He had already warned me not to give in to my *cheshm siyah's* demands. I looked away, but she didn't stop trying to climb onto my lap. Ali got up from his seat, pulled out a chair for Mojgan, lifted her, and sat her up on it. He held my *cheshm sefid's* hands back so she could not claw his face, which had suddenly turned red. One time she bit his ear, and, as a result, he confined her in a small storage room where he kept empty boxes. "This will teach her to sit on her seat," Ali told me. "You brought her up badly; she wants to hang from you all the time." I explained to him that my *cheshm siyah* was not really a *cheshm sefid*. She was just emotionally insecure because she had not had a stable home when she was very little. I'd kidnapped her from my husband and taken her out of Iran when she was one, and we'd lived in limbo for six months in Turkey. But Ali didn't listen to me when I told him, *"Vel kon zolfo."* It was as if I were speaking in a language he didn't know, not in Farsi. He asked me not to let her out of the closet. I had to continue with my dinner and converse with Ali while Mojgan was banging on the door, crying, and asking me to let her out. It was torture, which I had to get used to as Ali's education project continued. Mojgan learned to sit on the chair by herself, learned not to interrupt us every second while we talked, learned to say "thank you" to Ali after dinner or when he bought her something. But she never learned to let him carry her in his arms when we went out together, and she never learned to call him Dad. Ali still complained that I should teach her to accept him as a father. "I can't cut her head off for not loving you," I told him. "You should accept her as she is."

Ali asked me to marry him but I was not sure. I knew Mojgan hated him, and I wasn't attracted to him enough to put up with what he did to Mojgan, let alone to deal with the fact that he was traditional and boring. He didn't talk dirty in the bed, he wanted sex only twice a week, and he didn't go down on me. Our relationship was eventless. We spent most evenings at home, we ate Persian food every day, we went to the same parks and beaches every weekend. It was a stable relationship, though. He was committed to being my husband and to being my *cheshm siyah*'s dad. Didn't I long to have a family? Didn't I want to have security?

One Saturday when we were on our way to Lonsdale Quay to shop and go for a stroll, I told myself that once we returned home I'd tell Ali that I would marry him. I'd dressed Mojgan in a white dress with pink polka dots that Ali had bought, and tied her pigtails in pink ribbons. She looked adorable. It was sunny outside and we strolled down Lonsdale toward the quay. Mojgan didn't ask me to carry her in my arms, which was a good thing. Ali bought her an ice cream from the McDonald's by the Sea Bus station. "Thank you, Dad," I said, looking at Mojgan. When we came out of the shop and walked toward the water, she saw some children with their parents climbing up a tower in the middle of a cobblestone square. She said she wanted to go up too. I lifted her up and was about to climb the stairs after her when Ali stopped me. "This is too dangerous for you," he said. "I'll take her." And then, before I could say a word, he grabbed Mojgan from my arms and was on the first stair. "Daddy takes Mojgan," he said. But Mojgan started screaming and hitting him in his face. "Mommy," she cried, "Mommy," and I saw her yanking at one of her pigtails so hard that the pink ribbon fell off. I wanted to pull her out of Ali's arms, but it was too late. Ali was already out of my reach and there were two Chinese families following him. Each of Mojgan's shrills clawed at my heart. "Bring my daughter back," I shouted. My voice was so loud that people on the stairs turned around and looked at me. "That man has my girl! He is not her father," I yelled. The Chinese people who were in the middle of the stairs had to climb down first before Ali came down. A few seconds later, a furious Ali pushed a crying Mojgan with swollen face and flaring black eyes onto my chest. He brushed past me toward the quay. That was the end of our relationship. My *cheshm sefid* had done her thing: she'd brought to an end my relationship with Ali.

Mojgan didn't call Kevin Daddy, but Uncle. I met Kevin through Lavalife. After I broke up with Ali, I moved to Coquitlam and told myself that I was no longer going to date Iranian guys. "A new home, a new life" became my motto. I had heard about this phone-dating system on TV and decided to give it a try. Kevin was Caucasian, born back east. He was in his early forties and an engineer. He had a broken marriage and one son and he had put his ad in the category of "long-term romantic relationships." He said in his ad that he was looking for a relationship that could possibly lead to marriage. He also wanted to start anew. We were a great match, I thought.

At first, he was hesitant to meet me when I told him that I had a three-and-half-year-old daughter, but he changed his mind when he learned that I was Iranian and could make him Persian food. His colleague at work was Iranian, and Kevin had already tried our food and loved it. I spent the whole day cleaning and cooking. I got my *cheshm siyah* to help me organize her toys. She got so tired that by the time Kevin arrived she was sleeping like an angel, her long black lashes casting shadows on the area below her eyelids.

The quiet of my clean apartment made a good impression on Kevin. He said this was the home he was missing: warm food, peaceful environment, and good company. He had green eyes and curly light brown hair and was dressed like a real gentleman, wearing an elegant navy-blue suit and shiny black dress shoes. He brought me a bottle of expensive red wine.

He didn't stay over that first night. I knew it would be a great mistake to go that far on the first date. But then he never stayed with me for the night. He said he had to sleep in his own bed. I understood later that it was just an excuse. His real problem was my *cheshm siyah*; he was afraid she was going to wake him up in the middle of the night with her cries. "I had my days with a small baby," he once told me, "when his screams woke me up a hundred times at night."

I didn't want him to leave, though. "Kevin, please, *vel kon zolfo.*" I am sure, because of the imploring tone I applied to my voice, that he understood my words didn't mean anything bad. They just meant "Come on. Stay!" But he didn't listen. It was all right the first few times. But then I suddenly felt so lonely that I started to cry. As my psychiatrist said, this was my depressive mood emerging at night. It was as if it was me, not my *cheshm siyah*, who was three. And then I'd wake up in the middle of night feeling as if my mother had abandoned me and left me alone in an empty house. Even my *cheshm siyah* didn't exist anymore. She was lying there, but I couldn't see her. Only the walls existed — the walls that I clawed at while crying.

Nothing except booze could help me calm down. The wine Kevin brought with him from time to time was not enough. The welfare checks just sufficed to pay rent and buy ingredients for Kevin's favorite dinners. I had to shoplift dresses from the thrift store. The peaceful home with warm food and beautiful, well-dressed company that Kevin desired required money. And since I didn't have enough, I began to take Kevin's money to provide all this for him. The first time, I took twenty dollars. He didn't seem to notice. The second time I took fifty, and the third time it was a hundred-dollar bill. The next time he came over, he said he thought his son had stolen from him. I was safe. He didn't suspect me, so I continued taking money from his wallet when he was in the washroom to buy alcohol for my lonely nights. I saved face and never told him how much I cried every time he left me after he made love to me. He didn't even let me hold him for five minutes. He quickly got up, dressed himself, and said he was going to bed at his home.

Kevin and my *cheshm siyah* got along well. He took us out on the weekends. It seemed like a miracle; Mojgan was well-behaved during the six months that we dated. She listened to Kevin and said "Okay, Uncle Kevin" when he asked her to do something. She didn't cry or nag during the time he was with us. He played with her and kept her so busy that she always fell asleep in the car when we headed home. I wondered what so got under Kevin's skin at night that he needed to escape my *cheshm siyah*, whom he was so fond of during the day.

"She is not a newborn, Kevin," I kept telling him. "Please, *vel kon zolfo*. She is almost four—she doesn't cry at night anymore."

"I don't want to risk it," he answered. "I suffered from insomnia for a long time."

Even when he took Mojgan and me to his home, he
drove us back and dropped us at home at night. The
last time he invited us over was on my birthday. After
dinner, I tucked Mojgan into the bed that belonged to
Kevin's son. We had already finished two bottles of
wine before and during the dinner. I knew Kevin had
three more in reserve. I'd brought a CD of my favorite
Persian tunes and told Kevin that I'd dance for him if
he provided me with more wine. By the time we went
to bed, I was so drunk that I could hardly keep my
eyes open. I don't know what happened next, because
when I got up it was the next morning around ten.
Mojgan was pulling at my hair and crying. Her face
was puffy and red and her hair was a mess. When I
hugged her I noticed that her dress and stockings were
wet. Kevin was not at home. He came back at eleven.
It was obvious he hadn't slept all night. His face was
as white as a ghost, and the green of his eyes, which
had glowed last night when I'd danced for him, looked
mossy. "Hi, Uncle Kevin." Mojgan ran to him at the
door. He pushed her back with a cruel hand. Kevin took
out my keys and the hundred-dollar bill I'd nicked from
his pocket the previous night. He put the bill back in his
wallet, threw the keys in my face, and opened the door
for us to leave. My *cheshm siyah* had done her thing; she
had marked the end of my relationship with Kevin with
her crying that night.

Who says I haven't made sacrifices for my *cheshm siyah*? I have sacrificed my hope of having a stable relationship. Now I am stuck with casual dating. It doesn't matter, though, in which category guys put their profiles. I would never sacrifice my *cheshm siyah* to avoid being alone. I would never make her a *ghorbaani* to get what I want, even if it was to marry God himself. I am so unlike that crazy Ibrahim, who called himself a prophet.

"You don't make Mojgan a victim to get a man," I told myself. "You are not a *ghorbaani*. Understand? Don't you ever say it to yourself, Gisou. Not ever."

THIRD ARGUMENT

I am not a *ghorbaani*. *Ghorbaani* reminds me of Mohammad Hossein Fahmideh, the teenager who became a hero in the beginning of the Iran–Iraq War by throwing himself at an Iraqi tank and blowing both himself and the tank up. The government said that other men should take him as an example and sacrifice themselves for a greater cause. They should sacrifice their lives to push the invader from our land. By making themselves *ghorbaani*, they could save other lives, the lives of women and innocent children. I think my family took Mohammad Hossein's example and sacrificed themselves for me and my *cheshm siyah* to have a better life — a better future. Thinking about this, that my parents are *ghorbany*, makes me sick. I have no intention of taking after that teenager and being a *ghorbaani*. I don't know why it should be always the case that for one person to live another must become a victim.

My parents did everything, blew their savings and sold the house they had lived in for thirty years, to get me out of my bad marriage and out of the country. It didn't take me long to realize that I had married the wrong person. Hamid was not the businessman selling fabrics that he claimed to be. He was a drug addict who sat at home the whole day. He went out only to get his weed or hang out with other worthless, jobless addicts like himself whose families paid for their shit. My salary as a typist was barely covering the rent. If it were not for my father, we would have starved to death. My parents lived on my father's retirement money from the hydro company. It was a small pension, but he secretly gave me some part of it every month. My parents lived very poorly. As the proverb goes, they reddened their faces by slapping them. Their only advantage was that they already had a house to live in. Since they could not afford to buy things on the black market, my mother had to line up for hours to get the cheap meat and rice the government subsidized. Her knees became more swollen each day, but she still didn't complain. One day when I refused to take the money my father had saved for me from their household budget, my mother put it in my bag when I was in the bathroom. When I found the envelope with the money the next day and went to return it, my mother told me that they were hopeful Hamid would soon get over the depression caused by bankruptcy and go after a job.

He never did, though. Nor did he ever quit the shit he was smoking. He only worsened, stealing money from my purse—the money that could have bought medicine for my mother to help her with her osteoporosis, and that could have bought my father the new glasses he desperately needed, and that could have allowed my mother to throw parties and invite family and friends over so that she wouldn't be lonely. My mother also thought a child could save Hamid from the swamp of depression. When he knows he is a father, my mother told me, he will be motivated to go after a job or start a new business.

My *cheshm siyah*'s birth didn't motivate Hamid a bit; instead, it motivated my parents to make more sacrifices to get Mojgan fed. They lived on so little money—close to nothing. I didn't have enough milk, and the milk powder was so expensive. In addition to waiting in the other lines to get cheap food for themselves, my mother had to stand for hours in a line at the pharmacy to buy my *cheshm siyah* government-subsidized milk. One day

I decided I was no longer going to let Hamid turn the money my parents saved into smoke. I started hiding my money in different place around the house. But he always found it. Coming back from my parents' one day, I noticed that one of the bricks on the wall by our front door had become loose. I pulled the brick out, placed my money inside the crevice, and put the brick back.

After that, my wallet was always empty and there was no money hidden in the house to be found. This sent Hamid into a complete fury. One night when I was sleeping, he came to me, woke me up, and told me that he was going to kill me if I didn't tell him where I'd hidden my money. He had turned everything upside down to find the bills. He had even emptied the insides of all our cushions and spread out the stuffing on the floor. His continuous yelling finally woke my *cheshm siyah*. At that time, she was only six months old. She started screaming like crazy. I shouted, "*Vel kon zolfo*, Hamid." But he didn't stop his yelling, so I had to lie and say that I would give him the money only if he shut up and let me calm my baby down. He sat silently while I fed Mojgan. After I put her back in bed, I told Hamid that I was not going to give him the money that was for feeding our child. Not ever. This time he didn't shout. Instead, before I knew what was happening, he took my *cheshm siyah* from my arms and walked out the front door.

The next three days were the hardest of my life. Hamid disappeared. My father called Hamid's parents in Mashhad, a city six hundred miles away from Tehran, to inquire if they knew their son's whereabouts. They did not. He wasn't at their place, they swore. However, two days later, they called to tell us that Hamid had a message for us. They said he was somewhere in Tehran and that Mojgan was safe. He wanted a big sum of money to return her. We couldn't go to the police and say he had stolen my child. According to Islamic law, he was Mojgan's father and had full rights over her — he could sell her or even kill her if he decided to do so. My mother had to sell her own gold and jewelry from her marriage to provide money for Hamid. I had already sold the gold Hamid's parents and family had given me on my wedding.

Mojgan was very sick when my father brought her home. He told me to forget about Hamid from that moment on. He would help me divorce the bastard. My parents went to my home and got my things. I stayed with them. I turned completely paranoid. I was afraid that Hamid was going to sneak over to my parents' house and kidnap Mojgan again. I even took my *cheshm siyah* to the bathroom with me. My maternity leave was over. My father wanted me to go back to work. He said they would take care of Mojgan during the day, but I quit and never left the house. At night, I woke up

several times, checking to see if Mojgan was beside me.
I saw Hamid's shadow behind every window. The only
time I wasn't agitated was when I was breastfeeding
Mojgan and my mother would brush my disheveled
hair, as if I were a small child. My breast milk dried up
more every day as the shadow of Hamid grew bigger
and bigger in my mind. Finally, my father decided that
I had to leave the country.

My parents had to sacrifice their house to get us out
of the country. I needed Hamid's permission to get a
passport for me and Mojgan. He had disappeared again,
and if he came back, I knew he would probably ask for
a bigger sum than the person who forged a passport for
us. With the passport, I could travel to Turkey, but from
there I couldn't go anywhere, because every other country needed a visa. Through one of our distant acquaintances, my father found Abbas, who smuggled people
out to Turkey. There were eight other people with me
accompanying Abbas that day on the bus to Turkey.
We pretended not to know him. I sat with two women.
Neither of them had a baby. I was afraid that Hamid
was going to appear before the bus got to the border
and take my *cheshm siyah* away from me. During the
three-day journey, the bus stopped at least ten times
so that the passengers could eat, stretch, or go to the
bathroom. I stayed inside the bus most of the time, and
other times got one of the women to hold Mojgan and

stand behind the bathroom door while I was inside. I didn't care if they thought I was crazy.

Mojgan got a urinary infection twice during that year we lived in Turkey in the shitty accommodation Abbas provided. I didn't say a word to my parents about our condition when I called them. They had enough to deal with on their own. In their old age, they had become renters again. They couldn't afford a place in the same neighborhood they had lived in for thirty years. Then, after the Dutch police caught me at the border and sent us back to Turkey, they had to move to an even smaller house in a worse neighborhood to provide money for Abbas to forge a new passport for us.

I never told my parents that I paid Abbas too. He charged his female customers extra. We had no other way but to give ourselves to him; otherwise, he would send us back to Iran. When he came back drunk from the bars in the middle of the night, he made me kneel, stood in front of me, took out his dick, wrapped my long hair around his hand, and pushed my head close enough so I could suck it for him. There were a few times when Mojgan woke up and cried. I told my captor, "*Vel kon zolfo, Abbas agha*. The baby needs me." But he didn't let me attend to her. He said if I pulled his cock from my mouth, he would put it in Mojgan's.

My parents don't know about any of this. They are happy that their granddaughter and I live in the best city on earth—in Vancouver. Every time I call, I assure them that they haven't sold their house for nothing. If, one day, they were to find out about my real life—for example, that I was once caught shoplifting, or that I was in a complicated relationship with an Italian man—they would drop dead. Fortunately, my social worker got me out of the first mess. She convinced the police that I was on medication and wasn't aware of what I was doing. Fortunately, Mojgan is still with me. My mother still has her hopes that one of these days I'll become an immigrant, establish myself here, and bring her over to see my *cheshm siyah*. She told me that her only wish is to comb Mojgan's hair like she used to comb mine. She asked me to let it grow until she can be with us. I have not taken Mojgan for a haircut for years. I am determined to bring my parents to Canada to live with us in their last years. My parents didn't make themselves *ghorbaani* so that I could be one.

I cannot, under any circumstances, write and sign that I am a victim, as the people at Victim Services want me to. I am not a *ghorbaani*. And this is my last word.

Sign Language
as Second Language

There is no private language.
—Ludwig Wittgenstein

I AM IN LINE at the bank. The Brazilian and the Italian tellers are busy with customers who are craning their necks to grasp what the men are telling them in their thick accents. The quickest of the tellers at this branch— a short, stout young man who doesn't have an accent (a real Canadian) with short, dyed-blond spikes—is not in today. There is a sign on his counter: CLOSED. I look at my watch. The Italian and the Brazilian take their time. Keep talking. I'll have to grab something to eat on my rush to class. They don't care. They just shoot bland smiles at the impatient customers like me.

I see a hand waving at me from behind a desk at the other end of the counter. It belongs to a teller I've never seen before—a young Asian man. He must be new.

My turn. I take out my bank card and the student loan check. The words pour out of my mouth even before I sit down. "I want to deposit this and I need forty dollars in cash." I look up at the teller for a response. He smiles. I am confused. He waves his hand gently in front of my eyes and then points to a sign on his desk: I'M DEAF. PLEASE BE PREPARED TO COMMUNICATE IN WRITING.

"Oh, cool," I say out loud. "I am always prepared for writing." He winks a few times, but his eyes stay focused on my lips. *Oh, who am I talking to? He's deaf*, I tell myself. *But that's a good thing, because he won't hear my accent.*

I've never had my lips read. What's more, I love writing. Actually, I am a writer. Or want to be. A romance writer. Sure, I'm pursuing higher education — CAD drafting, which has nothing to do with love but is good for making money and a secure future — but my secret passion is the writing course at the local community center.

It might be too late for me. I may be a university student, but I am already thirty-six — "mature," they call me — and there isn't much English vocabulary in my word bank and my savings account is low on grammar. Nevertheless, I am more comfortable expressing myself in writing than I am speaking aloud. The same is true in my mother tongue, Farsi, a language that is said to be, as the old expression goes, as sweet as sugar. I have always felt this way. I didn't always hate talking, but now I get cramps in my gut when I hear myself speak with an accent. This is new. Post-immigration syndrome. Words lose their shape in my mouth.

While the teller's gaze is still pinned to my lips, I read the name-tag on his white button-up shirt and say, "Hello, John. I'd like to deposit a check, withdraw forty dollars, and pay my hydro bill."

He shakes his head, points at the paper, and jots down, "PLEASE WRITE THE THINGS YOU WANT TO DO, ONE AT A TIME." He draws a smile beside his words and passes the pen to me. I frown. I know the rule of "one thing at a time" from ESL class. "Don't cram too many ideas into your sentences. It is best if each sentence contains only one idea." Wherever you go in this country the same rule holds: one idea at a time — even at a bank with a deaf teller with a fake English name!

The paper in front of me is filled with scribbles and silly smiles. I find a blank space between two happy faces and write my first request: "DEPOSIT." Then I raise my head and try to pull my lips into a smile. He gives me back a grin so generous that it makes me let out a passionate "John" that has nothing to do with him, really. I remember how I once confused my former lover by moaning "John" the first time he went down on me. It took him a few months to ask who this "John" was whose name I'd screamed. I laughed so hard that I thought he would leave me on the spot, but I stopped in time to explain: "There is no John.

'John' is an utterance that springs from the heart to the tongue when we Iranians experience pleasure, feel joy, or when we become enthralled. Literally, it means 'life, soul, essence of existence,' something like this. We also use it to address our loved ones. For example, if I call you 'Richard John,' it means, 'Richard, my dear, my love, my whole life.'"

John the teller smiles patiently as I laugh at my funny memory. He holds up a finger to say, "one moment."

He takes my check and looks at the monitor. He seems the same age as me, maybe a few years younger. I like the way this man has dressed in a vest and a tie, and put on glasses with rectangular, shiny, black frames that fit well on his round face, and even add an extra charm to his look. His complexion is much darker than that of the Asian people I know. His black hair is spiked. He has the wide nose of a Filipino and the big eyes of a Vietnamese. Tiny freckles crowd around his nose. Under my gaze, he stands and turns. He has the build of a Japanese man — broad shoulders and short legs — but he does not walk in the short quick steps of the samurai I've seen in movies. He showcases all I find attractive about Asian men.

Finally, I manage a glance down at his handwriting on the page. Formal sentences that slant toward the edge of the paper. I like the way his *g*'s curl up and his *i*'s curve in the middle. His handwriting makes me think he is easygoing and warm. I'm so lucky it's Y2K, the year 2000, the year of the ILOVEYOU bug, when everyone had, so no one has to see my childish handwriting in English. Especially publishers.

He prints a receipt and with a gentle nod indicates he wants me to sign.

"All right." I catch myself speaking, and nod my head, yes. He grins. I can't take my eyes off the happy row of teeth he displays — or from the cute freckles on his wide nose. I shoot back a big smile, satisfied with my ability to interpret this visual language of his and express myself in the same language. Where and when have I learned this language? I have no idea. Speaking it feels soothing, easy, comfortable. I have never felt as confident in my English skills during these bloody challenging years in Canada as I do right now.

"John John" drops his head and I remind myself of the first rule of thumb: don't try writing until ideas have gelled in your mind. Do all Canadians do it this way? One thought at a time? And what is it that I want to express? He is still waiting for me to sign the papers in front of me. But all I want is to drop the pen in my hand and, instead, grab hold of his meaty fingers, nested together on the desk. However, as a writer I know that I should always hold onto a pen. My fingers should always remain faithful to the pen. Or nowadays, the keyboard.

"IS THERE ANYTHING ELSE I CAN DO FOR YOU?"
He writes on the only empty space left in the corner of
the page; his words, like the freckles on his nose, jam
together. I think of writing him an invitation for coffee.
In this way, I would use my pen to plot a romance story
for myself rather than for a made-up character. Yes, that's
what he can do—go out on a date with me ☺. My hands,
though, do not dare to express my wish. They stick not
only to the pen but to the original plan.

"I NEED $40 IN CASH," I write.

I wait for him to bring me the cash, the idea of initi-
ating a romance still fresh in my mind. Having found
the right male character, I am already developing a plot
for the story of our love affair. Love stories have always
been my favorite. My aunt, the cute, tiny old lady who
once was a teacher and never married, the woman who
took care of me during the day when my mother was at
work, got me started on them. I was only three when
she sat me on her lap and told me the story of Layla
and Majnun as she fed me. I'll never forget the spark in
her old virgin eyes when she narrated how much Layla
suffered, being apart from her lover. Persian literature is
full of love stories: Vis and Rāmin; Khosro and Shirin,
Bijan and Manije. The most admired, read, and mem-
orized form of poetry in Persia and today's Iran has
been *ghazel*, love poetry. Love is forbidden, but it has
nevertheless managed to survive a history of violence,

invasion, and atrocities—all those cruel kings, pools of blood, and eyes and tongues gouged out.

The first scene is starting to form in my head. We are sitting in the Starbucks coffee shop just around the corner. We are both deaf and, as such, live in voluntary exile in our imaginary world. Writing is a lifestyle we chose for ourselves when we realized we didn't belong to the real world but to the world of myths that no longer exists. We are, however, two productive members of a common past, constantly engaged in a serious discourse with a sweet future that never drops from the tree of possibility since it is not going to ripen, ever. We have no paper or pen with us at the café, where we sit in an intimate corner on the same side of a small table, so we pretend we are not only deaf but also blind. I take his glasses off and run my hand against his face where I know the freckles are—the same size and color as poppy seeds. Then I place my hand over his closed eyelids and listen to the words said by the movement of his pupils. My hands later slide down and rest on his latte-sweetened lips. They are sticky and give my fingertips a sudden tingle of excitement. He touches the bits of cupcake on the corner of my mouth as I nibble his finger. It tastes like berries. I imagine my mouth as a paintbrush. I paint his little freckles purple with my kisses. I scream in excitement, "John John!" Wrong move, for it brings the waiter over to our table. John pulls his face away. Although we're blind we still can feel the looming shadow of the waiter. He slams cash down on the table.

John the teller gently touches my arm through my jacket and points to two twenty-dollar bills laid down beside my hand. I take my time getting out my wallet and tucking the money inside. He looks over my shoulder and hesitates before handing me back my bank card. I turn around. A young girl, thin and blond, wearing tight jeans and a short tank top that frames her full breasts and displays her pierced belly button, is watching me. She shuffles every now and then. She wears a belt with large holes from which a set of chains hangs. I quickly turn back to the desk and thrust my bank card back into John's hand. Then I take the pen.

Yes, I am simply going to write to my teller that I am attracted to him before this girl takes my seat. I will use all the seductions of writing I've been taught. I will confess that I have always wished for a deaf lover, without being fully conscious of it. In this case, my accent won't bother my lover; on the contrary, he'll love it!

Besides, in bed I can talk as much as I want without fearing that it might jeopardize things. In the past, I started talking to my white lovers in my mother tongue when we were in bed, and the next morning they were gone. That's why I am blaming Canada for all my romantic failures, and for all the sweet men with bitter tongues whom I've let into my bed.

I wish all Canadians were deaf! Then I would feel like I belonged to this place. Then I could have remained silent as I took the oath of allegiance to the Queen at my citizenship ceremony. But what if they had asked us to make that oath in writing? I'd have been really screwed because I would not have been able to cheat, which I actually did. As the others were making their oath, I mumbled my favorite song in Farsi under my breath. I didn't flee my homeland and avoid making an oath to the Supreme Leader only to come to a country where they would force me to make such an oath to a monarch.

But I will not blame the Supreme Leader or the Queen for my landing in a foreign place nine years ago. The members of the writing group I used to attend in Iran were no less bossy or oppressive than the leaders of the revolution. They forced me to write dry literary stories that were not to my taste. They thought my romance writing was lowbrow, degrading, and superficial. Even worse, they called my stories "unimaginative," not "revolutionary" enough.

"Read Hemingway and Faulkner, not Danielle Steel," they said. To me, however, the simple act of loving in a place where young men and women who stroll side by side in parks are arrested and lashed for it is revolutionary. I was once arrested in Saei Park, sitting between two male friends and reading one of my stories to them. They put me in a solitary cell for one day because of my crime. I would have gotten lashes if my parents had not fabricated a story that I was the official fiancée of the man sitting on my left. His mother gave the same version to the morality police over the phone.

I did not consider sitting on a park bench with two male writer friends a revolutionary act, but I did consider it heroic to write romance in a land of no love. I view my writing as my most subversive act, even more revolutionary than the act of one of the female writers in our group, the tall, classy woman with short hair. What she did was acknowledged as a brave and subversive course of action by all male writers. She worked for the Institute for the Intellectual Development of Children and Young Adults before and after the revolution. One day she was called before the authorities in the morality office and was given a repentant letter to sign. She didn't wear hijab before the revolution and even for a short time after; she always talked with her male colleagues, and was seen laughing, indicating that she had counter-revolutionary, non-Islamic ideas. She should have been ashamed of her past and should have acknowledged her repentance by signing the letter provided. The classy virgin writer (by virgin, here, I mean unmarried) did sign the paper, but not the one the authorities wrote. She rewrote the entire letter, saying that she was proud of her past, yet she would comply with the new rules set out by the morality office.

At least in my romantic tales I didn't comply with any new rules in place at the writers' group. I left the group when I was asked to quit reading Danielle Steel and write sublime, worthy, literary stories. Although I'd never actually read any of Danielle Steel's books, I had read her Persian counterpart, R. Etemadi, which I kept a secret. I wouldn't have gotten admitted to the group in the first place if I'd ever mentioned R. Etemadi. What I liked the most about his books were their imaginative and "subversively futuristic" titles, written in Farsi on the front of the book and in French on the back—for example, *Ce soir une fille mourra* (*Tonight, a Girl is Going to Die*).

Like books such as Sadegh Hedayat's *Haji Agha*, Gholam-Hossein Sa'edi's *Fear and Trembling*, Shahrnush Parsipour's *Women Without Men*, and Salman Rushdie's *Shame*, translated into Persian by Mehdi Sahabi after Khomeini called for the writer's head, and many more, R. Etemadi's books were banned after the revolution. The only place one could buy an old copy was on the black market, which I did, once, when I climbed five flights of creepy stairs in a dilapidated building in front of the University of Tehran to get to a secondhand bookstore, leaving me out of breath in a room full of dust and old books. I first had to get my hands on the owner's wrinkly dick in order to get my hands on a copy of *Ce soir des larmes seront versées* (*Tonight, Tears Will Be*

Shed!). The most disgusting part was when he screamed "John" before coming.

I fiddle with the pen in my hand. *Ce soir*... There is no blank space left on the paper to write my proposal. But it doesn't matter anymore, because from now on I will communicate only in sign language. I have made up my mind to be a deaf writer. I will be much happier as such. I won't need to give lectures at my book presentations, if there are any. When I introduce myself as the author of the book, nobody will raise their eyebrows or screw up their faces, or look at me the way a sane person looks at the crazy ones. I know that look very well. Besides, I will be free of the question "Where are you from?" that is thrown at me everywhere I go. And I will tell people my Persian name. I will no longer be an eternal alien in the land where I am a citizen. Neither will my teller be known as "John"—he can have his real name back. Everyone will call him by that. Only I will add "John" after!

"Oh, John." I look my teller full in the face and put the pen down. I will communicate with him through his language. We are both deaf and will need no pen, paper, or even a keyboard. I have my hands and he has his, to lift me up and take me to bed. I will strip him of his clothes but leave his glasses on. Their shiny frames will wink at me in the dark, shedding light on his tiny freckles. We will pronounce every vowel with our fingers as we roll over one another. Our tongues curled into each other, we will talk till morning.

As I return to myself, John smiles, looking straight into my eyes. Is he reading what I am writing? Not from the way he's squinting at me with no smile on his lips. He looks down at his watch and points to the sentence he has written: "IS THERE ANYTHING ELSE I CAN DO FOR YOU TODAY?" Again my mind reels. *Yes. I want to pay a bill...* His smile is back for a moment, but I realize it is not meant for me. It passes close to my ears and flies over my slumped shoulders. It is aimed at the woman standing behind me: the blonde teenage girl who approaches to take my empty space.

So much for asking out my teller! Do I somehow have an accent even when I talk in sign language? Have I offended him? Haven't I gotten through?

To get even and to please myself at the same time, I stand up, lean forward, and yell into his deaf ears, "Thank you very much." I know he can't hear me. Let him be deaf. It's his loss. He could have been my lover. I gave him a chance. But no. He prefers this teenage girl over me: a girl wearing a ridiculously short tank top, too-tight jeans, and a belt with a set of ugly chains hanging from it. This girl who speaks fluently in English. Perhaps I should seek vengeance on both of them.

Although I still haven't walked away, the girl ignores me; her shoulder rubs against me as she sits down.

Should I shout out that I am not finished yet, pull on
the chain on her belt and knock her down? No, the girl
is sweet. At closer range I see that she too has small
freckles on her delicate nose. Besides, I don't want to
turn this story into a drama. Tonight, no tears will be
shed! Romance is my favorite genre. So maybe I should
come up with some peaceful diplomacy—a romantic
plot—and ask both of them out. Then the three of us
"Johns" will speak our own languages—English, sign
language, and Farsi. Yes, what about a *ménage à trois*?
Wouldn't that be perfect? *Ce soir, mes amies, nous con-
verserons d'amour en trois langues de toutes les langues du
Canada.* After all, we're living in a multicultural, multi-
lingual society, aren't we?

Saving the Dead

MARY SECRETLY MOVES HER air mattress and blanket from the Red Cross staff tent to the one where the bodies are laid out in plastic bags. She wants to keep an eye on things. Since there is no running water to give them a proper Islamic wash, someone will come tomorrow to give them ablution by earth before they are buried in a mass grave. She sets a cot sideways across the opening of the tent and peeks out to see if the pestering old man who was a nuisance the whole day is there. He is not. Mary draws a sigh of relief and lies with her back to the dead. It is better to breathe the freezing air of the desert winter than the odor of decaying bodies. Two bodies— a young woman and a young man partly wrapped in white cotton sheets—share a plastic bag as if asleep side by side. Mary feels a pang in her breast and gasps. She has come from Canada to her childhood city of Bam to save those still living after the earthquake in these last

days of 2003, but instead has ended up saving only the
dead. She hasn't even been here for twenty-four hours
and already she has seen enough.

Mary had to give the old man three shots in just
two hours. That many tranquilizers in such a short
time could put a camel to sleep for a week. Still he
kept trying to attack his daughter's body, finally tearing at the plastic with a knife, and in the end injuring
himself. He had hobbled away, through the ruins and
dust, toward the others trying to help pull survivors
from under the debris.

Now, exhausted from her struggle to quell the man's
rage, Mary fights to keep her eyes open. She hopes
that somebody got the knife away from the old man.
Surely by now the tranquilizers are doing their work.
Her eyelids are heavy, but she notices something moving outside, beside the lone palm tree just beyond the
tent — like a ghost, jerking periodically and moaning
like a dying animal. Mary is afraid it's the old man,
coming back, possibly still wielding a knife, probably
still set on using it on his daughter's lifeless body. She
sits up in the bed, hugs her knees, and rocks gently back
and forth, listening, terrified of the darkness. After a
while she lies down again and is overcome by sleep.

In her half-sleep, Mary sees the earth open and a
hand grab her. Then she recalls that she's in the tent
of the dead and shuts her eyes tight, hoping to dissolve

the vision. Even so, her heart races as she sees the old man's sharp knife right there, behind her eyelids. She gasps. Her mouth is dry with the taste of earth and she still feels the grip on her throat. She tries desperately to touch something—anything—but can't budge. It's as though, with the slightest movement, her bones will splinter. She wakes with a start—sits upright—remembers another time: the moment when she bent over her own father, just before his death.

He had spent all his strength in drawing that one last breath, the muscles of his face tensing with the effort. But he had never breathed out. Instead, a sudden shudder poured out from under his skin around his open mouth. The tremor expanded across his face from ear to ear, setting his flexed muscles free.

Mary exhales. She looks up and peers into the darkness. The ghostly figure is still there by the palm tree, whose topknot sways now in the dusty night. It can't be anyone other than that crazy old man. The same one who got Mary into all this trouble. She shouldn't have imposed on the Canadian aid team to help him—there must have been hundreds calling out for help—but the old man had reminded her so much of her own father. Even at a distance.

"HELP. MY DAUGHTER. Please. God," he bawled. He was tall and lanky and had a long, thin face, soft brown eyes, sunburned skin, and, just like her baba, deep furrows marking his forehead and face. Mary grabbed the old man by the shoulders. They felt so frail under her hands she was afraid they might break if she pressed a little harder.

"My daughter is here, please, for God's sake!" The man pulled away and pawed madly through the debris and broken mud bricks. "She was as dear to me as my eyes."

Mary trembled. Her own father used to say the same thing. Every time Mary had come back to visit him, he would sit her on his knees as if she were still a small child. His hand would move up and down the stream of her black hair. Mary's sisters used to make fun of them so much that she finally got a haircut, and her baba had stopped treating her as a child. But he had never stopped saying, "She is the apple of my eye."

Mary told the blond Canadian aid officer what the man had said. She translated everything except the part about how much the man loved his daughter. Moments later, four trained dogs in Red Cross vests sniffed through the dense rubble as the old man bustled about them. The aid officer shook his head—after a half hour of scouring the area, the dogs had not found even a whiff of life. He led the dogs away.

The old man remained in the middle of the debris and threw fistfuls of dust over his head. "I should not have let her stay. I wish I had broken my leg and not gone to the wedding of our far relative in Jiroft," he wailed. His bristle-headed scalp was layered with heavy dust—his liquid eyes were bloodshot. He didn't say anything when Mary gave him the first shot. But he resisted when she tried to move him out of the path of the approaching bulldozers, unearthing the dead. "I want to lift her with my own hands when she comes up," he said in a hoarse voice.

Mary noticed his burned eyelashes and felt like crying. She left the man and ran to the tent to shed her tears. Six years earlier, in Bam, when her own father was at death's door, she had rushed off in the same way—past the trees in the yard—stumbled thirty-two steps into the dark basement to sit by the pickle and jam jars, where she used to hide as a child. There, she had cried as loudly as she wanted. Then, as had been her childhood habit, she had opened a jar and fingered some jam into her mouth. She had returned to her father's side with red eyes, a wiped mouth, and sticky palms.

MARY LIES ON the inflatable mattress. Yesterday seems lifetimes away now. As soon as their group arrived from Canada, Mary told the supervisor that she needed to take care of some personal business first, and promised she'd rejoin them soon. Knowing that she used to be a local, the supervisor agreed right away. He even asked their driver to take her to the cemetery after dropping the rest of them at the site. The pallid, dead brilliance of the winter sky had made her dizzy for a while. She wandered around. Nobody was there. All the tombstones were broken, and the graveyard was nothing but churned ground. Mary found some bones regurgitated by the earth, but, thankfully, they weren't from her father's grave.

On the way back from the cemetery to the site, Mary cried. All of Bam had become one big burial ground. Every house they passed had turned to chunks of broken adobe, limed cement, and mortar blocks. When they reached her former neighborhood, she asked the driver to stop. As she stepped out of the suv, her heart was crushed by the sight of her childhood house, turned now into a crumpled mound of mud bricks, the base of its walls mapping out where the rooms had once been.

The most mortifying sight, however, was the trees; most had toppled and now lay beneath the rubble. Mary didn't even want to enter the yard. But she did want to see if the palm tree her father had planted when she was born was still standing. She walked into the yard and toward the entrance to the basement, now clogged by debris. And there, near the entrance, half-uprooted, her palm tree still stood.

She remembered how the tangerine trees bloomed every spring, even after the death of her mother, when

Mary and her older sisters had paid requent visits to their father near the end of his life. They always found him sitting in the garden on a threadbare carpet he had spread beneath the palm. A brazier sat in front of him, and he held an opium pipe in his hand. As they approached, the scent of orange blossoms in the air gave way to the smell of opium. Her sisters, who, like Mary, were all living abroad, couldn't hide their disappointment and scolded their baba, who had shrunk to the size of a child. "What kind of life is this, sitting here all day and smoking *taryak*?"

"I have nothing better to do," he said.

Only Mary accepted their father as he was. She was always more forgiving toward him than her sisters were. Perhaps because he was more forgiving with Mary than with them. When they were children, he wouldn't punish her in the same way he would punish her sisters for their wrongdoings. That aside, he had been right in what he said. If Mary's mother had been alive, she would have kept him busy picking orange blossoms for her, which she would have made into jam to send over to Mary in Toronto and to Mary's sisters in Phoenix, Arizona. Nevertheless, he always abandoned his pipe and opened his arms as soon as he saw Mary, his youngest child, approaching.

"Maryam," he'd call, using her Persian name. "Maryam Banoo."

To Mary, the house was the place where the memories of her father dwelled—a place she could always
return to, even if all other doors were closed to her.
The place where her palm tree still breathed. But after
his death, the house sold quickly. Mary was the only
one who hadn't wanted to sell. Her objections made
no sense to her sisters. They wanted their share of the
money. There was no point, they said, in keeping the
house after their parents had died.

Mary stared at the barren yard. Everything was covered by a thick coat of dust. She could not have come
out of her frozen state to go back to the car had she not
seen the young man carrying turquoise prayer beads
suddenly appear from what used to be the veranda, his
long, straight hair falling on his dust-caked shoulders.
The son of the new owner, Mary thought, watching
him stumble on the broken stairs and then recover.
The man looked at the ground, stirring the dust with
his heels. He wore a long and loose robe like a sack,
fastened with a rope at his waist. It had the same dull
hue as the white-tinged sky, and the soft skin under the
stubble on his face seemed burned.

Grainy bits and pieces crunched beneath his feet as
he ducked under the palm tree that sat at its awkward
diagonal angle and walked toward Mary, grinning. Like
Christ, his eyes were brown and suffering and he had
an elongated face. Mary didn't know him but she felt at

ease when the man saluted her, bowing his head while turning the blue beads around and around in his hand. She then headed back to the car to ask the driver, who was honking impatiently, to wait a little longer. She couldn't leave her childhood house before replanting the half-uprooted tree.

LATER, AMID THE rescue effort, Mary, dazed and fatigued and revisiting memories of her palm tree, found herself hugging a bundle of the clean sheets used to wrap the dead. She was surrounded by medical equipment, along with dozens of blankets and cans of food that two helicopters had brought in earlier that day. She wiped her face on the bundle of sheets and got up. What was she doing? Oh yes, medication. Go out there, help that old man. She wondered if his daughter had been found. She took two syringes from a black plastic bag and walked outside, ready to give him another shot in case he fainted at the sight of his dead daughter.

"Please be careful. She could be alive. Don't injure her body," the man screamed as the bulldozer moved forward.

A blue-eyed Quebecois aid officer wanted Mary to ask the man if there was only one person in the house. His eyes were clear against the dry background of earth.

"Yes," the old man replied emphatically.

On the seventh go, the bulldozer's scoop turned up the girl's body. Wailing, the old man ran toward the two aid workers, who took the body from among the rubble. He stood transfixed when he saw that she was naked. A man's blunt arm was in the scoop, too. The old man's face went as blank as his dead daughter's, and his pupils widened into the same shape as hers. Mary's knees began to tremble. The man stumbled forward, and Mary reached out and held him by the collar of his long khaki garment to prevent him from collapsing.

Her own father had looked this way before his death. He had shivered like the leaves of Mary's palm tree in the wind. "I'm sorry, Baba. We shouldn't have taken our mother abroad," Mary had choked.

"It's okay. The past is behind us all. Look into your future."

"I've talked to my sisters. We are going to come back here forever and live with you." A sudden cough had shaken her father; she waited until it passed. "Here is better for me. I can work as a doctor. In Canada, I'm only a nurse."

"You can't live here again. Your future is somewhere else. But your childhood stays here with me. My children have never left me. They are here and never grow up. You still roam in the rooms and run in the garden and hide in the basement." He had taken her hand in his own; it was very soft, nearly translucent to the point that Mary could see blue veins knotted together under the skin.

Mary knew she had gone too far. Her father had let her to go to Tehran to study medicine. Had he ever imagined she would emigrate to Canada after finishing her degree? He had thrown a big party for her graduation, but when she announced her plans, he'd left the party and hadn't come back until it was over.

Then Maryam had gone further still. She'd sponsored her sisters one by one and dragged them to Canada and pushed them through graduate school. Not being able to find a decent job in Tehran or to get admitted to a post-grad program, they had come back to Bam with bachelor's degrees to putter around the house. Mary's mother supported the idea of them leaving the country. Her sisters reported her words she'd told their baba over a long-distance call. "What kind of job are they going to get in this city? There's nothing. This garden doesn't need any more caretakers other than you. If they are idle all day, they will turn into spinsters, looking after their friends' children! And what kind of husbands are they going to get in this city? Men below them with no university education. You want that?"

Her words were effective, but their baba had not consented before she said, "I made them swear to my milk to come back after they've obtained their degrees. And I promised that, at that point, we'd all move to

Kerman together. Don't fight me on this. You're going to have to leave that garden behind."

Not only did her sisters not come back after finishing school, but they also found jobs in Arizona and moved there, where the weather was similar to Bam's. Worse, they brought Maryam's mother to live with them. "I want to be with my children and grandchildren," she had said. "I spent all my life raising them and now I have nothing to do in this house. I am no one without them." She'd pursed her lips. "My home is wherever they are."

Maryam's baba had let her mother remain with them so that her wish could come true. She had died, surrounded by her two older daughters, while Mary's father stayed back to die in his own home — in his orange grove, among the scent of tangerines — and to be buried in Bam's cemetery beside his ancestors. Only Mary, who had sensed their father was going to pass, had taken time off from work and come from Toronto to Bam to be present at his deathbed.

And now it was Mary who had come back to her ancestors' town only to help an old man who bore a shocking resemblance to her own baba. Even though, in reality, he was the father of this dead girl laid at his feet, naked and defenseless. Mary sat the old man down and turned him away from his daughter's body. The man's arm, torn at the elbow, that had turned up in the same scoop with the dead girl was stuck between two mud bricks, and the girl's body, turned on its right side, was leaning on it. Like a lever, the dismembered arm supported the body's weight, keeping it up and preventing the dead girl from falling face-down. Her small breasts hung, touching the ground.

"I think your daughter was taking a shower at five o'clock before the call to prayer when the earthquake happened," Mary said. She sat beside the man and gave him the second shot.

"We didn't have running water at home." The old man lowered his voice to a rasp. "We went to the public bathhouse once a week."

"These men who are working here are all doctors. They don't look at your daughter as ordinary men look at women, but I'll go and wrap her in white cloth." She tucked a wisp of hair on her brow under her scarf. "I'm a Muslim woman. My father was from here. We used to live on Ansari Street, close to Seyyid Mosque. He used to attend Friday prayers."

The man didn't seem to be listening. Crouched, he was rocking back and forth, mumbling something under his breath. Mary waved to the Canadian aid workers to take the body out of the man's sight. The aid officer walked over to Mary.

"Are you sure your daughter was alone at home?" Mary translated the officer's question.

"I don't know. She never came with us to Jiroft," the man stammered, biting his lips.

The bulldozer ran full throttle again, and the body of a young, naked man rolled out. He was missing an arm. The old man jerked up onto his feet and stared at the unearthed figure. He buried his face in his hands. "I am destroyed," he said. "Dust on my corpse. My dignity is ruined." He shuddered like the earth itself. His teeth hit against each other as he spoke.

Mary thought he would be better off dead. If only he hadn't seen what his eyes had dared to see. On an impulse she turned and embraced him, as tightly as she'd held her own father—nothing but a bag of rattling bones in the last days of his life. She didn't want to let go. The old man pushed her back. She was not a family member: a Muslim woman should never touch a man, except for her husband, her father, her brother, or her uncle.

"I am sorry," Mary said. The old man didn't seem to hear her. He had his gaze fixed on his own daughter.

The aid workers brought two plastic covers from the tent. As they lifted the girl's body to place her in the bag, the old man suddenly jerked forward and ran toward them. He ripped the plastic from the body and kicked his daughter's corpse back into the ruins. "Leave the girl who mortified me here to rot."

The girl's body fell on its back, her big brown eyes wide open.

"She has no shame." The old man gave a strangled yelp. "Look how she is looking into my eyes." He pushed the girl's face onto the ground with his right foot. Then he yanked at the young man's dismembered arm, pulled it out from between the mud bricks, and tossed the stump into the rubble. The arm landed on its severed end; the hand, stiff with rigor mortis, was turned up toward the low desert sky, its fingers wide open. The old man grabbed the arm and pushed it back into the earth the other way, so that the cut end, instead of the fingers, stood out.

Next, the old man attacked the man's body, grabbing his testicles in one hand and squeezing, while, with the nails of his other hand, he tried to pop out the boy's open eyes. The aid officer grabbed the man's arms and pulled him back, and Mary gave him a third shot. The other two aid workers lifted the girl's body again and placed her into the same plastic bag as her lover.

The plastic the old man had ripped from his daughter's body drifted on the ground among the rubble until a sudden breeze lifted it up into the air. It caught on the boy's torn arm where the meat and veins twisted into a knot, and flapped in the dusty air. With its brown skin peeling, the stump looked like the trunk of Mary's palm tree, half-uprooted by the earthquake. She shook her head at the bizarre idea.

. . .

MARYAM HAD PUT the roots of her half-fallen palm back in a hole she'd dug in the soil. Then, using her weight, she'd pushed the trunk up. It was a mature and heavy tree now. The Jesus-like young man who had surprised her when he'd walked into the yard of her childhood house had come to help her with the replanting of the tree. Once they had finished, he climbed the tree and hung his turquoise beads from a lower branch.

AT FIRST MARY stood still, staring at the stump of an arm, aghast at the old man's rage. He knocked the aid officer aside and clawed his way back to the body. Then she ran after him. She grabbed his arms from behind and yanked him back. When he fell on his back, she pressed him down and dug her fingernails into his arms as he struggled to get away. "You should let me tear her up!" he cried. "She sinned, and, as her father, I have every right to punish her. You know that, don't you?"

When Mary couldn't come up with an answer, the old man verbally attacked her. "Your father would have done the same with you, if he'd caught you sinning."

The mention of her father opened Mary's mouth, and the words poured out. "First of all, none of us is without sin. Secondly, leave it to Khoda to judge the dead. You're not allowed to sit in his place and determine their punishments before the Judgment Day. You know this, Baba. Don't you?"

Mary released his arms, not expecting that he would roll over in rage to quickly grab a kitchen knife gleaming amid the rubble. Mary's heart lurched as the man pushed himself up from the ground and ran. She quickly jumped forward and positioned herself between the old man and his daughter. In the split second before the knife's reflection caught her eye, she saw the Canadians running toward them. "No!" Mary shouted and threw herself on top of the girl. As she felt the man's hand grip her throat, she quickly turned and grasped at the boy's torn arm, using it like a stick to push the old man away. Finally, he fell on his side. Mary let go of the arm and tried to pull the knife out of the man's grasp. Again he pushed her back, but she grabbed the old man's wrist and twisted. They struggled until her Canadian co-workers separated them. Only then did she see that the man was bleeding from his side. There was a cut on his side where his shirt was torn and soaked in blood. She tasted salt and earth, and blood in her mouth.

"You have become like these blond outsiders who don't have a God," he said. "I bet you have done every wrong you desired abroad. Good your father did not see you disgracing him like this." The man got up and spat on his dead girl. "She is not my daughter."

Mary sat in silence. Seeing her unmoved, he turned and left.

. . .

NOW IN THE early morning, she stirs. Gazes into the dawn. The suffering figure is gone from outside the tent and all is peaceful. She lies on her back and thinks about her father. If it weren't for him, Maryam would have run after the wretched old man, but this time only to throttle him. She wished to God he hadn't looked so much like her father, with his same tone of voice, soft, liquid eyes, and long, thin face marked by furrows. She rolls onto her side and thinks about the robed man who had helped her by holding up the trunk of her palm tree as she scraped fistfuls of soil into the hole and then evened out the earth at the base of the tree. They hadn't even spoken to each other. Not a word.

Divided Loyalties

I ARRIVE IN TEHRAN two days after my brother calls to inform me about my father's death. "A car hit Papa," Milaad says, his voice cracking like phone static. "It happened close to his home. He died on the spot. The driver fled the scene — we couldn't find him. There is also something else, which I'll tell you when I see you."

Thankfully, Milaad accompanies Maman to meet me at the airport. Maman and I had a fight on the phone six months ago and we haven't talked since. That was the night I came back from Paris, the last place I saw my father alive. Our squabble doesn't matter now. I am here to be with my mother during the forty-day mourning period. I might even stay longer — for six months, a year, or, who knows, the rest of my life — if Maman and I can get along now that the source of our separation is gone.

Nor does it matter that my mother wrongly accused

me of siding with my father. In truth, Papa and I had a row at the end of our trip and he accused me of exactly the same thing: of supporting her. This is what our parents did to me and Milaad all our lives. Each wanted us in their camp when they fought with each other. And once they made peace, they would divide their children between them. Milaad was hers and I was his.

My situation was much worse than my brother's during the times when our parents quarreled. As a girl, I was supposed to side with my mother. This wouldn't have been difficult, if her true reason for being angry was that my father was a miser. We lived very close to poverty because the only money that came into the home was from our mother's meager salary. Papa used all of his money to buy property. However, the real reason behind my mother's anger was her desire to control my father and keep him, like Milaad, under her thumb. I believed my father should have his independence as much as I wanted to have mine. I wanted to have freedom of association — to like, love, and assemble with whomever I chose, including my aunt Raazi, Papa's younger sister.

Entering the arrivals area and dragging my suitcase behind me, I look around for my mother and see her, along with Milaad, walking toward me. In her black winter coat, slacks, and wimple hijab, she looks slim and miserable. I speed up and we meet halfway. She throws herself into my embrace and wails. "You see, Maana, your mother is a widow now."

People standing nearby look at us with compassion. "Sorry for your loss," they whisper as they pass. The other passengers laugh with joy as they reunite with their loved ones. Their families, dressed mostly in bright colors, shower them with flowers and kisses. I pass Maman a clean napkin I've saved for my own crying and hold her until her sobbing subsides.

"Let's go," Milaad says, grabbing the handle of my luggage. I am startled by how much, with his sideburns and goatee, he looks like our father when he was young. Milaad has come without his wife, Shabnam. Perhaps he didn't want to put her through the ordeal of witnessing an unpleasant exchange between our mother and me.

Hugging Maman around her shoulder, I walk with her out of arrivals and up the road to the parking lot. She continues shivering all the way to Milaad's white Renault, which belonged to her before she gave it to Milaad as a wedding gift.

As Milaad drives us out of the airport, I wonder where we are going: To Papa's house or Maman's? They are separated but not divorced. Maman and I are sitting at the back, and Milaad checks us in the rearview mirror from time to time, as if he can't believe he is seeing us so close together again. Holding onto my hand, my mother is no longer crying.

She had made up with Papa shortly before he died. She'd even taken him to visit her home. Six months earlier, she had refused to even give me the address. This was what began our fight over the phone; she'd said she was afraid I'd give it to my father.

Maman stares out the car window, her face swollen and her eyes foggy. Milaad turns on to the Chamran Expressway. So we are heading to Papa's place. He lived in the Atisaz Residential Complex, in one of the old towers that were part of phase one of the development project. When Papa first saw me in Paris, where we both went to vacation this past summer, he told me that he had made a down payment on the pre-sale of a unit in phase two. He also said he intended to put the property in my name.

My father's compulsion to buy real estate started during the construction era after the end of the Iran–Iraq War and never slackened. He became greedier with every new possession, which he immediately rented out, using the money toward his next purchase. Recently, he'd even thought of investing in real estate in Vancouver through me. I'd been an architect in Iran, but, unable to find a job in my field in Canada, I became a realtor. I didn't say no when Papa brought up the idea, but I didn't want to have anything to do with his real estate ventures, not in Canada or in Iran.

As I think about my father and our difficult

relationship, I set my sights on the marvelous Atisaz buildings, a mixture of cubical and triangular structures that have become landmarks in Tehran's northwest. I wish I could live in Iran, work in my field, designing constructions like these, and build a future for myself in my country. I haven't been here for four years — not since 2002, when Milaad married Shabnam and I attended their wedding. Unlike with my last visits, this time there's no rush to go back to Canada. I closed my latest real estate deal the day before Milaad called. "Can you come right away?" he said. "If you'll leave tomorrow, you can make it to Papa's third-day memorial. Maman needs you here. You're her only daughter."

"I'll be there in two days."

"Thank you. You know Shabnam gets along with Maman very well, but she cannot replace you."

After I hung up, I immediately called the RE/MAX Lougheed Mall office and told them I would be off for a while; they could give my office to another realtor.

Milaad pulls into the parking spot assigned to my father. He had no car. I squeeze my mother's hand and then let it go to open the passenger door. Milaad opens the door for her on the other side and it squeaks. As I take my suitcase from the front seat, I know I must decide if I'll stay with my mother for good. I can call my landlord and terminate my rental agreement in Vancouver. I can ask a friend who's got my keys to send me the items I want to keep and sell the rest. In Iran, I will have both a family and a job of my choice. I can buy Maman and Milaad out and have Papa's apartment to myself. I'll renovate it, buy new furniture, and turn it into the home I always wanted. I'll throw parties, inviting Maman and my favorite aunt, Raazi... of course on separate nights!

The security guard at Papa's building recognizes Milaad and rises from his seat, putting his hand on his heart, and greets Maman and Milaad. "*Salam*, Malak Khanoom. *Salam*, Milaad Khan." He is a middle-aged, bearded man with large, rough hands, unlike Papa's, with their long, shapely fingers. "This is my sister who lives abroad," Milaad says, and slips a few banknotes into his hand as we pass.

"Thank you, and my condolences, again," he says. His loud greetings set Maman crying again. I hold her in the elevator during our ride up to the tenth floor, where she and my father lived together until one year ago. It is as if I've become her mother.

She separates herself from me when the elevator doors open, pulls a set of keys from her coat pocket, and strides forward to Papa's apartment at the end of the hall on the left. We troop after her. I enter first and Milaad, carrying my suitcase, follows me.

I put my boots beside my mother's shoes on the upper shelf of the shoe rack in the foyer. My father's brown shoes are on the bottom shelf. He was wearing that particular pair in Paris when he and I visited some old, flirtatious Persian woman he introduced as one of his clients.

Papa's scent still hangs in the living room. It is the same smell that filled the room we shared in my cousins' house in Paris—a mixture of the aromas of Aunt Raazi's cooking and the scent of the Old Spice aftershave I'd mailed him from Vancouver. Even though he was a rich man, he lived on his loved ones' charity so that he could purchase more properties.

The room looks the same as when I saw it four years ago. The walls desperately need painting—Maman had demanded this continuously ever since they'd moved to the apartment—and the heavy, mismatched furniture needs to be changed. This apartment doesn't look like a rich lawyer's residence. I recall Maman shouting at Papa, her voice bouncing from the walls, "I'm embarrassed to invite our daughter-in-law's family to this place."

I look around for my father. Is he in the bedroom, his ears stuffed with cotton balls, and a heavy blanket pulled up over his head so he can't hear the echo of my mother's bitter tirade over issues mostly related to household expenses and money? No, he is dead, I realize, as Milaad enters the room. And Maman is not on her way to the bedroom to pull the blanket from him, addressing him in an old-fashioned and respectful way by using his last name, but insulting him by yelling in his face. "I'm talking to you, Ashrafi, and you're hiding like Milaad did when he was a teenager. Shame on you!"

Maman is in the kitchen; I can tell from the sound of cups banging on the counter. She must be making us tea.

"Why are you standing?" Milaad taps my shoulder. "Sit down." He lounges on the sofa. "I know you must still be in shock."

I sit beside him only to find that the coffee table is covered with the land title documents from my father's properties. "Oh, these?" The words jump out of my mouth.

"Yes, these," Milaad exclaims. "Maman seems in a hurry to sort things out. She is afraid you'll leave suddenly, like last time."

As soon as he mentions her, like the genie out of the bottle, our mother appears. She stands over us, holding a tray. "Please put those papers to the side. I brought tea."

She places the tray on the table and takes a seat in an armchair on the other side. "Have some halva, Maana, dear. I cooked it for you today. Or, if you are hungry, I can make you something."

"No, thanks. I ate on the plane."

Before taking the halva, I first offer it to Maman. She waves the back of her hand at the plate and says with a hoarse voice, "Can't eat." Her lips are white and dry. She wets them with the tip of her tongue and pleads, "Let's send your father's soul a salutation."

I nod and chant after Maman. *"Allah-o-ma sale ala Mohammad va ale Mohammad."*

Milaad's voice joins ours for the second and third salutation. He turns to me after the ritual and announces that he has to go. "Don't stay up. We have a big day tomorrow. I'll be here at 8:30 to take you to the cemetery."

"Finish your tea before you leave," Maman says.

"Shabnam is waiting for me."

"One cup of tea doesn't take that much time."

Reluctantly, Milaad sits back down. I give him his cup and then take mine and start sipping slowly.

"I wanted to discuss this." My mother points at the land titles beside the tray. "You need to be present."

"Some other time, Maman," Milaad objects. "Let's leave this for after the seventh-day memorial."

I nod in approval and smile as my mother turns toward me. She smiles back for the first time tonight. I am glad we don't have time to discuss Papa's inheritance. If it turns out he did put Atisaz II in my name, it might create another rift among the three of us. My father had already put his first house in my name when I was born, and gave my brother nothing on his birth. Maman used this as an example of his unfair treatment of his children, and turned Milaad against Papa and me. When I sold the house to transfer the money to Canada as a requirement for my immigration visa, she claimed that half of the house belonged to her. It was the same claim she had made a hundred times before—that she had loaned her entire savings to Papa to purchase the house when they got engaged. This time, however, she asked me to pay her share so that she could pass it to Milaad to undo my father's injustice. I refused to give her anything.

As my mother's sweet halva melts in my mouth, I feel embarrassed about my selfish behavior. But I had to be selfish. If I had given Maman half of my money, how would I have escaped from my parents and their troubles? I'm sure if I told people that the reason for my immigration to Canada was to escape my family, no one would believe me.

To calm my uneasy feeling about my past actions, I make a promise to myself: if we find out that the Atisaz II apartment is in my name and my mother wants me to give a share to her and to Milaad to be just, I will do this. Hopefully, nobody will do anything that could tear us apart. It is so good to be a family again, sitting around in one home, sipping tea.

Maman offers to refill Milaad's cup, but he stands up and says he really has to go now. I accompany him outside. "How is Aunt Raazi?"

"Good," he whispers. In an even more hushed voice, he asks me to come downstairs with him. "I need to quickly talk to you."

As the elevator closes, Milaad starts. "I'd like to ask you not to mention Raazi in front of Maman. Pretend our aunt doesn't exist."

"Isn't she going to be at the cemetery tomorrow?"

"She will."

"Then I shouldn't talk to her? Shouldn't even greet her? Why? What's the matter?" I feel stupid, as if I need to ask permission to talk to my own relatives.

"Of course you can greet her. But stay by our mother instead of socializing with Raazi and others from our father's side."

I raise my eyebrows in disbelief.

"You know that our father spent a lot of time at Aunt Raazi's after he came back from Paris. Maman thinks that she was trying to set him up with some woman, the same way she did twenty years ago. I am sure you remember."

Not wanting to hear one more word about the past, I raise my objections. "It was her husband who arranged those meetings between Papa and the woman who worked at his bank. Aunt Raazi was actually against it. You were only a child, so maybe you don't know, but I went over to her house and asked her flat out. She put her hand on the Koran and swore that it wasn't her."

"Anyways, Maman thinks that this time Raazi discouraged Papa from making up with her. Even after Maman brought him over to her new place, he refused to move back in together. Maman thinks that's because our aunt found him a woman in Paris. Somebody from the time when Raazi and her husband lived there with our cousins. Did you notice anything suspicious when you were there together?"

"No," I lie, and to cover it up I put on a surprised face and add, "Notice anything suspicious like what?"

Before Milaad can continue, the elevator door opens and we step out into the lobby. The concierge jumps to his feet. Milaad waves at him to sit down. He obeys, but his eyes are glued to us. I am about to continue our conversation when Milaad stops me, shaking his head and nodding toward the main entrance.

I walk with him outside. He pulls at my sleeve to continue walking to his car, and then motions for me to get in. Once I'm settled in the passenger seat, he turns to face me. "You remember I told you on the phone that there was something about Papa's accident that I'd tell you later?"

I nod, already feeling troubled.

"I'll say it quickly and then you should go back. Maman will think we are talking behind her back."

I nod again and sit back silently, letting him talk.

"You know how super-sensitive Maman is about

Aunt Raazi. If you hang around with her during Papa's memorials, Maman might cause a scene. I want to prevent this, because if she does, other things might be revealed—things we don't want our extended family and friends to know. Things that would cause our mother to lose face."

"What things?" I hear my heart thumping loudly while Milaad takes a breath and continues talking.

As he speaks, he looks at the rearview mirror instead of at me. "Papa had the accident and died twelve days ago, but we learned about it only on the day that I called you. When Maman didn't hear from him for days, she sent me to his building. The concierge—who, if you didn't notice, I paid earlier—told me Papa was dead. It was awful to find out from a stranger like that. But anyway, Raazi did the same thing earlier on the same day. She had also come to check up on Papa, and the concierge informed her about what had happened to him. When we arrived at the coroner's to identify the body, she was already there."

"Oh my!" I gasp.

Milaad turns to me. "I am sorry, sister. You don't know how guilty I feel. Papa called me two weeks before his death. It was my birthday, and he wanted to come visit us. I turned him down. Then, a week later, when I saw Aunt Raazi's number on my phone, I thought she wanted to ask me to be nicer to Papa, so

I didn't answer. Only when Maman told me that Raazi was also trying to get hold of her did I think it must be something important." He shakes his head in despair. "I was a bad son to Papa."

I reach out my hand to grasp his shoulder, which is trembling as he silently cries. I notice his hair has gone gray in the front.

I wait for him to wipe his face before asking the question that's on my mind. "I wonder why Raazi didn't call me?"

"Perhaps she didn't want to distress you. You know how much she loves you."

My brother's tears pour down his face again. I don't tell him how distressed I feel, how upsetting it is to be so baffled by the actions of my family members. No, I still don't have the understanding required for living with and among them.

Milaad drops his head. "Our father's corpse lay at the coroner's for ten days before we learned about his death from a complete stranger. If this leaks out to others in our family, not only Maman but also you and me will lose face. Nobody can know. People don't even know our parents were separated and living apart."

"I understand," I say faintly, even though I don't. "Raazi won't tell anyone," I add. "Unlike our mother, she usually keeps her lips sealed."

Milaad nods. "You should go back," he says. "Please

be extra kind to our mother until her nerves settle. She's gone through a lot. We don't want her to remain depressed for the rest of her life."

"I will," I say as I get out of the car. I wave at Milaad as he drives away. Before going back into the building, I take a few deep breaths, letting the crisp air calm my head, which is still buzzing from the stifling heat in the car.

The security guard gets up when I enter the building. I look away and walk straight for the elevators.

During the ride up to our floor, I try to calm myself. I decide that the story Milaad just told me, like other bad stories, belongs to the past. I am going to look to the future, to a different future for our family. Hopefully, Maman will also let the past be history, once all of the memorials are finished. Hopefully, in a near future, like all normal people in the world, we too will have a normal relationship with our relatives, including our father's side of the family. With that thought in my head, I barge into our apartment and throw myself on the sofa.

"You look exhausted." My mother's raspy voice pulls me out of my wishful thinking. "Go to sleep to be ready for tomorrow." I cower as I realize she is sitting beside me, gazing at the wall, lost in her own thoughts. She has taken off her hijab, and hasn't touched her cup of tea.

"Yes, let's go to sleep." I caress her thin gray hair

before standing and offering a hand to lift her up to her feet.

"Yes, let's go." Her voice is as hoarse as it used to be in those times after a bad fight with my father. We trudge together through the foyer to the bedrooms. "You can sleep with me in the master bedroom or in the guest room. I changed the sheets this morning."

I am tempted to go with her, but decide on the guest room instead.

Milaad has placed my suitcase at the foot of the bed, where my favorite red velvet blanket is still spread out. I put on my nightgown, turn off the lights, and slip under the covers, hoping that I can finally rest. I cannot.

The tension between my mother and Raazi goes back a long way. As the story goes, Maman once kidnapped me from Raazi's arms. It was the first time she left Papa. Milaad wasn't born yet, and I, at two and a half, had been left in the care of Papa's younger sister, who was married but hadn't yet given birth to her sons. After ten days of separation, my mother was a mess — crying all the time and going crazy. One night, she disguised herself in a chador, rang the doorbell, and, when Raazi opened the door, snatched me and dashed to a waiting taxi. Apparently, I cried nonstop and was so frightened that I bit her. She occasionally reminds me of that — as if I am a villain in that story. I roll over. The room is warm, but still I shiver.

When I open my eyes again, the room is brightened by sunlight and Maman is shaking me. "Wake up! Milaad will be here soon."

"Good morning." I sit up, noticing that the window is open.

"I opened it. It was like a sauna in here. I'm still having a hard time breathing. I wonder how your father lived with you for a month in the same room!"

"I'm not used to the weather here anymore."

"You will be if you stay long enough."

"For sure."

"Now come to the table for breakfast. I hope you still enjoy our food."

AN HOUR LATER, I am once again sitting at the back of Milaad's Renault, this time beside my sister-in-law, Shabnam, a slender young woman wrapped in an expensive fur coat. It is the first time I have seen her since her wedding. Elegant leather boots cover her delicate legs up to the knee. She has large hazel eyes and long eyelashes like rays of sun. A large tray of halva, on which Papa's name is written, sits on her lap. There is a bouquet of gladioli between us.

Maman sits in front and holds a Koran. She starts reading it aloud halfway through the long ride to Behesht-e Zahra Cemetery, forty-five minutes outside of Tehran. I feel like a kidnapped child being taken to a place she doesn't want to go. But unlike in my childhood, I don't cry. I cannot cry, because in a way, I don't believe Papa is dead. Unlike my brother, I haven't seen his corpse. My last image of him is from Charles de Gaulle Airport, just before I headed for customs. He was staying one more week in Paris at my cousins' house. He was looking so skinny, even though he'd gained several pounds during our time together. I'd taught him how to cook rice to add to the canned fish or beans he bought for daily consumption. "Don't forget to practice cooking once you're back home. I'll test you when you come to visit me in Canada," I said, hugging the bag of bones he'd become during his short separation from my mother. "I'll wait until you're back and then send you an invitation letter."

Maman's melancholic voice reciting the Koran makes Shabnam sob quietly. Not wanting her soft crying to seep into me, I concentrate on looking down at the gladioli on the seat. Once I can no longer bear the thoughts of my hands pulling apart their petals, I look up, past Shabnam, and watch the road. The closer we get to the graveyard, the more poor local children selling flowers and rose water gather by the road.

Shabnam's sobs get louder. A small puddle of her tears starts to form on the plastic that covers the halva. I touch my mother's shoulder and shake her slightly.

"What?"

"Can you finish your reading, please?"

She turns around. "Oh," she addresses Shabnam. "Don't cry, my poor girl."

"I won't, Malak Khanoom," Shabnam utters with a broken voice.

I also look at my sister-in-law with pity. With two tough women in the family, it makes sense that Milaad has chosen this fragile wife with the sensitivity of a high-school girl.

"Sorry," Shabnam murmurs, "but the sight of your father's face at the coroner haunts me night and day." I tremble as an image of my father's face, dead and gray, replaces the image of torn flowers in my mind. Feeling guilty for judging my sister-in-law in my thoughts, I think about how lucky I am to live in Canada, and not to have experienced the horrible ordeal that she has. I move the bouquet to my right side and slide toward her. "Do you want me to massage your shoulders?"

"Yes," she says softly and presses her eyelids together, a few more tears falling on her high cheekbones before she turns her back toward me. I rub her shoulders until her sobbing subsides. Milaad looks at me in the rearview mirror with appreciation. I nod at him, a replica of the Papa of my childhood, sit back, and look out the window.

We are at the cemetery entrance. There is a long walk from the parking lot to Papa's grave. Behesht-e Zahra has grown into a small town. Maman leads the way, carrying the bouquet. Shabnam, Milaad, and I each carry dishes of halva, dates, and fruit. We try to keep pace with my mother but it is not easy; Shabnam cannot walk fast in her high heels and she avoids walking on the flat slabs of stone that mark the graves through the old part of the cemetery. We can still see Maman at a distance. It is a weekday in a cold January, and the cemetery is almost empty.

In ten minutes we pass the central morgue and reach the area where new graves are dug. A procession of a few *Allah-o-Akbar*–chanting men, followed by a group of women and children, take their shrouded dead on a stretcher to his grave. I lose sight of Maman as she mingles with the women but then find her again as the throng moves off in the direction of an open grave.

Farther down the field, my steps slacken when my mother arrives at Papa's grave and a few people clad in black rush forward to hug her. They must be Milaad's in-laws. They step back when we arrive and greet them. Shabnam throws herself into the embrace of her father and cries like a baby.

Maman pushes aside the bouquets from Shabnam's family and places the bouquet we brought at the center of the pile of fresh dirt that stands a bit higher than the surrounding ground. She crouches down, sprays rose water on the parched soil, and sobs loudly. Shivering in my bones, I am about to join her when I see Raazi and her husband arrive. I put the dish of dates I am holding down on the grave beside the flowers and go over to greet my aunt. My mother seems too absorbed in her mourning to notice what I am doing.

Raazi opens her black chador and shelters me in her embrace. Wrapped in the same cover, we are now one. She holds me for a long time, crying on my shoulder. "It's so good to have you back. You smell like your father. My poor brother."

Her bosom is as consoling as it was on the day when, crying, I went to her house after Maman and Milaad barged into my room and beat me for siding with my father. I was a teenager then, and Milaad only a child. I knew it was Maman who had manipulated him like a puppet; nevertheless, I couldn't forget the way he stomped on the architectural model of a house I had made as a school project and destroyed it while Maman knocked me down to the floor, sat on me, held my hands with one hand, and repeatedly slapped me across the face with the other. My mother's blows hurt, but Milaad's actions broke my heart. I cried all the way to Raazi's on the bus, and decided to take revenge on my brother by hurting the person he loved the most — who else but Maman?

After few seconds, I separate myself from my aunt and step back. Milaad, standing among his in-laws at our father's grave, is raising his thick eyebrows at me and pointing with his head to Maman, a signal to leave Raazi's side. His sunken cheeks, covered by light stubble, show how much he is suffering inside, struggling to ensure that this event goes as smoothly as possible.

"I should go and serve the guests halva and dates," I tell Raazi.

"Go, dear. I should also go to your mother and Milaad to offer my condolences."

As Raazi moves toward the grave, I walk in the opposite direction, pick up a dish of dates, and start serving our distant relatives, who have made a cluster on the left. I am alert, imagining that something dramatic might happen between Maman and Raazi, but as I hear no commotion, I decide to turn and assess the situation. Raazi and her husband are now standing with Papa's other relatives, and Maman, back on her feet, is surrounded by her siblings and her mother, our grandma Aziz, who sits calmly in her wheelchair. I greet my grandmother and my aunt and uncles. I offer them dates. They each take one and send their blessings to Papa's soul.

Meanwhile, the Koran reader Milaad has hired arrives. He is a thin-bearded man with thick-framed glasses. We make room for him to stand beside Maman over the grave. She picks up her Koran, which is lying beside the flowers, and hands it to the man so he can recite a few verses and bring the third-day memorial to a happy end. I look over at my brother, who is among his in-laws and is holding his wife around the shoulders. We exchange a secret smile of victory. Now everyone can go back to his or her home in peace to get some rest before leaving for the afternoon gathering at the mosque. As Maman made a point of explaining to me in the car, assuming I'd forgotten our rituals and needed a refresher, this afternoon's memorial service will be open to the public. The following memorial, on the seventh day, will be a more intimate gathering where only family will be present at a dinner. If my mother were to cause a scene, I didn't know whether it would be worse for a large or a small audience to witness it.

WE ARRIVE AT the Jahmeh Vanak Mosque for the afternoon memorial service an hour before it starts. To greet those who arrive, I stand with my mother at the women's entrance, and Milaad stands with my uncle from Papa's side at the men's. When the mullah comes and bows his turbaned head to us, we move inside. The women-only hall is large, and the walls are decorated by black banners with inscriptions from the Koran and religious texts in white and green. There is a table in front with a few bouquets of white flowers Milaad has ordered. A photo of my father taken by me at Deep Cove, enlarged and in black and white, sits beside them.

Women from my father's family sit together on the right side of the room, and women from my mother's family on the left. I sit beside Maman during the mullah's speech to the men, which is broadcast over the four loudspeakers at the corners of the room. As the man goes on about what a nice, kind, and generous husband and father Papa was to Maman and us, women weep under their chadors or scarves, pulled forward to cover their brows and eyes.

Once the mullah finishes his sermon about my father, Agha-ye Aadel Ashrafi, he starts reading the names of those my father has left behind. He says that my mother, Malak Khanoom, was a faithful wife who remained at her husband's side until his last breath. I fear somebody will say that this is a lie, but nobody does.

As he speaks about how much Maman and Papa cared about each other, my thoughts wander and I remember a story my father told me in Paris. I steal a glance at Aunt Raazi from the corner of my eye. The only part of her that is visible is her hands, which she constantly rubs together. Is that because, like me, she is recalling the same terrible story? Beside Milaad and me, Raazi is the only one who knows about what happened on the night, only eight months ago, when my mother and father came back from their pilgrimage to Papa's birthplace in the holy city of Mashhad. And she only knows because my father told her in an effort to convince her to search for a new wife for him.

As the story goes, following their return trip from Mashhad, Maman and Papa took a taxi from the bus terminal. My mother insisted that the cabbie should first drop my father at his place, while Papa wanted him to drive Maman home first. He was so eager to know where she lived that he was willing to pay the taxi fare. But Maman wouldn't give her address to the driver. This is when my father got more aggressive, telling the driver that Maman had a lover and was guilty of adultery. My mother demanded that the driver pull over in the middle of the trip, which he did, and as she got out of the taxi, my father called her a whore in front of a crowd of pedestrians. I've heard this story from both of my parents. Neither of them answered my question about why the hell they still traveled together, even though they were separated. As usual, it seemed they could live neither together nor apart.

The mullah says my name: Maana Khanoom. He has finished his speech about Maman and is moving on to talk about me. He says that I am an architect living in Canada but, as a good daughter, have put my job and life on hold and come back to be present here today. I lower my head, but I can still feel everybody's eyes on me. I am grateful that my father told everyone I am an architect, not a real estate agent, but I also feel a bit like a hypocrite for endorsing his lie. Next, the mullah talks about Milaad. He starts by addressing the stereotype that daughters are usually the ones who take care of their parents even after they marry, whereas sons belong to their wives' families. In this respect, Milaad is an exceptional son. He works at Iran Railways, where our mother used to work, is Maman's helper, and has a loving wife.

After the mullah finishes and everybody hails to the Prophet Mohammad and his household, I stand up to go around the room and greet our relatives and friends. Everybody tells me how proud Papa was of my success as an architect overseas and how much he enjoyed his two visits to Vancouver.

On the last day of his second trip in 2004, just before I drove him to the airport to return home, I invited Papa to come back to Canada. I said that the next time he came it could be for good, and he could live with me. This invitation is something I will never reveal to my mother, who would be devastated. Of course, before I made the proposal, I had asked myself whether I could live with my father, given my great annoyance at cleaning up the bathroom after him during that visit. But then I thought it was all right; I should take care of my father. At least it would put a stop to him dropping in at Aunt Raazi's every other day, asking her to find him another wife.

Of course, I was appalled by his behavior, calling

my mother a whore. Maman had a right not to give her address to him. But at the same time, I pitied my father. I pitied him because he was an old man — twenty years older than Maman — and I feared he would starve himself to death without her. I pitied him in spite of my concerns for women's rights and in spite of all the bad things he had done to Maman. I pitied him simply because I loved him.

In response to my offer, Papa said he first needed to finish a few law cases he still had on his hands and to complete his purchase of the Atisaz II condo and rent it out. As a token of his appreciation, he was planning to put the condo in my name. I thanked him, but was not happy about what he wanted from me in return: to become his real estate agent in Vancouver.

ON THE DRIVE back, Milaad reminds us that the next gathering will be the seventh-day memorial dinner at the Railways Restaurant. I am happy that I'll see Raazi there. There was no time at the mosque to sit with her and catch up with the news about her and my cousins in Paris.

Milaad drops our mother and me at Papa's place and leaves to go home with Shabnam. We each carry one of the baskets of flowers. A security guard beside the front desk steps forward to help as we enter the building. "I can take it for you upstairs, ma'am," he tells my mother.

I enter the apartment before the man, put my basket down, and hurry to collect the land titles, which are still lying on the coffee table. I scramble down the hallway to my room. It's not that I think the man is going to steal them, but that I see this as a good opportunity to review them in private. I want to see if Papa has put the Atisaz II condo in my name. This is something that could ruin my new relationship with my mother. She'll surely grill me about what I offered Papa to get the condo in exchange. If I tell her the truth, she won't believe that I didn't want anything in return when I told him he was welcome to come live with me. I simply thought that if they lived very far from one another, each on one side of the globe, it might help my mother to ask for divorce and start a new life for herself, for real.

"Where are you?" I hear Maman calling me.

"In my room. Coming."

Sitting on the edge of my bed, I continue shuffling the documents in my hands until I finally find the one related to Atisaz II. My name is nowhere in the presale agreement. Strangely, I first feel upset, thinking that my father has been disloyal to me, but then deep relief replaces disappointment. Things would be much more difficult for me now if my parents had divorced. If I decided to stay in Iran, I'd have no other choice than to drop Papa's entire family. In the order of family loyalty, Maman is first, before an aunt.

"Maana." My mother's voice is closer to my room now. "Have you seen the land titles that were on the coffee table?"

Before she opens the door, I quickly glance at the date the document was signed—just after Papa returned from France. Now I know why he changed his mind: because of the fight we had after visiting the old woman he introduced as his client. Fine, I think. I wouldn't approve of his behavior and plans with regard to that woman for any reward, even ten properties in my name.

I insert the document among the others, stand up, and walk to Maman, who has just opened the door. "I brought these in here to keep them out of the concierge's reach."

"Oh!" Maman exhales. "You've been smart since childhood, much more forward-thinking than your brother. Like me, he is very emotional. He—"

My mother's words are interrupted by the door buzzer sounding in the living room.

When I answer, Milaad's voice comes through the intercom. "You forgot the bag of groceries. Come downstairs and get them."

In the lobby, Milaad passes me the bag. "I probably won't be able to visit for a few days. Take care of our mother."

"Don't worry," I assure him. "We are getting along very well."

Milaad beams, and I cannot resist hugging him. I hold him for a good long time in spite of the presence of the security guard. The man looks away, the corners of his lips pulled down in a grimace.

The grin is still lingering on my lips when I reach our floor and come face to face with Maman, who is waiting for me in the hallway by the elevators.

"I missed you." She suddenly grabs me and pulls me into her embrace. Her breath blowing in my face is foul. I want to pull back but she keeps me in place. Her dry lips rub against my face while she speaks in a voice that sounds like barbed wire. "You're finally mine. Entirely mine."

My heart drops and my stomach starts to churn, yet I cannot muster a force from within me to move away from her. I am about to break into tears when she herself lets me go. "Give this to me." She takes the plastic bag from my hand. "It's good Milaad brought this back! Otherwise I couldn't make you your favorite food tomorrow. I should give him credit for being smart like you."

Immediately after we step inside the apartment, I tell my mother I am tired and want to go back to bed. Afraid that she'll ask me to sleep in her room for tonight, I disappear into the guest room before she can say anything. Like the previous night, I roll over and over in distress, but I am extremely hot this time instead of cold, as if I've somehow been thrown into hell.

You're finally mine. Entirely mine.

My mother's words swirl in my head. I push the blanket off and get up to open the window. A rush of cold air cools the hot tears streaming down my face. I stick my head out the window; I don't want my crying to bring Maman to the room so she can claim me again, as if I were one of my father's properties.

When my face is again dry, I go back to bed where I continue to toss, resisting the orders from a voice in my head that tells me I should pack right away and leave for Canada.

COVERED IN SWEAT, I wake up thinking I am back in Burnaby. The guest room is dead silent, just like my bachelor suite in the new OMA 2 building on Dawson Street. The room is cold and my red velvet blanket lies on the floor. I shiver, wondering if Maman has gone to her own apartment, leaving me here all by myself. I spring to my feet and dash to the living room to find out.

I am relieved when I find Maman in the kitchen, cooking. Her back is toward me. I stand at the threshold, watching her for a while, and I feel like a fool for thinking of leaving. "Good morning." I walk to her and hug her as she turns around.

"Good morning." Her voice indicates surprise at my sudden show of affection.

"What time is it?"

"It is almost noon. I made tea earlier, but since you didn't wake up, I turned off the samovar."

"Sorry."

"It is all right, dear. Go sit at the table and I'll bring the breakfast. I went out this morning and bought you fresh bread."

I am on my way to the dining table when the phone rings. I tell Maman that I will get it.

There is a pause before a woman's voice comes through the receiver. "Hello?" It sounds familiar.

"Hello. Who is calling?"

"Is this you, Ms. Maana?"

"Yes."

"Good to hear your voice. Your father didn't say anything about you visiting him."

I struggle to attach the voice to a familiar face.

"Hello?"

"I'm sorry, but I don't know who this is." I don't know why, but something about this woman's voice is frightening me.

"Of course you do! You came with your father for lunch to my place in Paris."

I feel like I've been stabbed in the heart. This is the last person I want to hear from. I look around to check if Maman is listening. When I don't see her, I cup my hand around the receiver and whisper into it. "My father passed a few days ago. I am here for his memorial." I am careful not to say "ma'am," for it would reveal the gender of the caller.

The woman gives a yelp like a wounded dog. "Oh, my! How is it possible? He was in perfect health."

"He died in a car accident."

"That's horrible! I can't believe it."

I don't let the woman continue. "I am sorry, but my mother and I were just about to go out. I have to go. Can I call you from Canada after I return? I'm sure you understand."

"Yes, but..."

I cut the woman short, this time with a firmer voice. "Please don't call again. We are already devastated by my father's death." I hang up before she can say another word. Just then, Maman enters the room. She is holding a tray. "Who was it?"

"A realtor. He had a deal for Papa. I told him to leave us alone." I am surprised by myself, coming up with such a perfect lie.

"Ah, one of those! They won't leave us in peace as long as we stay here. They're going to call every day to talk Ashrafi into new deals, thinking he is still alive."

"You're right! Why don't you go back to your place?" When she doesn't answer, I add, "I don't mean to suggest that this is not your home."

Maman looks at me with no sign of hurt in her eyes. "I'll take you there after the seventh-day memorial is over," she says decisively. "Even though I am here, our relatives have started to talk behind my back. Imagine what they would say if I left!"

"Nobody can say anything bad about you, Maman."

"You forget how people are in this country—always after sabotaging your life and splitting you from your loved ones. But they cannot harm us as long as we stick together."

I decide that I'll never let Maman know about the woman and Papa. It would tear her apart. I walk to her and put my arm around her shoulder. "We stand together, Maman."

"I believe you," she says happily. "Now, let's go eat."

AFTER BREAKFAST, MAMAN says she has a task for me. "I'm going to give you the files for your father's law cases. You can go through them and separate those that are still active. We need to call his clients to let them know he died. You'll be good at this."

While Maman goes to collect the files, I clean the table. When she returns, she lays the documents on the other side of the table. "I'll be in the bedroom, going through Ashrafi's clothes and personal stuff to separate what I want to give away to charity. Call me if you need me," she says before leaving the room.

I have ten large folders in front of me. Happy that my mother has given this task to me, I am determined to

first find the files related to the woman in Paris. She was
his client, but was she only his client? I recall her flirting
with Papa. My mother, like most women of her genera-
tion, always used Papa's last name to address him. But
on the day I visited the woman in Paris, she called my
father by his first name, Aadel, and with such affection
that one might have thought she was already his wife.
She made me so nervous with her ostentatious hospi-
tality that, the moment we stepped out of her place,
I scolded Papa for promising to go with her and her
daughter to visit the Palace of Versailles the next day.
He said her daughter was rich and had bought the small
apartment where the old widow had entertained us. She
also paid him to represent her mother, who wished to
take back her family house that had been confiscated
by the Mostazafan Foundation of the Oppressed and
Disabled at the beginning of the revolution.

She had come around the table and tapped on Papa's
shoulder when he pretended a morsel was stuck in his
throat and coughed. I told my father that I hated her
cooking, even though the four dishes and the dessert
she prepared for us were delicious. I ate very little,
though, pretending I had no appetite. She suggested I
was perhaps suffering from sunstroke and pulled the
curtains, obstructing my view and forcing me to watch
as she continued to swoon over Papa. This made me
more irritated by the minute. I could see she was very

lonely, and willing to do whatever it took to marry my father. She was even willing to put half of her house in his name if he won the lawsuit for her. Imagining them moving in together made me want to throw up her food. So this was why Papa was after this woman: he would have a place to live for free and he could rent out his own apartment and use the money for some future purchase.

I finally got fed up with her flirting, pushed my plate away, turned to my father, and announced: "I am not feeling good. Let's go."

Once in the street, to lighten my mood, Papa made a funny remark about being scared by the looks I had thrown at him during lunch. "You rolled your eyes the way a mother does when she catches her teenage son talking to the girl next door."

He underestimated my irritation with the situation and was taken aback when instead of laughing I lashed out at him. "I forbid you to fool around with other women while still married to Maman!"

He went white in the face but tried to improve my mood with another joke, recalling the game we'd played on the two occasions he'd visited me in Vancouver, in which I would pretend to play Papa's mother. "Am I allowed to pursue romantic relationships if I divorce my wife?" he asked. "Please permit me, Maman."

I'd found it an amusing routine in Vancouver, but

in this moment it was awful and improper. "Hell, no!" I shouted.

Realizing how furious I was, he took a step back. When a minute passed without another word from him, I once again started snapping. "Perhaps you *should* divorce Maman," I told him. "If one day I hear you have taken a second wife—this woman or any other woman—I won't talk to you for the rest of my life."

Now it was my father's turn to become serious. "Stop mothering me. I allowed you to do that when I was in Vancouver, but not here."

"Shame on you. You dared to call my mother a prostitute, but it is you who is acting in that way!"

He froze.

"Do whatever you want, but leave me out of it!" I stormed off to the Gare du Nord metro entrance and descended the stairs.

Papa followed me, but kept his distance while we waited for the train. When it arrived, we both boarded and he sat beside me. I looked out the window, my back to him, as if I were absorbed by something exciting projected on the empty walls of the tunnel. However, it was only when the doors closed and the train began to move that a scene from the past came to life on the dark screen of my mind. Following my seventeenth birthday, we moved to a new house. Shortly after, my mother and father had one of their worst fights ever. It ended with Papa beating Maman next to the staircase that connected the living room to our bedrooms on the second floor. It was the first time he'd physically hurt her, and he immediately realized how wounded I was also, standing there watching. He reached down and lifted her from the floor with surprising gentleness.

Their battles didn't end that day, and Papa never apologized for the things he did. Later, he adopted Maman's strategy of going over to the houses of family members to complain about my mother and her behavior. He told everyone that he was the real victim and that he had filed for a divorce. It was around this time that I heard that Raazi's husband had set up a date between my father and one of his colleagues at the bank, an old maid from a good family.

The story infuriated me so much that I planned an attack on my father. One afternoon, I waited behind the front door of our house for his arrival. As soon as he opened the door and set foot inside, I lashed out at him. I'll never forget how my father's eyes opened wide behind his glasses as he saw me jumping toward him and bringing my fist down in his face.

I took Papa's arm when we got off the train. "I'm sorry for shouting at you."

"You scare me sometimes," he said as we proceeded to the exit.

· · ·

"ARE YOU SLEEPING over there? You haven't touched half of the files yet." Maman's gruff voice brings me back to present as she pops her gray head into the dining room.

"I'm almost done with this one."

"Good. I just put on the rice and the stew is simmering. I'll continue my sorting until they are ready."

When she disappears into the bedroom, I look down at the folder in my hand. The name on the sticker confuses me. I read it three times over before I realize it is my mother's name. The folder contains two files, one from twenty years ago, around the time I hit Papa in the face by the front door, and one from six months ago. I open the old file first. The page on the top says that my father had dropped his divorce lawsuit against Maman. I put it back in the folder. Smoldering inside, I open the new file and read the first page. It is a court verdict, authorizing my father to dissolve their marriage anytime he wishes, without requiring my mother's presence. It is dated right after Papa returned from Paris. I tremble, thinking that my comment—that he should divorce Maman if he intended to marry another woman—might have caused him to obtain the authorization. I feel lucky that only very shortly after, Maman made up with Papa and took him to her place.

I take both files, the one related to the old woman in Paris and the one concerning Maman, and tiptoe to the guest room. I put the files in a plastic bag and hide the bag at the bottom of my suitcase. I will shred the file related to Maman once I am in Canada and dump the other file after I call the woman to tell her to get herself another lawyer and forget about my father.

I sneak out of the room. Before going back to the table, I check on Maman, only to find she has fallen asleep among Papa's clothing spread out on their bed.

This time, I don't let memories disturb me, and I finish the job in an hour. I put all the current lawsuits in one file and take the old ones to the kitchen and toss them in the garbage bin.

The good smell of rice and *ghormeh sabzi* stew has changed the stale air in the kitchen. I am extremely hungry. Nobody can make this stew like my mother. And nobody can make *gheymeh* stew like Aunt Raazi. I cannot wait to visit her one day soon and taste her food.

I set the table and go to wake up Maman, who has snuggled up with the thin, lace bedcover. Thinking that old troubles are finally behind us, I feel relieved of the stress of reviewing Papa's files. Tonight, I am going to sleep in Maman's room. She must not suffer from loneliness while she has her daughter in Iran.

I WAKE UP fresh the next morning from a deep sleep. My mother is not by my side. I pull open the curtains to bask in the sunlight, something I could not do at this time of year in rainy Vancouver.

When I bound into the living room, singing loudly to myself, I see Shabnam lounging on the sofa, dressed in a neat black embroidered shirt and skirt. Today, her long chestnut hair is down. "What a good surprise!" I say.

"I asked Milaad to drop me here before going to work. I thought you and Maman might need a hand making the halva for the memorial."

"You are so thoughtful! Better to do the cooking today than to leave it to the very last day. Actually, my plan is to dye Maman's hair tomorrow." In appreciation, I give my sister-in-law a peck on the cheek; her long eyelashes caress my face. At the same time, my mother appears in the room. "Before cooking, you need a good breakfast. Come to the table."

We move to the dining room. Maman has bought fresh lavash and made a scrumptious Persian breakfast for us. The table, from which she has removed the lawsuits folder, is set colorfully with butter, feta cheese, sour-cherry jam, scrambled eggs, tea, and freshly squeezed orange juice. "Thank you, Maman," Shabnam and I say together as we sit down.

I present the idea of coloring Maman's hair at the table. At first she objects, but later, when Shabnam says that social norms have changed and it is no longer inappropriate for the family of the deceased to freshen up their look, she agrees.

After breakfast, we go to the kitchen and start

making halva. I feel joyful being around my family. The day passes pleasantly as we put the halva and dates on trays, decorating the halva with pistachio and almond slivers and sprinkling shredded coconut on the dates.

"May Ashrafi's soul rest in peace," Maman says once we are finished. "Let's recite a Fatiha for him."

As we go into the living room, I notice that Maman has set flowers from the memorial in the mosque in every corner. We sit around the coffee table and together recite by heart the first chapter of the Koran. I glance at the flowers and wonder how much longer they are going to last. The air is full of their sweet aroma, even though their petals are about to fall apart.

After the prayer, Shabnam leaves. "I leave you two now to rest. Enjoy your time together tomorrow and make yourselves beautiful." She winks at Maman. "Milaad and I will pick you up around four the day after tomorrow."

"She is right," I tell my mother after she's gone. "We have forgotten all about ourselves. Look at us. We are both such a mess."

"We have all day tomorrow to look after ourselves. I am tired now," Maman says before retiring herself to her bedroom.

The next day I sleep until noon, only to find Maman as grungy as the day before. "You didn't even take shower?" I ask her.

"Didn't you say you wanted to dye my hair? Normal people shower after."

"Oh, sorry. I am still groggy." I head to the bathroom. After washing my face, I invite Maman to bring over her hair color.

"What about breakfast?" she shouts from the living room.

"I'll have it later while you are taking your shower."

When Maman comes out of the bathroom, she is wearing a white cotton dress. I draw a sigh of relief. "I don't like to see you in black."

"I must wear black in public until the day after the forty-day mourning period is over."

"I know."

"We'll go to my place after the restaurant tomorrow. There, I can wear whatever color you'd like me to."

"I can't wait," I say, aware of the excitement in my own voice. "Now, let me blow-dry your hair."

I bring a chair from the dining room and set it in front of the dressing table in the master bedroom for Maman to sit on while I dry and style her hair.

When I'm done, I look at her image in the mirror. "Now you are as beautiful as ever."

She flashes one of those smiles she used to give when she and Papa were at peace.

We take it easy for the rest of the day and watch TV. Around nine, Maman says she is tired. I put the TV on mute and accompany her to her bedroom. I reach forward and pull away the blanket covering her bed. "Slide in, Your Majesty."

She lies down and grins again as I tuck her in.

"Don't go back to Canada," she pleads as I climb into the bed and lie where my father used to sleep. "Stay here and live with me."

"I'll look into it, Maman." I kiss her cheek. Unlike the other day, when she squeezed me into herself by the elevators, her breath is pleasant.

THE NEXT DAY, I pack some of my clothes and other accessories in a suitcase my father had with him in Paris. I plan to take them with me when Maman and I go to her place.

I bring the suitcase to the living room and show it to Maman. "My suitcase is too big and will take up the whole trunk. I'm leaving it here. We'll come back here again, won't we?" I ask.

She nods. "This apartment is also ours."

I busy myself with wiping the dust from my luggage. It is not a proper time to speak of my enthusiasm for buying out her and Milaad and making Papa's place my new home.

My brother is going to pick us up in an hour. Maman is ready to go. She is wearing the black coat and skirt and the crêpe georgette headscarf I suggested she put on. Her dyed golden hair shining from under the veil gives her the appearance of a queen. Unlike the last few days, when she was so depressed and hunched over, she is sitting upright. As I am about to go back to the guest room to get ready, she taps on the seat beside her and orders me to sit down. "I want to tell you something." Perhaps she really believes she is a queen and I am a lowly subject.

I sit down obediently and turn my face toward her, my heart pounding hard with premonition. She moves closer so that our knees touch. Then she holds onto my shoulder. Her gaze is inescapable. "I want to ask you something, Maana. Something that will prove you are loyal to me. If Raazi invites you to her place, turn her down. She has always wanted to steal you from me. Your aunt should submit to God's will for not giving her a daughter. The Almighty knows what's best for each of his creatures."

Even though my mother is pressing my shoulder in her hand, it feels as if she is tightly gripping my heart, trying to rip it out of my breast. I want to tell her she has no right to ban me from seeing my relatives and that my relationship with Aunt Raazi has nothing to do with being disloyal to her, but I am afraid to open my mouth. If I do, I might start crying instead.

I nod so that she lets go of me.

"Good," she says and releases my shoulder. "Now go and get ready. We must arrive before our guests do."

As I dash down the foyer leading to the bedrooms, I feel the first tingling of fever blisters on my lip—my body's typical response to stress and upset. My hopeful heart has once again misled me into thinking the past is behind us. I see it now: Maman will try to control all my socializing. I am not sure if I can stay in Iran.

I burst into my room, sit on my luggage in the corner, and sob for a short while. I try to calm myself when I hear the ticking of the clock on the wall. Tomorrow we will be at Maman's place, I tell myself. I can talk to her then. Now I need to get ready before Milaad buzzes from downstairs. I don't want to worry him and his wife, showing up like a total mess.

Entering the living room, I see Maman pulling Papa's suitcase filled with my belongings after her toward the door. She balances a dish of halva in her other hand. "Please bring the other dishes and lock the door. The keys are there on the table."

"OH MY GOD, what happened to your lips?" Shabnam says as she sees me approaching the car, her lashes flapping like the wings of a lost and scared butterfly.

"It's nothing," I say, wetting the fever blisters with my tongue. "This sometimes happens to me when my environment changes."

My brother makes no comment. He knows me well enough to know that something has happened between

Maman and me. He throws concerned glances my way in the rearview mirror throughout the drive to the restaurant. What bothers me the most is not the insistent question in his eyes but my own reflection. Like everyone said when they saw me at the mosque, I look so much like my mother. No wonder she sees me as an extension of herself!

When we get there, Milaad asks his wife to help Maman take four trays of halva and dates into the women's section. "You stay, sister. I need a hand to take the rest to the men's section."

I know he wants to talk with me in private. He takes his time removing the dishes from the trunk and placing them on the roof of the car. Once our mother is out of sight, my brother turns to face me, his pitiful stare getting on my nerves. "Are you okay, sister? Did you have a fight with Maman?"

"There has been no fight. She asked me to ignore Raazi. She doesn't get that I'm an adult." I start rubbing my hands against each other in the same way as my aunt does when she is under stress.

"I know," Milaad says in a hushed voice. "But we need to do all we can at this moment to fulfil her wishes, at least for a short while. She's gone through a lot."

"So have we."

"True, but she is old. We are still young and can bear extra pain."

"I don't know. I'm tired of being afraid of her, and of taking care of her unreasonable wishes. What if I cut off relations with our aunt and she suddenly dies? Don't you now regret that you listened to Maman and abandoned Papa in the last while before his death?"

Milaad drops his head.

"I don't mean to shame you, brother, but we both need to grow up if we want to be independent."

When Milaad raises his eyes again, his lashes flutter like Papa's when we said goodbye at Charles de Gaulle. "All I'm asking is that you grant her wish for tonight. Do it for me. Shabnam's mother and sister will be in the women's section. They don't know anything about what's going in our family. They have no idea Maman and Papa were separated. You're not married and don't know what it takes—"

Maman's voice cuts Milaan's words short. "You said you wanted your sister to help you carry the dishes! What are you talking about, standing here in the cold?"

"About how much we love you," Milaad answers hastily. He's an expert when it comes to pleasing our mother.

I leave Milaad to deal with the trays and go inside with Maman. The large hall holds several round tables covered by white tablecloths with black napkins. The head waitress has transferred the halva and dates we've brought to small dishes and is distributing them to each table. I sit with my mother and Shabnam at a table close to the entrance, waiting for our guests to arrive.

The first group includes Auntie Raazi with my uncle's wife, Ati, and her daughter, donned in black chadors. Shabnam and I jump to our feet but Maman remains seated. Before kissing us, the women approach her. Ati throws a surprised look at Maman's golden, coiffed hair, partly covered under her thin scarf. Widows should look miserable when in public. She herself stands out with her tattooed eyebrows. The women bend forward to kiss Maman on both cheeks and express their condolences. Their courteous gesture makes her stand up and greet them.

"Sit wherever you like," she says, gesturing to the still-empty hall.

"We came a bit early to help. Is there something we can do?" Raazi gently asks.

"I have arranged everything by myself. Like I did throughout my life with Ashrafi. Your brother kept his hands off everything related to the daily work and children. I even paid for the household. He couldn't have found such a devoted wife and servant even on the moon. You know that, don't you?"

I tense up, hoping Raazi won't express her opinion. Fortunately, she doesn't. I even notice her discreetly pulling at the side of Ati's chador to keep her silent.

They choose a table in the middle of the hall. Maman

sits down with her back to them, facing the entrance.
I sit half-facing the door and half-facing Raazi and Ati,
exchanging smiles with them until the guests suddenly
pour in and I get busy.

Grandma Aziz and Maman's sisters and their daughters arrive later. "Where have you been?" Maman yells
at them. "Did you not think we might need a hand?"
I quickly glance at the tables nearby to see if she has
drawn anyone's attention. Since Raazi and Ati arrived,
my mother has been getting progressively more nervous. It is good they are over in the middle of the hall,
where Papa's relatives have gathered.

"Don't you know how hard it is to get Aziz moving?"
my oldest aunt snaps.

I ask a guest sitting at a nearby table to move to
another spot to accommodate Grandma Aziz, who is
leaning on her walker. I pull out my own chair for my
aunt, who still looks angry at my mother, so she can sit
and calm down. "Thank you, sweetheart. It's so good
to have you back in Iran with us. I hope your mother's
bad temper won't push you away to the other side of
globe again. Now bring a chair and sit here with your
auntie. I miss you."

"Okay, but later," I say, forcing a smile. "I should
greet our guests at their tables before the food is
served." Afraid that this aunt, who is as controlling and
quarrelsome as Maman and has a history of getting into

arguments with her, is going to say something that will agitate my mother, I quickly stride toward the back of the hall.

When I reach the table at which Aunt Raazi is sitting, Ati pulls at my sleeve. "Sit here! We haven't seen much of you."

She taps on her daughter's shoulder, indicating that she should get up and give her seat to me. As soon as I sit down, all of the pressure I've been holding in suddenly releases itself; bursting into tears, I throw myself into my aunt's arms. Raazi embraces me and presses my head against the large breasts that fed four boys. I cry even louder. "Poor child. You were Aadel's love."

As it used to be in my childhood, Raazi's embrace is so warm that I soon relax. Maman is busy squabbling with her sisters on the other side of the room and does not seem to have noticed my absence yet. "Don't go back to Canada," Raazi whispers in my ear. "Stay here and I'll find you a good husband. It's time for you to get settled in your own country."

I nod, pulling away from my aunt.

Bringing a chair and setting it down beside her mother, Ati's daughter joins us at the table. She, too, resembles her mother, at least before Ati got herself those fake eyebrows. "Uncle Aadel told us that you were a great host when he visited you in Canada," she says, looking at my swollen lips.

"He also told us how much fun he had with you during your time together in France," Ati adds.

I grin, feeling acknowledged by at least one of my parents.

As they start serving the food, I am happy to be sitting with Raazi and her family instead of with the confrontational women from my mother's side. "In the name of God," Ati murmurs, before she starts to eat. Her daughter and Raazi do the same, and I follow their custom.

It is only later, when a server comes to clear the table, that I glance over and realize Maman is sitting alone. My heart drops. Partly turned toward the entrance, she is not engaging with her family at the adjacent table. I look around for Shabnam and find her sitting with her own family. Fortunately, everyone is so busy with themselves that nobody realizes I have abandoned my mother.

I decide to risk another five minutes with Raazi. After that, I'll quietly move myself to the other side and sit by Maman, as if I have been there the whole time. Soon, Raazi senses my restlessness. "If you wish to depart, dear, go," she whispers in my ear. "We'll see each other again soon."

I nod and kiss her before getting up. Once I am on my feet, ready to excuse myself to Ati, I notice that Maman is standing now, and watching me. As soon as our eyes meet, she rushes forward and stops me on my way to her. She grabs me by the arm and turns me to face Raazi. "This is *my* daughter," she says. "Stop separating her from me!"

"Me?" Raazi's face pales and she starts rubbing her hands together. "I swear by the bread and salt we've shared that I have done anything against you."

"Do not deny it. You have been talking to her for a long time. Were you bad-mouthing me? What did you tell her to make her throw herself into your embrace and cry, hmm?"

Maman still clutches my arm. I am afraid to budge, afraid that it will only aggravate the situation. Raazi is also silent, so Ati stands up for her. "What are you talking about, Mrs. Malak?" she asks. "Raazi is an angel." She tries to keep her voice down, but it's loud enough to draw the attention of the whole hall.

"'Angel,'" Maman scoffs. "She was always trying to separate my husband from me, to no avail. And now she is after my daughter."

"You're mistaken." Ati grimaces, joining together her thin, painted-on eyebrows. "Our family always wanted the best for you. We saved your marriage many times."

"Really?" My mother's voice is incredulous. "You think I've forgotten Raazi and her husband plotting a second wife for Ashrafi?"

"Do you want me to tell in front of everyone that

you left your husband nine months ago and moved to a place of your own? That his body lay . . ."

"That's enough, Ati. Please." Raazi puts a stop to Ati's speech.

I free my arm and start picking at my lips, but they burn so badly that I leave them alone and look around for someone who might be able to stop Maman. Fortunately, Grandma Aziz is wobbling forward with the aid of her walker to warn her daughter. "Malak, calm down. You're dishonoring our whole family in front of our guests."

But Maman has gone mad. She lunges at her mother, practically spitting her words. "How come you don't think of family honor when you sit there talking behind my back with your other daughters, saying that I was a bad wife and that Ashrafi should have divorced me a long time ago? I know what you're thinking. You think that I am wearing a sad mask but that in my heart I am having a party, because I am a rich widow who now has her children under her thumb." She points at her sisters and yells. "Are you in my heart to know? Shame on each one of you!"

This time, it is Shabnam who comes forward to calm our mother down, her face reddened, her blinking eyes darkened. "I beg you to sit down, Maman. You're not well."

Shabnam is trembling so badly that I hold her with

my free hand so she won't collapse. Only then does Maman let go of my arm and sprawl on a chair. Shabnam desperately looks over at her mother and sister, who have hung their heads in shame.

Women circle around Maman as Aziz sprinkles rose water on her face. I know her well enough to know she has not passed out; this is another one of her acts.

I am right; soon enough, tears start to stream from the corners of her closed eyes.

Raazi brings a napkin and wipes Maman's face. "Please don't cry, Mrs. Malak. We are leaving."

Before departing, she passes me a napkin to clean the blood from my upper lip. "Take care, dear," she murmurs without hugging me.

Maman sits there even after Raazi and Ati are gone. The guests come to her one by one to say goodbye. When Shabnam's family approaches, she turns her back to me, puts on a victim's face, and clutches Shabnam's arm. "Thank God, I've got you," she says. "You are like a daughter to me."

I walk with Grandma Aziz to the exit and apologize to her on my mother's behalf.

"You don't worry, dear," she says. "I know my daughter very well."

I also want to apologize to my older aunt but she has disappeared.

We leave the restaurant once everybody is gone.

I SIT WITH Maman in the rear of the car but, imitating her, turn my back to her and look out the window. Milaad is driving us toward the north of Tehran, to Maman's home. We go through the neighborhood where I grew up and pass by the street where we lived. My childhood home, to which all of my good memories are attached, has been replaced by an apartment building. Maman and Papa fought once in a while in that house, but their rows were never as caustic as the ones they had in the other houses we moved to over the years.

I close my eyes as we exit the neighborhood and open them only when the car stops. Maman lives in a four-storey white building at the end of a dead-end street. "I am on the first floor," she says.

I turn to her, and when she is about to open the car door, I put a hand on her shoulder. "Wait. I need to tell you something."

"Tell what? You're not coming?" I can read the panic in her voice. Her swollen red eyes, lit by the faint light coming off the street, beg me to deny it.

"I'd rather stay with Milaad—if he doesn't mind, of course." I turn to look at my brother, who is facing us from the front seat. "Do you mind?"

He cringes, his eyes also pleading with me to go with Maman. I turn to his wife. "Do you mind, Shab-nam, dear? Only for a few days before I leave. Also, if you don't mind, I'd like to pick up my suitcase from

Atisaz before we go home. I don't wish to return to my father's home again."

"It's not a problem for us, but Maman..."

I turn to my mother before she can say a word. "I'll come and visit you with Milaad and Shabnam, but... you need to get used to living by yourself. It's better for all of us if I don't stay with you."

"I knew it. You are so much like your father! I'm not going to beg for your love." Crying, Maman storms out of the car. Shabnam and Milaad rush after her, but I sit back and look away so as not to witness her departure. Even though the window is closed and the engine is running, I can still hear her talking loudly. It seems from the commotion that she cannot find her keys and is rummaging for them in her bag. I know she always keeps her keys in her coat pocket, and I am inclined to get out and tell her where they are, but instead I slide along the seat to the other side of the car, to where she was sitting. Most probably she, too, knows where her keys are, and this is just her way of delaying a lonely entry to her home.

Two or three long minutes pass before the door to Maman's building is finally opened. I remember the promise I made to myself on the day I arrived: that I would be with my mother and support her during the forty-day mourning period. Clenching my teeth, I muster all my courage to resist getting out and following her into her home. I hold my gaze steady on the wall of the next house until the engine sputters and dies and absolute silence fills the car.

Family Reunion
in the Mirror

Who has drunk the poison of separation, knows
For those who hope against all hope, the same goes.
　　　　　　　—From a *ghazel* by Saadi Shirazi

BOTH LEGS OF HER flight were delayed, so Homa left the airplane more tired than usual. Nevertheless, her exhaustion dissipated as soon as she saw her daughter, Roya, along with her own mother running to greet her in the arrival hall. Her ex-husband, Abol-Fazl, had given his permission for Roya to stay with her at her Grandma Soraya's house. It was a wonderful surprise, though she wished it was for more than one night. Homa placed her luggage on the front seat of her mother's car and climbed into the back with her daughter to talk to her about her immigration plans. But as soon as Soraya began driving, Homa fell asleep, holding hands with Roya. By the time they got back to her mother's apartment, it was late in the evening.

After dinner, when Soraya went to do the dishes, Roya sat herself in front of the TV and began flipping channels. Homa approached her. "Let's go to the other room to talk."

"About what?" Roya asked, with her eyes still on the screen.

"About the meeting with your father this weekend."

"Meeting with Papa? Oh . . . okay." Roya reluctantly turned off the TV and followed Homa. In the guest room, Homa's luggage lay on a stand beside a tall mirror in a silver scrollwork frame, a gift from her wedding. The mirror sat on the floor and was tilted up against the wall, standing taller than any of the three women. Homa had put the mirror up for sale before leaving the country in 1998. A buyer had come to pick it up, but Soraya had plucked it from his hands as she wanted it for herself.

Roya sat down on the single bed and tucked one leg underneath herself, dangling the other off the side. Homa sat on a *poshti*, cushioning her sore bottom and supporting her tired back, and watched her daughter, who had grown into a beautiful seventeen-year-old during her absence. This was Homa's third visit in ten years. But this trip was like no other; she was here specifically to speak with Abol-Fazl and his wife, Effat, about Roya's wish to emigrate to Canada.

Roya was silent. She wore a white shirt that framed her slender body. She resembled Homa when Homa had been her age, and fallen in love with Abol-Fazl. The same large brown eyes, the same frown, the same black curls shadowing her brow. She was also as withdrawn as Homa had been before starting university. Her quietness at this moment bothered Homa more than all of the times she had asked questions about Roya's life on the phone. Why cut herself off now, Homa wondered. The whole emigration plan was Roya's idea. It was she who had asked Homa to come and negotiate with her father on her behalf.

"As you asked, I have come to Iran for you." Homa began. "I've traveled thousands of miles to help you fulfil your wish. Now, tell me more about your plan."

Roya clasped her hands on her lap. "I want to come to Canada to attend university there. That's it. There is no more to what you call 'my plan.'"

Roya's straightforward answer was more hurtful than Homa could have imagined; she'd almost have preferred it if her daughter had slapped her across the face. "So, this has nothing to do with reuniting with me?" It was an unsettling thought, but Homa did her best to keep her composure as she continued. "This will not be enough for your father. You are a good student; you can easily pass the entrance exam and attend a university in Iran."

"My parents want me to study medicine. I want to study cognitive science, and they don't have that program at the bachelor's level here."

"But our only option is to apply under the family—"

Roya cut her short. "And what if I cannot pass the exam? There are thousands of students who fail every year..." She let her words trail off, and began to swing her leg back and forth nervously.

"I hear you." Homa said. She knew her disappointment could be heard in her voice. "But part of me was hoping you wanted to come to Canada to join me as well."

"I don't know," Roya said. "I'm sorry. I'm so confused."

Homa nodded. "You need to understand that for the Canadian government the only acceptable reason for you to apply for immigration is family unification."

"I know. I want to go to the University of British Columbia, and live with you in Vancouver."

"Okay, but we also need to make a solid argument to your father. We will need his consent in order for you to live with me." Homa raised her voice slightly, which made Roya look away. Homa could feel her daughter's anxiety. She berated herself for not expressing these uncertainties earlier.

Perhaps this is my fault, Homa thought. *I shouldn't have assumed that she has the same feelings for me that I have for my mother.* No longer able to suppress her disappointment, she snapped at her daughter. "Please stop bobbing your leg like that! It was also your father's habit, and it makes me very uncomfortable."

Roya uncrossed her legs and snapped back. "I already

told Papa that you have come to talk to them! You cannot pull out now."

"I am not pulling out, Roya," Homa said quietly. "I am here for you. My only problem is you wanting me to pretend it was my idea."

"You don't want me to live with you?"

At first, Homa did not understand her daughter's question, but once she did, anger started boiling in her. How could the girl think like this? Homa turned from Roya and focused her gaze on the green color of the carpet to calm down.

Roya was quiet. She stared down at her hands on her lap, fingers knitted together. Perhaps she did understand how Homa felt inside.

Homa drew a deep breath, raised her head, and looked toward the mirror. When she began to speak, she addressed her daughter's image. "You know how much I want us to be together. But to make it possible, you need to be as involved in the process as I am. The first step is to tell your parents that you are one hundred percent sure you want to come to Canada and live with me, and you need to do this when I'm there at their home to talk to them. You should say, in front of them, what you told me on the phone. Do you hear me?"

The loud thumping of Homa's heart in her ears contrasted with Roya's silence. She was afraid that her daughter's obvious indecisiveness would prevail and she would withdraw. What if Roya pulled out of the plan now, before they even had a chance to talk to Abol-Fazl and Effat? Homa felt a sharp pain in her chest that stopped her breathing for a moment. She thought about the day, so long ago now, that she'd given up custody. Back then, she could never have imagined a time when she would be so frightened at the prospect of Roya's rejection. She wished Soraya would come and save her.

Homa continued to watch Roya in the mirror, and Roya continued to stare at her hands. Long moments passed before Roya finally raised her head and gave a quick nod.

Her lips were violet. It reminded Homa of the times when Roya was just a few months old and she'd get so upset that her breath would catch inside her and she couldn't cry. Homa immediately stood up and tapped on Roya's shoulder before realizing that Roya wasn't a choking child but a grownup pondering a grave decision: a grownup who had just nodded her head to indicate that she was choosing to live with Homa. Homa felt like shaking her for a clearer answer. Instead, she sat beside her on the bed and put her arm around her daughter. "Don't worry. Everything will be fine."

THE NEXT MORNING, Homa woke up to the sound of Soraya's voice. "Wake up, children! Let's go to the park and exercise together." Soraya looked exuberant in her navy-blue velvet track pants with red stripes on the sides, purchased from Zara; Homa had brought them from Canada. She wore a matching shawl on her dyed burgundy hair.

"Maman, I'm going to wear the tracksuit you brought me, too!" Roya jumped out of bed.

"Perfect," Homa said. "I will wear mine as well, so we can match."

THE PARK WAS on the street just behind Soraya's building. Soraya walked between Homa and Roya and held their hands. As they entered the park through the cypress hedges surrounding it, Homa saw a group of women doing stretches in the distance, behind the children's playground. As they got closer, all heads turned toward the trio. Even the instructor, with the knotted ends of her scarf on her back and a whistle around her neck, stole a glance. Several of the women cheered and one called out, "Wow, Soraya! You three look like triplets."

"It's true," the instructor agreed with a grin. "Now come and join us, beautiful ladies."

Homa, Soraya, and Roya made a new line at the front of the group for the remaining fifteen minutes of cardio. Homa didn't mind that at times during the jumping jacks Roya's hand brushed against hers.

After the cool-down stretches, everyone gathered around, asking questions about Roya's plans to join

Homa in Canada. Roya mumbled unclear answers, just a word or two, and tilted her head right and then left. Homa could see she was holding her breath. Sensing that her daughter was overwhelmed and wanting to return home, Homa intervened.

"Excuse me, ladies, but I have jet lag and need to lie down." She nodded her head toward the park exit, indicating that the women should open the circle they had formed around them to let them leave.

"Thanks, Maman," Roya whispered softly in Homa's ear as they walked away from the crowd toward the carefully trimmed hedges.

"No problem." Homa smiled, grateful for the small kindness and the hope it instilled in her. The sound of the instructor blowing her whistle behind them confirmed her optimism and gave her the courage to extend her arm and hold her daughter's hand.

Today is my lucky day, she thought as they walked. *I should try to talk to Roya about our meeting again.* But as they walked past the hedges, her thoughts were interrupted by the appearance of a large woman in a black overcoat and scarf who was entering the park, nearly knocking into them. She addressed them in a loud and surprised voice. "Soraya? . . . Roya?"

The trio and the burly woman stopped and faced each other. Roya jerked her hand away from Homa's and dropped her head to the path.

"Soraya?...Roya?" the woman repeated, her curious eyes moving from one to the other and then to the woman she did not recognize. She stood over them like a principal who had caught a group of children sneaking out of school.

Homa detected a subtle quiver under the skin of Roya's face as her daughter pulled gently at the sleeve of Homa's matching tracksuit. What was she trying to tell her? The towering woman's next question did not give her enough time to figure it out.

"You three look so much alike. Are you related?" The woman was looking directly at Homa.

"Yes. I am Homa—Soraya's daughter who lives in Canada. And Roya is my daughter.

"I had no idea," the woman said. "But I always thought it strange that Roya looks neither like her father nor Mrs. Effat." She continued talking, explaining her own relationship to Roya. "Roya and Saba, my daughter, go to the same school." She turned her intense gaze on Roya, who refused to look up at her. "I see Roya's father, Mr. Mir, every month in the Parents' Council, and once saw his wife. I always wondered if she was Roya's real mother—"

"Mrs. Effat is also her mother," Homa explained, cutting off the woman's words. "She is the one who raised her."

Roya stared blankly at the ground, as if what Homa was saying had nothing to do with her.

. . .

ONCE HOME, HOMA followed her still-sullen daughter into the guest room. "Can you leave me alone?" Roya snapped. "I want to change my clothes. I am sweaty."

Homa stood behind the door. She didn't go to the kitchen because Soraya was there. *It would be awful to burst out crying in front of Maman*, Homa thought. *She'll know right away that I am not in control of the situation.*

Homa hovered in the hallway, pressing her back to the wall and her fingers into her palms to push away the tears welling up in her eyes. As she had done a thousand times before, she started reevaluating her reason for giving up custody of Roya at the time of her divorce, when Roya was two. According to Islamic law, she could only have her daughter for seven years. After that, if Abol-Fazl insisted on taking Roya back, Homa would have had to turn her over. That could have been more devastating to Roya, let alone to Homa herself, than giving custody to Abol-Fazl from day one. Nevertheless, Roya had probably felt abandoned, no matter how logical Homa's reasoning had been. And that feeling had likely grown, when four and half years later, Homa chose to leave Iran for good. Like Abol-Fazl and Effat, Roya probably thought of her as selfish and irresponsible.

Perhaps that's why she didn't want her classmate's mother to know I was her birth mother, Homa thought, realizing too late what Roya's tug on her sleeve had likely meant. *What kind of mother would leave her child?*

Good mothers stayed with even the most abusive husbands to be with their kids. After all, motherhood still meant self-sacrifice in Iran, although this was not something Homa believed. This was why she was not willing to admit guilt. Leaving her bad marriage had been the right thing to do. The myth of what makes a good mother was made by men. Abol-Fazl had no idea of the postpartum depression Homa had suffered through. Only many years later, in Canada, had she learned that it was a common experience that had nothing whatsoever to do with being an unfit or unloving mother.

Homa could still feel the trauma of those days gnawing away at her. She'd been a nineteen-year-old girl, alone with a constantly crying newborn in an apartment without a phone to call her mother for help. There were days when she'd paced the rooms, crying along with Roya, scared to death that she was going to lose her mind. Abol-Fazl would leave early in the morning and not come back until ten at night, expecting his food to be warm and on the table. He wouldn't close his bookstore early — not even by a few minutes — and he never allowed Homa to visit her mother.

"You are my wife and you must be at my home," he'd say, leaving no room for argument.

Homa had been in her last year at university when she gave birth to Roya. Abol-Fazl didn't wish her to finish her studies, but he did not want to order her to quit, either. "You can attend your classes, but you should take Roya with you. I am not paying for a babysitter."

Homa knew that getting Soraya to look after the baby while she was at school was out of question. Abol-Fazl was not shy about expressing his hatred of Soraya. Homa had left him on a Friday, after a particularly bad fight. They had just returned from a weekend visit with Soraya. Her mother had bought Roya a golden pendant with the image of a mother and her child. As soon as they got back home, Abol-Fazl ripped off the thin golden chain that held the pendant loosely around Roya's neck, jerking the baby out of her sleep. "Your idiot superficial mother cares only about appearance and beauty," he shouted. "This will give my daughter a rash."

Roya had cried, and a red mark instantly formed from the tug at the right side of her neck. Homa looked at it and realized that it was time to go. If she allowed her husband to insult her mother, she would be setting a bad example for Roya; her daughter would grow up believing that it was acceptable to allow her future husband to insult her.

No, Homa did not regret her decision to leave him and ask for a divorce. Neither did she regret wanting to continue her education and to work as a professional outside the home. She wanted to be a good mother and to make something of herself.

"Subservient mothers raise subservient daughters. This is not what I wish for Roya," she'd told Soraya when her mother had opened the door, surprised to find her daughter back without Abol-Fazl.

After she left the country, she'd kept in touch with Roya through phone calls and letters, imagining the day when a grown-up Roya would tell her father that she wanted to emigrate and live with her mother—the independent woman who had made something of herself. Her hope, she told herself now, had not been false. It had already happened, and she was not going to let the opportunity slip through her fingers. *I will win my daughter back. I'm not going to be defeated this time.*

Homa pushed open the door to the guest room only to notice that Roya had dropped her track pants on top of Homa's suitcase bearing an Air Canada logo.

"You no longer want them?" Homa asked, shivering. The cold anger she'd felt behind the door had abated, and her sweaty body had started to cool down.

"I pulled at your sleeve so you would keep quiet and not say anything to that woman," Roya said, her voice breaking. "But you did."

"I don't understand you! Was I supposed to lie and hide that I am the mother who gave you life?"

"Silence is not the same as a lie."

"Maybe. But I refuse to be silent. I am so tired of this game of hiding that you and your family have been playing for years. Why should I hide that I am your mother? And that my mother is your grandmother. Why?"

"You don't understand."

"No, I don't."

"Now everybody in the Parents' Council will know things about me. And soon the whole school will know. Starting tomorrow, they'll say—"

"Will say what? 'Poor Roya! Her real mother abandoned her'?"

"No! They'll say, 'Poor Roya! She lives with a stepmother'!" Roya shouted.

Homa raised her eyebrows. "What's wrong with living with a stepmother, if she is a decent woman?"

"You don't understand," Roya said again, biting her lip.

"How is anyone supposed to understand you when you don't express yourself?"

When Roya remained silent, Homa pushed harder. "It is not right that you sacrifice me for your own comfort to hide the fact that Effat is—"

She stopped speaking when Roya's sealed lips began to quiver.

Homa waited until Roya took a deep breath before continuing. "I understand how this society views stepmothers. But, first of all, it is not your responsibility to protect Effat against others. Second, the way to change this biased view is to not hide the reality. You should—"

"I am not you. Why don't you understand?" Roya said under her breath, staring at the wall. Feeling hurt once again, Homa watched her daughter's scrunched-up face in the mirror. "If you are not going to acknowledge me as your mother, how is it that you want to live with me in the future? It seems that you have not thought through what it means to emigrate. You do not even have a concrete plan."

"So, you are not coming to talk to them?" Roya's words were addressed to Homa's own reflection.

Homa stared at her daughter's image. *In her white shirt*, she thought, *Roya looks exactly like me on my wedding day.* She remembered how uncertain she had suddenly felt when, eighteen years ago, the mullah sitting to the left of the groom had asked for her consent to marry her to Abol-Fazl. They had been sitting side by side on two short stools—facing this very same mirror, set between two long candle holders on an embroidered satin spread on the floor. The women standing behind them and holding a white cloth over their heads had gone silent. Abol-Fazl's sisters, who had been rubbing sugar cones against one another while the mullah recited verses from the Koran, stopped what they were doing and waited for her answer. When Homa did not at first reply, as was the custom, one of the sisters chanted, "The bride has gone to the meadow to pick flowers. Ask again." The second time, her groom's other sister repeated the same thing.

The third time, Homa knew she had to answer, but somehow, she could not bring herself to say yes to the man beside her, the man who was impatiently bouncing his knee up and down. She had only snapped out of it when the mullah had prompted her. "Ma'am?"

Ma'am?

It was actually Roya's voice calling her. "Maman?"

Homa turned to her daughter, who stopped bobbing her leg. "Yes."

"Yes, what?" Roya asked.

"Yes, I am coming to talk to your father," Homa announced. "You are my daughter, and I love you." As she hugged Roya, the door opened and Soraya stepped in. "What about me? Please take me to Canada too," she said, joining their embrace, framed in the silver-rimmed mirror.

"You are next on my list, Maman." Homa laughed. "But there is one condition."

"And what is that?" Soraya chuckled.

"You must bring my mirror with you."

"And also your track pants, Grandma," Roya added. "So we can join a cardio class and exercise together."

Acknowledgements

Parts of the stories within this collection remember and pay homage to the lives of people from the Iranian community I have befriended or known in Iran and Canada. Three decades of Iranian history from 1978 to 2008, in addition to my life history in my homeland and in migration, echo in the pages of this book; nonetheless, it is a work of fiction.

My deepest gratitude belongs to my one and only, my husband, Pter Straka, who never stopped believing in me even in the difficult times when I was about to give in. With unparalleled patience, he travelled along with me through the ups and downs of writing. His love and kindness gave me strength and hope and his genuine sense of humor and encouraging smile lifted my spirit through my journey of composing each tale.

I would like to thank the members of A Drift Collective, especially Ken Klonsky and Dr. William

Ellis, for their comments on different drafts of the stories. I am hugely indebted to Dianne Maguire for her editorial help and to Tom Gorman for his substantial feedback on the finished manuscript.

Special thanks to my publishers, Sarah MacLachlan and Janie Yoon at House of Anansi Press, for giving me the opportunity to publish this collection. My greatest regards go to my editor Michelle MacAleese for her wisdom and editorial rigor and for being a fantastic guide and advocate for this book. She nurtured the stories in a way that showed deep compassion for their female protagonists and profound insight into their lives. Thank you to Linda Pruessen for a remarkable copyedit and to Maria Golikova, managing editor, for a smooth navigation of the editing process. I also owe thanks to Alysia Shewchuk for designing the beautiful cover and to Laura Meyer, my publicist, for outstanding guidance and ongoing promotion of the book.

Last but not least, I would like to acknowledge the financial support of the Regina Public Library and the Canada Council for the Arts for the period of time I served as the library's 2015–2016 Writer in Residence, during which I completed this collection.

Author photograph: SFU

NILOFAR SHIDMEHR is a poet, essayist, and scholar, and the author of six books in English and Farsi, including *Between Lives* and *Shirin and Salt Man*, a BC Book Prize finalist. She writes and delivers lectures on women's rights, migration and diaspora, and social and political issues in Iran. A specialist in the literature and cinema of modern Iran, she teaches in the Continuing Studies program at Simon Fraser University in Vancouver, Canada, where she lives with her husband.